# PRAISE FOR

## BLUESTONE FOLKLORE

"A tender hymn to the fragile pulse between creation and decay… prose razor sharp in small, sensory truths."

—*Independent Book Review*

"Stoddard expertly entwines religious symbolism and nature in this haunting, artistic debut."

—*BookLife Reviews*

"There are shining moments… grotesquely horrific as the boundary between human and flora blurs."

—*Kirkus Reviews*

# BLUESTONE FOLKLORE

# BLUESTONE FOLKLORE

TIMOTHY STODDARD

**Bluestone Folklore**

Copyright © 2023 by Timothy Stoddard.

All rights reserved. No part of this book may be used or reproduced in any manner whatsoever without written permission of the author.

This book is a work of fiction. Excepting those where prior permission has been obtained, the names, characters, places, and incidents are the product of the author's imagination or are used fictitiously. Any resemblance to actual events, locales, or persons, living or dead, is coincidental.

*Art:* Alexis Anne Marino
*Cover:* Theresa M. Evangelista
*Editing:* Martin McHugh
*Layout:* Jason Price

ISBN 979-8-9884351-3-6
Library of Congress Control Number: 2023950660

*Published by*

*In gratitude to my parents,*
*my grandmothers, Brian, and Bea*

The apples were bitter, but that didn't trouble the does. They arched their lithe necks to pluck the unripe fruit. Even the white-faced Yearling stood on her hindquarters to snag as many as she could. The long-lived apple tree on the acreage was contorted. Each limb was inflected and curved so peculiarly as if it had been trained to grow that way. It was strange, but it was also sacred. The tree had fed the deer of this bluestone land for ages.

When the Yearling left the coyote den as a fawn, the apple tree was first to greet her. Its silhouette was rooted in her earliest memories. There was something about this tree; it anchored the land. It was the core of existence around which all life there pivoted.

Nobody knew the exact age of the tree or who had planted it. Yet there it stood impaling the tip of the east-facing field. The does were bound to the apple tree through a forgotten covenant made by their forebears. They were indentured to it without knowing exactly why.

They labored about its base, reaping its harvests, warming its roots with their bedded bodies, and nourishing it with their droppings.

The sprawl where the apple tree stood was bordered by clusters of trees and bluestone outcroppings. It was on the top of a grade at the end of a winding dirt road; the view was unobscured. The stretch of field gave way to an overlook of hills and valleys beyond, which incrementally shaded from green to lavender the farther the eye went.

The Yearling and her mother along with the others had free roam to slip in and out of the protection of the woods. In the Bluestone Woodland, days melted into each other effortlessly. Grazing gave way to languid resting in a clockwork gesture. Mouthfuls of sour apples, tender greens, and fungus flavored the even-tempered passing of days.

The Yearling wandered freely about the acreage listening to the wind mourn through the tightly knit topiary and watching the wild turkey glide down the wooded ledge to the meadow's opening. Her play was solitary as she traveled about the forest floor with hooves cushioned by fat pads of moss and mounds of yellow pine needles.

As yearlings were apt to be, she was curious. The complex world intrigued her. She watched riveted as a mother robin regurgitated gelatinous bits down her chicks' throats. And if nothing swayed her attention, she might crouch in the tall brush to startle the older, sedentary does who'd grunt in response. She was mesmerized by their mouths. They never stopped. They were an endless rippling of mastication.

Life had been mostly easy for the white-faced Yearling at her mother's side. It was an idyllic existence. Yet there was pain, and it grew every day. The does felt its force pull like the sea's undertow. When would it sweep them away into the unknown depths? It carried with it the weight of trauma cracking the bedrock with its heft. The outlying trails, meadows, slopes—all were littered with scores of bluestone fragments. What was the origin of all this pain that made the land fracture and shatter so many times?

This was not yet the case on the acreage, however. The roots of the apple tree, deep and expansive, were holding everything together. It stretched its roots out wide like open hands that cradled the earth, its powerful limbs the buttresses of heaven. It stood tall and strong. It was the axis mundi of the Bluestone Woodland.

This refuge was the only reality the Yearling and her mother knew, but it was more than just a dwelling place; it was a reflection of their being. They were just as much a part of the acreage as it was a part of them. The woodland and the does were the same though perception was like a cosmic trick mirror presenting an incongruous reflection. It was the great conundrum of life, the deceptive array of distinct individuals being one entity.

Life had its own rhythm on the acreage pulsating from the apple tree. It whirled and spun illusions as organized and as patterned as music. Mothers and offspring came and went like apple blossoms and fruit always returning to earth. Only the daughters remained as the sons ventured to the outskirts of the Bluestone Woodland returning in autumn to breed. Spring would bring speckled fawns wobbling on stilted legs and suckling teats. Old deer would venture off alone into the depths of the woods to die with dignity.

Things had dramatically changed, however. Sons stopped returning. The doe clan began diminishing. The white-faced Yearling was the first fawn to have been born in many springs. From across the river in the land of man came a dark adversary, a great shadow carrying with it anger, hatred, hopelessness—none of which the doe clan could understand.

And when the Yearling was conceived under a veil of blood, the gravity of the situation began to overwhelm the doe clan. The steps they took, once graceful and light, seemed to sink into the earth. They felt as though the ground were turned on its side and they were sliding away into the unknown. They drew even nearer the tree to keep themselves moored to the land.

Unsure of how to face their predicament, the doe clan buried their faces in their grazing keeping their most ominous thoughts just before the precipice. What could they do? They were as bound to the land as the roots of the tree were. As night settled in and covered them, they huddled colorless and vulnerable in the tree line.

However, the land had a gift bestowed upon it that lit the gloom as much as Venus did in midwinter. The little Yearling with the white face had brought the promise of new life. Her mother, the Elder Doe of the clan, cherished the fawn. She grew quickly under her mother's watchful eye. Before the Elder Doe knew it, her babe too would ripen into a doe.

As a tiny fawn, the Yearling had had visions. In waking hours, old memories from another life would spring up but then slip away. There were recurring images and feelings. Pain, always pain. And then as she slept, she dreamed strange and unusual things. In the rising of the sun, she realized it had all been carried away with the moon, and she remembered only having the memories and nothing more.

That's when she started to hear the noise.

There had been evenings when from afar, likely somewhere over a hill, the Yearling had heard a strident tone cut through the blackness. It was a squealing, the sound of ice as it splits. Then it morphed into something percussive like a farm cat walking over the hood of a car pressing into the thin metal with fleshy paws. Ultimately, it would flatten out into a long wail punctuated by a snap, a sound akin to the cracking of a bone-dry stick. And then silence.

None of the does had been alarmed or even awakened by the noise, but their disinterest didn't do much to calm the Yearling. She edged closer to her mother. She let her head drop to the ground as she moved inward to take shelter abut the warm, strong flank lying next to her.

Her mother's metered breathing always lulled her back to sleep. But the strange sound returned on later nights, a sound so shrill that it roused her from rest into feverish fear. She never did understand why none of the others heard this noise or how her mother could slumber so serenely while it shot over the range. All she knew was that each time it resounded, one thing was certain: it was moving closer.

She became resigned to the idea that this sound carried with it the weight of things to come. It was an echo of the future if echoes could ever travel backward through time and space. And this echo certainly reverberated the windows of the little Cape Cod where the Old Man, who dwelled within its white clapboard walls, listened to the rattling glass with wariness.

The Old Man was the guardian of the acreage, and he considered himself the steward of the does. He was a retired physician who looked more like a dockworker—barrel-chested with generous features and virtually bald with stubbles of white hair. For many years, he lived on his property as a near-recluse. He had few friends in the area—most he never saw in person—and no family. Contact with the outside world had become limited to material objects whether they were his prized artifacts from years of traveling or the endless stream of propaganda pamphlets he found stuffed in his mailbox. Straight into the trash they went, the unchanging slogan, Thin the Herd! peeking out above the wastepaper basket.

One person with whom he did speak often was the Woman across the river, who found herself in a similar position as he. She wasn't a widower like the Old Man. She was married to a cruel man—the overlord of their little woodland community. And though there had been a large age gap between the Old Man and the Woman, they were still very fond of each other. Their friendship was like the tying arm of a galaxy that bridged the space between their lonely universes.

They had met four years earlier when she was a newlywed. While driving back from the market down the Bluestone highway, he'd seen a figure in the trees outside her home—had glimpsed arms flagging down his sedan like the wings of a game bird. He doubled back and pulled into the drive, relieved to see that her husband's car was gone. When he could find nothing in the trees at the side of the house, he shuffled to the front door and knocked. The Woman answered. Sunshine floodlighted her large, tree-sap eyes. Earthtone fabrics covered her like buckskin. She denied having been in the trees but was glad to make his acquaintance nonetheless. She reached her hand out to shake his, and they were bound by shivering, clasped hands.

After that, he often paid her a visit on days when he dared venture to town for groceries or medications. He'd tell her of his deer and his garden, and they'd exchange gifts of canned goods or sit at her chrome-legged dinette table and swap stories. He'd share a funny anecdote about Fay, his deceased partner, or she'd offer an old thread of her grandmother Ava's, also gone. They spoke of their dearly departed so candidly, with such care and vitality that it was alchemy. The two extra chairs at the Woman's secondhand kitchen table were never truly empty.

He never could stay long visiting with her in her house or garden shed. It was uncertain whether it was the thought of her husband coming home early or simply being outside the safety of the acreage, but being there always filled him with a sense of doom. The psychological and physical trauma that hung about the property was as thick as the Virginia creeper that was strangling the front porch. It spurted from out an old hunting shanty atop the hill and wept down the ridge at the back of the house. Along an old foot trail it trickled until it pooled at the base of the deck. Through the mesh of the screen door, it spattered the stacked propaganda leaflets on the dinette table waiting to be circulated by her husband.

It was a dangerous environment, and the Woman's welfare was a constant worry for the Old Man—especially after he had found her in the bathroom covered in her own blood. She had no access to a vehicle, yet he insisted she run far away from her husband. She could flee during the full moon when it was light enough to find one's footing in the dark forest. He could meet her somewhere and pick her up, hide her on the acreage. But she reasoned it was too dangerous for both of them, and she insisted he stop suggesting it.

Her husband was no stranger to the Old Man. He remembered him as a shy, sensitive boy who was sometimes brought to the acreage by his mother to pick apples. On one visit on a cloudy day, his mother plucked apples while wearing large sunglasses. The next, she held the basket for the boy as she couldn't lift her arm high enough to pick fruit or even raise a glass to her broken lip.

"You ought to let me look at that," the Old Man whispered to her while the boy fought with a stubborn apple. He was at that time a semi-retired physician. "I might be able to treat it."

"Treat? Oh heavens, Doc. There's no treatment for clumsiness."

There had been a long stretch of time when the boy was absent from the Old Man's life. The boy's father felt the world was moving too fast, losing touch with the values that kept society zipped up and contained. He didn't approve of the Old Man's lifestyle.

Then the boy returned to the acreage as a teenager. He needed help—wanted someone to see him for who he was. However, the Old Man could never grasp what the boy had tried to tell him. It was something the Old Man had come to regret. But as Fay had pointed out time and time again, it was probably too late. The young man had already been molded into the image of his father—angry and violent.

The boy grew into a wicked man. He came to have a crooked pointer finger. No one knew how he'd gotten it, nor did anyone dare ask. He had remained in his childhood home after his parents died—even brought the Woman to live there after they'd married. Nothing good ever came from that property. The promise of new life the Woman had been given by the Man with the Crooked Finger had instead turned out to be imprisonment.

Whenever the Old Man returned home from the Woman's place, he finally felt as though he could breathe. The does served as a sort of welcoming committee huddled around the apple tree. They grazed or rested in its shade, the white face of the Yearling beaming like quartz in clay. She was the prized gem of his herd. Often, she had found herself the subject of his paintings. Once he'd hoisted himself out of his sedan, he would head indoors to begin a new composition with a superstitious compulsivity.

He had taken up painting during his career as a physician to find calm in the relentless stress of his vocation, but the root of the passion was that it was his way of creating infinite worlds. He had come to enjoy capturing the deer on his canvas first in acrylic and later in watercolor. He had stationed his painting desk in his east-facing living room window, which offered a stunning vista: the apple tree superimposed on an endless horizon. In good weather, he chose to work *en plein air* on the porch.

When they weren't bedded down in the grass bower, the does were under the apple tree. Its contorted majesty was picturesque and grave. In early spring, the tree was pregnant with milky blossoms effervescent with pollinator hordes. In winter, it was a shadow of arthritic fingers scratching at the sky. From summer to fall, its branches wept with an abundance of medium-sized fruit. It was the favored food of the doe clan. Its bounty kept them tied to the place, the Old Man, and his canvases.

Compositions of realism dominated his earlier output, but his later depictions, especially his recent ones, were principally marked by the abstract. Lush, bold colors and discomposed shapes covered the blank space his brushes caressed. He worked with urgency; he believed his canvases were prophetic. Painting his land and the does in scenes of beauty were akin to the power of designing new realities or sustaining the order of things. He had even painted his friend, the Woman, safe beneath the apple tree with the white-faced Yearling. He put his hope in it—willed it to come true. The Spirit worked through him in this manner.

Yet the dark power of the Woman's husband, the Man with the Crooked Finger, was gripping all the woodland. His influence could be felt even on the acreage. An ache worked its way down the Old Man's arm. Was something possessing him? He began to notice things he'd never seen in his paintings—murky tones, smudges like charcoal, scrapings and splattering of scarlet. He feared days of violence.

The Old Man was influenced by all the cultures he'd studied as an anthropology student prior to his medical training. He searched in desperation for a meaning to the universe; to find comfort in a mortal condition. He had traveled the world to witness healing rituals and observe the ways of old religions. It was a background for which he was grateful; it had taught him to revere the earth. It shaped his view of nature—a sacred blanket of which he was a mere thread of even now as it unraveled. And it was in this season of unknotting and fraying in which the Old Man awaited death. He didn't know why; he just felt it in his bones.

The wilderness was full of healers and ghosts in the form of animals. That's what the Old Man had learned in his spiritual pursuits. Therefore, he respected the autonomy of nature including his resident herd of does. He kept a boundary as best he could between himself and them. He honored their wild essence; he revered them as the sacred beings they were.

He often liked to think of his relationship to his does as a motto taught to him in his medical school days: *Primum non nocere*—First, do no harm. He knew in this context that the meaning was different than it was in medicine. To him, it was a mantra of a hands-off approach, to interfere only as necessary. But the deer were in danger. The community had come to see them as a nuisance, a threat. They were being slaughtered and discarded as rubbish.

It wasn't only the deer that faced destruction. The Old Man remembered some years earlier seeing a large she-coyote in the trees near the field. He knew coyotes could eat deer, but he didn't intrude. It was the order of things. Nature kept its balance. Besides, the she-coyote's teats were engorged with milk, and its pups were coming any day. Through his binoculars, he had watched it prepare a bluestone den at the eastern end of the field.

A group of men, which included the father of the Man with the Crooked Finger, had spotted the she-coyote hunting in the woods for cottontail rabbits. They pushed it away from the acreage, chased it as it flashed far from its den. The Old Man had looked for it in the tree line, but it was as if it had vanished.

On a walk a few days later, he found its mangled body dumped in the trees near his field. It had been left in such a way that the Old Man knew it was intended to be a threat. That silvery shadow with yellow eyes darting like meadowlarks … He vowed to never forget them. He painted it resplendent in moonlight, pregnant and cunning. He hoped it gave power to its spirit.

However, the she-coyote's absence in turn served a purpose. Her vacant den offered a safe space for the white-faced Yearling to be born. The Yearling's conception was something the Old Man recalled with vividness. The Buck who had sired her was shot near the old service road at the edge of his property. He could still see the Elder Doe at his door, her back sopped with blood as she entreated him for help. As violence against animals escalated, the Old Man often wondered when his time would come.

The Old Man and the Woman had suspected that it was her husband who had shot the Buck though they had no proof. It was unwise to accuse the Man with the Crooked Finger of wrongdoing. The woods were wide and deep, and a body could go missing for years, even generations. Old trees grew up and out of the buried bodies of early settlers—The forest covered over many secrets.

The Old Man sometimes felt eyes on him. He paused his gardening to survey the tree line from the safety of a joe-pye weed rampart. He would have liked to feel safe as most of his time was spent at home. His estate was his sanctuary, and he took pride in it. Spaces had been cultivated to serve his interests and the encircling ecosystem alike. The woodland had suffered extensive damage in recent decades due to climate change and pollution. His property had been formed as a place of healing and balance—a rustic utopia.

In summer, the beds were full of masses of azure delphinium matched in splendor only by sprawls of rose. There was also ample foxglove—tubular blossoms an array of colors he likened to Neapolitan ice cream—but they were poisonous and remained unscathed. Lilies he cherished the most; exotic oriental varieties that climbed as high as a man only to be nipped at the long-awaited bud by a hungry doe. He offered his cottage-style plantings to the does, and they sampled it all.

In early summer, while lapping up the sparse remnants of an old salt block, the Yearling observed him as he sat outside before her. He kept his customary distance from the porch and was half-hidden behind a canvas. His rotund head flitted in and out while he reappraised his subject. She cocked her head in consideration. He spoke loudly to her in a tone she sensed to be benign.

The doe clan was a stunning sight in his gardens, their auburn coats damp from leaf dew. Most radiant beneath the sun was the Elder Doe, thick-necked and cream-muzzled. *Gratia plena!* Every movement she made was at a dignified tempo. She was salt of the earth.

Her daughter, the Yearling, was also of a sturdier build with large, inquisitive eyes. Beginning atop her right eye, an irregular white patch of hair stretched to the top of her head. The piebald feature made her easily identifiable by the Old Man. He felt this trait was something she had carried from a former life, as if a tragic event had removed her from her last incarnation. It was like how a glass of falling red wine becomes the future stain on a carpet. How many lives had she lived? For this, he favored her—He called her Saint. To him, a divine aura radiated from her crown. On his canvas, he likened her to a mystical vision among the herd of does under the apple tree.

As he watched them feast upon the sumptuous gardens, he thought of them as the fattening, pampered objects of a strange and pointless sacrificial ritual.

The sun traveled the length of the field, and the sky reddened. It was an unsettling color, more of an inflammation than a blushing, the summer clouds rubbing and chafing along their course. The Old Man spent the evening watching the sun sink into nothingness from the rocker on his front porch; it always seemed as if the land just fell off at skyline's edge. Time was running quickly. Time was running thin.

The Yearling paused from her activity to look at the stout, silver-headed figure wobbling from his perch. She'd never had close interaction with the Old Man, yet there was something homely about him. But as she had regarded him only from a distance, there always seemed to be an air of enigma about him. As such, her wildness never allowed her to truly feel at ease around him.

After the sun had vanished, the Old Man stiffly rose to head indoors. The kitchen light flipped on, and the sudden glare reflected off the many deer eyes, yellowish-orange embers blinking from the abyss. This prompted them to start their trek to the bower. They once delighted in the thought of collapsing into the tall brush conquered by the exhaustion of the day's luxurious idleness. Now, they feared sleep.

Cricket chittering filled the air as the swish of hooves sounded toward the tree line. The Yearling kept pace with her mother at the back. Then the whole lot slowed to the blotch of billowy brush at the wooded opening. Once there, each doe found her spot, some curling while others protracting their spindly bodies. The maturing Yearling planted herself aside her mother, who gave her a few cleansing licks. She shook her spit-damp head and grunted in exasperation. Mother deer licked their fawns because it was instinctual. But in her old age, the Elder Doe licked her babe in case there'd be no tomorrow.

The Yearling was growing up and began defying coddling gestures, but she secretly treasured nestling next to her mother. The Elder Doe too treasured this routine—All things in the Bluestone Woodland were impermanent, fleeting. The Elder Doe knew soon it would be her turn to make the one-way journey to the mysterious end of the woods.

The lights of the house migrated from one window to the next as the Old Man made his way to bed. Inside the Cape Cod were wall-to-wall wood paneling, floors covered over with jewel-toned Turkish rugs, and art and artifact at almost every turn. It resembled the cabin of a mythical pirate ship. At least, that's what Fay had always said.

The Old Man was lonely. Once, there had been two who shared this nightly ritual. Normally, when he reached his bedroom, the light stayed on for a short time and he'd speak to the portrait on the nightstand—the image of the one now gone—and would pull the chain of the old glass lamp. Its final snap thus cast the acreage in total darkness.

Not that night, however. The phone's ringing drew him from his bedtime habits.

His stretch of land was lit only if the moon was large enough and the sky was clear. Nighttime was mostly peaceful. The sounds of infinite insects and amphibians lifted in the air just as the musty perfume of the damp earth rose. Winter runoff could be heard trickling from afar.

From the swath of tall brush where the does slept, the Old Man's white Cape Cod remained visible. It glowed in the distance with an unearthly radiance. It appeared through a clearing of trees like a will-o'-the-wisp. Its iridescence drew dark things toward it like a flame calls to moths.

It was high summer, and the Yearling struggled to sleep. The herd's collective fear made it a difficult task. At night, the does feared the return of the shooter who had wounded the Buck. It was as palpable as the breeze, as sharp as the grass tips that stabbed the Yearling regardless of the position she lay.

Rattled, she stretched her limbs. Her eyes ached for rest. Crickets scratched away at their melodies while the blade of the Milky Way slashed the sky behind cracks in clouds. Even the gentle wind's touch seemed to aggravate her. She wanted it all to stop.

But the crickets went silent. Her racing mind halted. Thick air stagnated about her. The hairs of her coat began to stand on end. She heard a branch snap. She held her breath to listen. Her heart was throbbing. She lifted her snout to catch any scent. No breeze. Nothing moved. Her ears rang in the silence.

Again, the cracking of deadwood. It picked up speed and ventured closer. She had heard squirrels and small creatures going about the wood, but this approaching entity was much larger. She discerned its considerable weight by the depth of the fracturing under each step. Peering toward the direction of the sound was futile in the pitch of night. She wanted to nudge her mother but was too terrified to do so.

She couldn't rotate her clenched neck. Her throat was constricted—She couldn't swallow let alone cry out in fear.

The entity was so close that she could hear its breathing—a cavernous, labored gasping. Its gait had an unusual quality; it was unmetered. Then it began to reveal itself. She watched tree limbs move from their place. Their leafless branches twisted up then rocked from one side to the other. Floating through the moonless backdrop, this ghostly tree drew itself toward the Yearling. She seized frantically against her mother.

The other does were alerted to the presence, and they cowered together unprotected in the brush where they found repose. They grunted and pointed their snouts skyward like a nest of hungry fledglings. And when they couldn't find danger's scent, they flattened their ears to their heads and tucked their snouts down to conceal their glaring white throats. They kept still like a scattering of tawny-breasted stones.

At last, the entity broke through the barricade of pines just behind the bower. It stood behind them, a black shape before the sightless, soundless forest. The Yearling shivered in its presence, and she leaned into the Elder Doe. She curled up to make herself smaller hoping to disappear aside her mother's flank. There wasn't time to flee. No defense. No lights on in the Cape Cod. The Old Man's phone call had ended. He was now in a heavy sleep and plagued by nightmares.

The intruder rasped, and the voice of the owl sent up a warning.

The Elder Doe raised herself up to square off with the intruder. The others kept still as they watched. The intruder's rasping accelerated, the air sweeping through a mucous-lined windpipe. The does saw a shape being lowered within its silhouette. It skimmed the soil as the intruder drew close. To the doe clan in the dark, it looked long and thin, like a weapon. *A man with a gun!* a few does murmured.

No sooner than the Elder Doe had stood had her gaze shifted and lightened, her flicking tail slowing to a swish. She crept closer to the shadow, a faint gleam banding her eye. Clouds were beginning to break; the moon was lighting the woods. The Yearling let loose a tiny welp still curled tightly on the matting of brush. The Elder Doe turned to softly scold her.

A breeze picked up reeling the hardwood leaves that mimicked a babbling brook. Cloud cover parted to reveal an enormous moon almost as bright as the sun. The forest was bathed in a pearlescent sheen revealing the intruder.

What stood before them was a being of imposing stature yet neither a beast nor a menace. It was his bad front leg with which he struggled, out of keeping with the general shape and movement of the rest of his body. His nontypical antlers were draped in lush velvet. Each of the fourteen tips leaped in all directions, a flaming crown. His coat glimmered, moonshine coaxing out its red undertones causing it to glisten with the luster of wet blood. The light came as if from another world—neon, electric—giving a radioactive glow to the woodland. It presented the intruder as wraithlike.

*Beloved*, the Elder Doe whispered. *Where have you been?*

Backward in time, two autumns past. A memory still echoed. Into morning's cantaloupe light the Elder Doe sang out, *Awake, north wind. Come south. Blow on my garden so the spices may flow out.*

October. The time of the breeding rut was at hand again, yet it'd been many autumns without a visiting buck. Dwindling opportunities to breathe life into the herd had become a dour reality. The does spread out beneath the apple tree unaffected by the sour odor of fallen apples, fruit that was caving in on itself and deteriorating into mush.

Life on the acreage was well insulated. It gave the illusion of timelessness. However, the does never allowed themselves to be seduced by this illusion. Old does had wandered off to die unbothered; mortality was simply a part of life. But trouble was stirring. It had been for a few years now. The doe clan sensed this. They smelled it as it blew from the north. It smelled of decay.

The community had evolved to view deer as competitors in survival. As the climate shifted, crops failed and storms battered the Bluestone Woodland. Residents took it upon themselves to thin herds to spare yields. But none hated deer more than the Man with the Crooked Finger. Such loathing was as mysterious as his deformed pointer finger.

Nevertheless, it was simple for him to convince the community that the whitetail population was a conglomerate of unclean, dangerous beasts. Most didn't think further than the tips of their noses, so none batted an eye at the slaughtering. And as none would eat what they considered pestilent meat, the piles of kill blackened, fizzling with flies.

There were no traces of living deer on the breeze. Those bucks who had once resided in nearby ravines and meadows had vanished. The does had chosen to remain on the Old Man's land simply because it was the land their ancestors had promised them. The hardwood fortress atop the grade provided safety, yet the question left unspoken was always *For how much longer*? They were stuck there anticipating their fate—to die and leave no trace, to return to earth like the dropped fruit strewn about them, unloosening their rotting to the wind.

It was during that time there had come an unseasonably warm afternoon for mid-October. The Old Man's garden was still crammed with summer squash. On this particular day, he sat from his kitchen glued to binoculars. He watched as a falcon bobbed and lunged around the vines hunting chipmunks that burrowed in his beds. Birds were holy to the Old Man—they held court in a divine echelon high above the dying earth. This was the first falcon on his land as he could recall. He absorbed every detail: its milky breast that graduated to a stippled black, its ombre head coloring that had an uncanny shape. It reminded him of an executioner's mask.

Squealing from its shelter, a creature appeared from under the parasoled gourd canopy. The falcon held the writhing thing in its beak as it tried to free itself. It was not a chipmunk but rather a fat little cottontail. The pitch of its screeching climbed as the falcon pinned it below, its squirming body once again concealed. Finally, the rabbit ceased to pip. The bird had lowered its beak toward its meal and severed its spine. Rising with it grasped tightly, the falcon winged upward and disappeared into the tree line. All the while, the does looked on chewing and swatting from the apple wasteland.

Hours passed as the sun burned its way across the turquoise sky. The falcon returned. It perched on a pine branch and began squawking pointedly at the does. They noticed, but they quickly became disinterested and returned to their lazing, all except the Elder Doe, whose attention was fixed on the unusual sight.

Sputtering another sequence, the falcon spread its voluminous wings creating a *V* shape from tip to tip. It held its wings in this position for some time as if it were in an act of oblation. Then it began to beat with fury about the air each flap resounding in a series of thumps. The Elder Doe approached, falcon eyes searing into her own.

The pounding wings began to knock loose a number of feathers. They swiveled to the floor below pirouetting like snowflakes in alabaster and mahogany. Time slowed. The downy shower played about the doe's greying snout. She snorted while feathers were collecting at her feet, forming into a fan shape. This was her gift, a flabellum born of falcon wings.

When the final feather touched the earth, an explosion of movement caused leaves and brush to quiver. A sound of stampeding rushed toward the Elder Doe, her ears pressed against her head and her limbs poised to fly.

The doe clan threw up their heads. The Elder Doe retreated toward the apple tree but stumbled on her way. She turned back, tail held high, and glanced at the emerging force racing through the wooded edge.

A towering creature barged in, his asymmetrical antlers a coronet atop his skull. Much like the Elder Doe, his snout was also ashen-white. Brawny and wide set, his body was strapping from the haunches to the nape. His breath was quick. The speed and power of his arrival caused the feather formation below to mushroom up in a reverse shower. It clothed the Elder Doe in plumage—She was a bird but for a moment. Overhead, the falcon took its leave and faded into the forest once more.

The Buck's sprint abated into a trot, and he surveyed the Old Man's estate. Another house of man, and yet it didn't trouble him. Once his breath had steadied and his nostrils had grown lax, he made his way to the Elder Doe. His was not the body language of a stranger idling in an unfamiliar place but rather that of an individual busting onto the scene filled with resolve. He behaved as one with a fully formed objective.

The other does had risen from their resting spots in anticipation of his first move. Some of them snorted alluringly to the Buck, while others scrutinized him. It would have been customary for the Buck to familiarize himself with all the females of a clan, but he approached only the Elder Doe. He grunted and moved around to her backside, sniffing behind her upraised tail. It was there that she emitted the aroma of her body in heat. The brashness of the gesture caused some of the does to pace. The dance of the rut had become foreign after so many absent seasons.

The Buck needed go no farther. He knew with certainty that this was the singular odor that had guided him across the land, whisked off falcon wings. And while the Elder Doe could have been disturbed by his assertive display, her insight allowed her to plumb his character. He was neither cavalier nor threatening. She was drawn to him—to his odor. He was as old as she and as distinguished; he too had quiet wisdom. His eyes were dark pools she let herself slip into, and in them, she saw a point of light growing outward. It blossomed like tansy flowers—all of him in fact smelled of tansy.

The other does had encircled the Buck under the apple tree. They too wanted to cooly draw in his essence, to ascertain as much critical information as possible. Each step he took perfumed the grass with the glands beneath his hooves. The rosette of his flared tarsals, which stained the back of his legs dark-brown, wafted a fine cologne of urine and pheromones and sebaceous oil. Blood rushed hot through doe veins.

From the small kitchen yards away, the Old Man sat riveted. He thought to capture the vignette with scuffing and deliberate brushstrokes—a doe, a buck, and a falcon in the apple tree. But something specific stirred his passion. The Buck's antlers, as unpredictable and curving as the old apple tree's branches, was arousing in him new possibilities for his canvas.

It never crossed his mind, however, what kind of danger it would also arouse.

The Yearling's eyes widened. The two darksome medallions reflected the Buck as he hobbled forward on injured leg. It had been two years since he had been shot, and the limb had never healed. He kept it hoisted upward when not hobbling on it, his once stately gait reduced to a stagger. There was no time to waste in fear, so the Elder Doe approached to sniff about him. Once she was sure it was him, she buried her muzzle into his coat to caress the length of his beautiful neck. Over her shoulder, he eyed the Yearling whilst tilting his head. It was unclear whether it was an evaluation or a greeting, but nevertheless, it appeared amiable enough. The Yearling nodded back, her taut neck muscles causing her head to tremble.

Bending his neck down, the Buck latched onto something. Employing an easy thrust, he tossed it toward the Yearling. It hit the ground with a thud and bounced. She looked at the round thing, its waxen peel striped with a glimmer of moonlight and dirt adhered to smears of saliva. It was a small, ruby-gold apple. The Buck gestured with his snout, which quickened his haggard breathing. The Yearling froze. She referred to her mother, who in return gave her reassurance.

The Yearling wavered only momentarily before sinking her teeth into the firm fruit. It surprised her; it was silky against the spongy flesh of her mouth. The season was still early for apples, but this particular fruit had a honeyed tartness. She chomped it down to a pulp and swallowed it while her mother and the strange visitor stood side by side keeping watch. The aftertaste ripened on her palette like a mouthful of rain-soaked rosebuds giving way to bitterness.

The Buck pulled himself past the other does, now recovering from the initial shock of it all. Through the bower, the Buck's essence glossed the brush and grasses along his path. It was no longer the musk of a once-virile being but a redolence twisted with fear and sickness. Where had he been all this time? What news did he bring from the surrounding woods? The moment of quiet reunion pounded with the soundless carillon of warning. One doe with eyes glimmering asked, *And what of the shooter?*

Before the Yearling was born, at the peak of the deer vanishings, it was rumored that herds had begun migrating across the great river to the North Territory, a land of considerable elevation untouched by humankind. To reach it required a difficult trek up a life-threatening ascent. Yet it was to be between a rock and a hard place. Those deer who remained in the Bluestone Woodland were being obliterated. The Man with the Crooked Finger and his lackeys took the feat upon themselves. It was the advent of the Thin the Herd movement; countless deer were shot, piled, and discarded along old logging roads. In a land where deer had outnumbered men, the woodland had become eerily void of them.

Bucks had learned that living close to men came with a season of killing, when hunters set out to harvest deer for food and trophies. It was an ancient ceremony that occurred during the breeding rut when bucks had to remain vigilant while heeding their reproductive urges. Now, however, the killing was accelerating regardless of season. A creek that had once been a watering spot for many deer had been reduced to a trickle. Upstream, the area had become littered with bloated deer carcasses that had dammed the flow.

The grey-faced Buck had decided to risk the journey north, though he wasn't certain of the route. Fortifying himself as best he could, he foraged for food rich in fat and protein. He needed to keep himself sustained if the trek forward offered limited feeding opportunities yet required brute physical exertion. His velvet still clung in tatters. Either it was his age or the tumultuous times, but he seemed to shed it later and later each year. He paused underneath a white oak to rub loose the leathery remains from his rack and then nosed about the generous cache of acorns the oak had spilled.

The forest shade was skewered by spears of nacreous sunlight puncturing tendril upon tendril of fern. The Buck worked diligently, his summer coat a titian blush in the haze of afternoon. He ground his teeth about a few acorns, sometimes loosening the caps, but mostly ingesting them whole. He gave his jaw a rest, pausing to scratch off more lashes of velvet.

In the midst of his efforts, the Buck hadn't noticed the figure who'd drawn near floating along the forest floor with the stealth of a shadow. From a clump of wild grasses, the Man with the Crooked Finger had positioned himself upwind of the Buck. He watched the deer with a sharp eye that he could dispatch as an evil spirit at his target. He gripped a rifle he'd carefully swung loose from its strap. He mounted it against his hardened shoulder to take aim, to fire.

The Man with the Crooked Finger, a sharpshooter, had a gift for hitting the prey that found themselves in his scope. He called this power the evil eye. However, the storm-laden summer days were now at the highest point of humidity, and the rifle's wood stock had soaked up the wetness. The result was a firearm that was no longer accurately sighted in. And when he squeezed the trigger with his hooked right finger, the shot missed the Buck by inches. It wounded the oak tree instead, wood splintering about the air in a sawdust shower.

With that, the Buck was off at high speed through the woods. He barreled through thick patches of undergrowth and hurdled over downed trees. The light from above was intermittent, and the landscape all about him became indecipherable. He passed through dim glades only to be blinded by the solar flares of October sun that plunged through cracks in treetops.

The Man with the Crooked Finger fired again. The shot embedded itself in a heap of underbrush. The Buck disappeared over the ridge line, his unusual antlers lowering beneath the horizon. The angry shooter roared, but the sound refused to ring. All of nature worked against him, and his voice was swallowed by greenery. He paused in the silence, his ears burning, the bluestone underfoot splintering.

The Man, like the Buck, traveled the Bluestone Woodland as swiftly as the dead. Indeed, a large part of him had died. He couldn't recall that life or why he hated deer. His memories played as silhouettes against a wall that stood in a place he feared, where he dared not tread. It was the origin of his pain and his anger. It loomed high over his house atop a hill, a dilapidated shanty tucked into the tree line.

Each time he killed, he tranquilized his growing rage for a while, but no kill was ever enough. The sleeping devil inside him soon awoke starving for blood. It drove him to acts of inconceivable cruelty. *Kill, beloved. Kill*, it cooed.

Once he'd found a fawn bedded in a briar while its mother went out to feed. Its helplessness triggered something vulnerable in him. He imagined putting his steel-toed boot on its head and neck to crush its spine—and so he did. He wiped the killing boot clean. It pierced him with an agonizing euphoria that lasted the drive home, where he sat for a quiet supper before his hunched wife.

He was darkly dynamic, and his strength grew each day. He was a storm swirling and twisting outward and drawing in anything in sight. Some people had this power by birthright or circumstance, where their trauma and pain were so tremendous that it pulled all others into the center of their personal hell—Such a hell was a lonely home.

This was the way and the magick of the Man with the Crooked Finger. He was no ordinary man. He was obsessed with pain and devoid of compassion. Once his evil eye had latched onto an object, it would be his in the end.

Even after all this time, the Buck didn't dare utter the name of the Man with the Crooked Finger. He had shared little of his life during the previous two years, how he had been a ghost passing through the gloom. Danger was overwhelming every corner of the woodland. Humans had gone mad. They had joined the Man with the Crooked Finger in his blood crusade.

The Buck told them that he had spent much of his absence healing from the gunshot wound, enduring bouts of infection and periods of unconsciousness. Little by little, he'd regained some strength and began scouting the many paths that wove about the woodland. He didn't move well, so he'd kept his search by night. The land was littered with carcasses, weeds growing through pelvises, hair clinging to carrion mounds that resembled sprouting cheatgrass. There were no more deer.

Soon, the Man with the Crooked Finger would return with his sycophants in tow and bring destruction. The Buck would use what breath he had left to lead the doe clan to a higher elevation. It was certain to be risky, yet no other options remained at this late hour. They'd migrate across the river, mud-brown and raging from storm after storm, and climb north. The waterway's barrier still held men at bay but not for long. He'd seen the camps of men on its shores, and the infiltration was beginning to show—cans and trash buoyed upon the river's whitecaps.

Another warning came from the distant owl.

With a turn of his neck, the Buck faced north holding his snout high, his antlers scraping low-hanging branches. His presence endangered them all and especially the white-faced Yearling whom he'd protect at all costs. He feared the Man was drawing near with crooked finger trembling on a trigger. At the next full moon, they were to go north, deep inside the trees near the trench where winter runoff made a pool. There, the Buck would be waiting.

He signaled his departure with a gesture of the head and limped back into the recesses. The breeze shifted directions, and the blazing moon, having traveled a short distance, was again shrouded. The Elder Doe returned to her bed aside the Yearling still watching about the darkness.

The Yearling spotted his antlers in a clearing of timber and saw him pause to turn back and regard her. He stayed there for some time, and she felt comforted by his protective silhouette. His image appeared fixed in the near distance. Perhaps tonight, sleep would find her more easily. The visit was obvious. She didn't even have to ask her mother who he was. Maybe it was the apple soothing her belly or the subduing release of adrenaline, but she grew drowsy.

The lone owl again sounded from the depths, now a lullaby. Her father's watchful eye surely would guard her soul while she slept—would surely guard her from the strange sound that at times had haunted the midnight hours. At last, the Yearling was overcome by an irresistible sleep. She drifted away, her last vision being the outline of her father's antlers in the trees.

After escaping the barrel of the Man with the Crooked Finger's gun, the Buck hurled himself down an uncertain path flying through unknown country. Hooves slipped on shale as he tried to career up a rocky slope. The incline crescendoed into a flurry of birch. Fear overcame him when breaking through the white-trunked grove; a community of houses splattered the land. He dropped down a ravine and followed a ditch until he arrived at a field of sweet corn.

He positioned himself near the center of the spread. A high black cloud hovered in the distance. Sitting just outside the tree line, a farmhouse with a mud yard caused the Buck to fret. Inside farmhouses lived men, and that meant the risk of getting shot at again. He knew neither where he was nor in which direction he should go.

A pounding suddenly percussed all about him. He cowered about the soil; a snaking breeze rattled the husks as it slipped between rows of corn. Poised atop a weathered post was a flecked-breast falcon. It flapped its wings steadily as if to stoke an invisible flame. As it fanned, the clouds rose and swelled above like incense. It then stopped and stared at the Buck with citrine eyes. Rotating its head along an impressive circumference, the bird surveyed the field. A crack of thunder resounded from the horizon, and the falcon chirped in response.

Edging closer to the field, the high black anvil flashed with lightning. The green blades of corn deepened to blue. The falcon dove down their lengths to the clay below landing in front of the Buck. It once again flapped furiously stirring the hothouse atmosphere. Through its fluttering, a pungent odor blew about the Buck's snout; it was the musk of a doe in estrus. It caused his blood to rush and roar like a river in his ears. He entered an ecstatic trance divorced from his senses.

The falcon was Polaris. Rising into the air, it released a final sequence of calls. It spread its wings against the backdrop of the storm and set course. Beguiled, the Buck followed full tilt, setting a blue-green tidal wave of corn sheaths beneath the black sky.

The route was seemingly predestined. The falcon swept the breeze as the two creatures coasted from terrain to terrain; they raced through meadow and flew over ridge. And before long, they were once more in the protection of forest. The course was long and drawn out, but it guaranteed the Buck safe passage. He was unaware of the destination, but the indescribable odor pulled him along. It whispered to him from falcon wings.

Now in the depths of the woodland, the falcon flew behind a grouping of pine. The Buck slowed, and then stood idle. He scanned all about. He tilted his head up to sniff. He looked toward the clearings, where the sky gleamed with the cinnabar of dusk. The bird didn't circle back—perhaps it wouldn't return. He felt foolish for having blindly followed it to this bit of unfamiliar forest. He was at an impasse.

Then came a surge of the sensuous odor. He breathed it in, tasted it in its potency. It seemed to radiate from some undergrowth. When he went to nuzzle about it, he discovered therein an apple spotless and ripe. He took it into his mouth, the flavor savory and bittersweet like molasses. Nectar dripped down his large neck. He devoured the whole of it, but it didn't satisfy.

The scent brushed along his flank. His eyes followed its course as it rustled the greenery upon its passing. The apple tree peeked through the grouping of firs. All at once, it was as if the sky had opened and flooded everything below like the black cloud over the cornfield that sopped the red earth. But this was a shower of plumage. And with that, he charged through the trees into a flurry of feathers.

There he beheld the does on the Old Man's field, the Elder Doe before him, the source of the erotic fragrance. They all joined beneath the cragged apple tree, which had formed as a chuppah in the center of the acreage. The tree, crux of the woodland, was a place of high power. It was the mother of the forest, and the only sacred object that the Old Man hadn't collected himself.

Long before the Buck had arrived on the acreage two years earlier, the Old Man had bedecked his home with holy objects. The most prized were on a rosewood coffee table pushed against the living room wall. There, he placed his paintings and two religious cards, one of which was a gilded icon of Our Lady of Perpetual Help. She held the Infant King flanked by two angels: Gabriel bearing the cross and Michael carrying the wormwood-doused sponge and spear. The other was an image of the Christ Child, his crucified hands raised and bleeding onto the white lilies thrust at his feet.

The Old Man had an amalgamated system of beliefs. He had been raised Catholic, and though that had had a profound effect on the way he viewed the spiritual realm, he also borrowed from many other theological and cultural branches. As a doctor, *curanderismo* and shamanism resonated with him. Even quantum physics spoke to his existential theories. If energy was neither created nor destroyed, it was certainly repurposed. Thus, reincarnation weighed heavily on his mind. All one had to do was look at the precipitation system to understand such a process. And if Christ, the Holy Spirit, and God were all one and separate beings, he was certain the wave and the particle model could help explain such a conundrum.

In old age, he often meditated on the notion of the communion of saints, something he had learned in catechism class. The dead and the living were not separate but were united in one spiritual body aiding and praying for one another via the divine presence. It was something he and Fay had discussed. It helped his grief to believe that Fay was not gone—that they were somehow still together. Nothing died, only transitioned—like people moving from one unit to another in the same apartment complex. Or maybe it was like dying and becoming the apartment building in which everyone lived.

The Old Man took his medicine and brushed his teeth. He was lost in thought. Some things have no theological explanation. Take the Man with the Crooked Finger for example. It was hard to understand how someone so contrary to himself in belief and principle could also be included in a divine, universal body. Or how the community had followed such a man, who had aided them in liberating themselves of critical thinking. They hadn't always been that way. Aligning with the Man with the Crooked Finger had allowed them to become the worst versions of themselves. He tried to reconsider without judgment—Taoism says at any given moment, everyone is doing the best they can. It was tough medicine to swallow.

The phone rang. He staggered down the hall to the living room. "Hello? … My word yes, it's been years. How can I help you at this hour, Crane?" He used his toes to straighten a bunched Turkish rug flattening it like setting a broken bone. "I'm sorry, what? He did what? … They burned it?" He traveled quickly to the window catching his own reflection.

"When did you hear this? … Yesterday? … Did you inform the sheriff?"

He went to his desk and rested his body against it. "Did nothing? He did nothing? … My God! He *thanked* him?" He slapped a palm flat on the desktop and again faced the window. His left arm began to ache.

"Protecting the community from danger? Absolute insanity. It's murder!"

He tucked the receiver into the crook of his neck. His idle mouth hung open like a ventriloquist's doll. The voice on the other end of the line was audible in the small living room: "Just be careful. They're targeting anything deemed dangerous."

"Dangerous? What on earth is happening? No words … No, I'm not okay." His tongue searched for the right vowel shape. "*Ahhh …*

I'm in shock. I … I have to go now … Yes … More soon … Good-night, Crane."

As soon as the phone was out of his hand, the Old Man was back to his reflection—a white effigy in a black square. The Bluestone Woodland had become a madman's paradise, and it brought news of murder, a rationalized murder. The killing was out of control, and it was cause for commendation no less.

He inched toward his room with shuffling feet, his joints swollen with arthritis. His head throbbed. He crawled into bed without undressing. He shut out the light to drift into a vacant sleep. He couldn't even spare one word for Fay's portrait on the nightstand.

While the Old Man slept, the Buck, at last having met his daughter, took his leave from the acreage. The Buck—symbol of Bluestone Woodland brutality and the prelude to danger.

All night, the Old Man had such nightmares that were underscored by the call of a solitary owl. He dreamed that the devil that dwelled inside the Man with the Crooked Finger visited his window. It proclaimed, *I grow strong like the cuckoo in the robin's nest!* It danced among the burning marigolds, its footwork extinguishing their beauty. It sung a simple song while scraping a fiddle:

> *Soon, old man, you too will rest*
> *On the top of a fiery nest.*
> *Soon, old man, you too will see*
> *What the inside of an oven shall bring.*

**T**he devil had gone. Something struck the Old Man's head. And again. A rain of apples. A light grew. Red dawn. A hand held a broken robin's egg. They were in the field under the apple tree. The field was bursting with irises, shades of purple shooting through the sod. He began to cut some for Fay.

Fay grabbed his hand. He could not see his face. Fay commanded, "Wake up! Put the coffee on. The devil's in the woods!"

The Old Man's room was warm and quiet as he awoke; beams coming through the window cast slanting light against the dresser like the side of a sandstone pyramid. He rolled himself free from a twist of brutally crisp linens still smelling of outdoor line drying.

He went through the dream's symbols like a bullet-point list. "Eggs, apples—round things, life, eternity, fertility. The devil's in the woods? Jesus Christ." He crossed himself, which he immediately found strange as he hadn't done it in years. "But purple irises coming out of the soil? *Hmmm*."

He recalled the Mesopotamian irises he'd seen in the Middle East. They were deep lavender, the naturalized flowers of some old graveyards.

"Something bad is coming."

While the Old Man was dissecting his dreams, the Yearling was out in her bed of flat-laid grass doing the same. Had it all been a dream? Mere seconds it seemed had passed, but it was dawn. The sun drenched everything. She had awoken refreshed. She looked toward the clearing. The figure of her father still remained, yet in daylight, it was the limbs of a dead hardwood. She studied it a moment and couldn't be sure. It was truth. He had passed through the night as a ghost.

She took leave of the bower and joined the herd beneath the apple tree. The Elder Doe nudged her playfully. The others had been up and moving since before dawn while the young one slept.

However, none of it was a dream. The Buck had returned, and though there should have been hope emanating from the doe clan, their morning caucus beneath the apple tree was solemn. The many grazing faces with worrisome eyes peered at the tree line. A crow laughed from the forest, and the does flinched.

They'd be departing soon, when the moon was at its ripest. What of the Old Man? The Yearling could sense the danger surging around him. She turned toward the Cape Cod especially anemic in cone-flower season. Inside, he was standing in the living room making knot-shaped motions as he rubbed his face and eyes. He moved to massaging the back of his oak-stump neck with liver-spotted hands.

Behind her, the other does had made their way toward the tree line. The sun was beginning to beat down on them. Its heat caused a sleeping jealousy they carried to grow restless. Seeing the Buck again had awakened this feeling that had dwelled in them for nearly two years. In the shade of the pines, they sat with a resentment they'd not felt since the courtship of the Buck and the Elder Doe.

Two years had fallen through time and space like a broken-winged bird. Thus, it seemed only yesterday that the Buck had tended to the Elder Doe. Alone, they browsed for nourishment in the wooded depths. Often, the grazing turned into a lusty sort of play. They used her odor to guide their desires, and together, they would wait until her estrous cycle peaked. At night, the Buck chose to go farther into the woods to sleep. It was distracting for him to sprawl near the herd as the other does had entered heat and the fragrance disturbed his rest. Tossing about the brush, he groaned and moved farther, finally slumping in a spot where all he could smell was pine sap and dirt.

Bucks tended to breed with many does in a clan, but this male chose to pursue the Elder Doe exclusively. After all, she was the matriarch of the herd. Nonetheless, there were does among them who felt a longing, a yearning for fawns of their own, for a love of their own. Desire was an open door.

In the shade of the imposing pines, a soft murmuring began to sound in the does' ears. Jealousy spoke in shadows and invited itself to enter them. It didn't so much as wholly overtake them; it merely weakened them. It gave a chill of ice in the brain as it waited for the most opportune moment to break their goodwill and set fire to their reason.

Then on the night of the full moon, the Elder Doe's fertility reached its pinnacle. She would be ready to receive the Buck. As the last of the day slipped beneath the horizon, the Buck made his way to his bedding area.

Upon a well-worn rocker, the Old Man watched as the Buck turned his head and paused at the field's edge. The orb of the moon was lifting between his wide-set antlers framing itself at the center of all fourteen tips. It magnified the moon's radiance and distilled the light into a single powerful point. It was as if it had ignited the Old Man's face in a mystical flame.

For a moment, the Old Man shaded his eyes that were blinded by the intensity. He then stood from the chair in a daze unaware of the slowing rocker smacking the back of his legs. The Buck was a holy vision like that of the hart-hunting St. Hubertus. The Old Man was transfixed. "My God," he whispered as he hid his face from the light.

Shaken by the vision, he went about the Cape Cod with a joint in his mouth. He searched through closets wrestling like a gladiator with a Herculean row of outerwear. He threw clothes and ties out of dressers drawers until they hung like sheets of drying pasta. At last, slipped underneath the bureau in the spare room, he found the cigar box he used as a childhood time capsule. Nestled inside was a bundle wrapped in a pristine handkerchief. He opened it revealing a deer figurine, a carving he'd fashioned as a boy scout. He held the figurine with reverence. The moment had an air of fate about it. It was indescribable. He felt that the arrival of the Elder Doe's suitor signaled a change for the deer of the Bluestone Woodland. This creature was a divine being in the guise of a whitetail buck.

His joint went dark; a match scrape birthed a ceremonial wisp of sulfuric incense. He inhaled deeply hoping the high would induce more psychic visions. Yet it only put him to sleep.

Early the next morning, the Old Man came rushing out of the Cape Cod with two overflowing bags of summer squash. He doubled back for a few that had fallen, and he loaded the bounty into the sedan. The October sun was barely lighting the sky when he got into his car. He started the sleepy motor. He sat idling as the combusting gasoline and pistons heated the engine. His friend, the Woman, would be awake by then, and her husband, the Man with the Crooked Finger, would be off to work. How long since they'd seen an old buck in the Bluestone Woodland? He could hardly wait to tell her.

The does were already up and moving about to keep warm as he drove past. Each morning had become more and more cool. Before they knew it, the killing freeze would be upon them. The Elder Doe had separated herself from the herd anticipating the arrival of her suitor. They had but a slender opportunity to breed. Soon, she'd regress and have to wait for the estrous cycle to begin anew. In her old age, she wasn't confident in her ability to become pregnant or to rely on another window of opportunity. This could well be the last door closing.

An hour went by, and the Buck had yet to come for her. Over the field, the Elder Doe watched the shape of the falcon soar. It crossed the ice-white sun forcing her to avert her gaze. At the last moment, she caught a glimpse of it as it took a steep dive into the treetops. The light spread about the field, but its warmth never manifested. A hush fell over the acreage.

Then from out of the north a shot rang out, its echo tearing in all directions. The does, all lowered in their grazing, snapped their heads up. The blast reverberated in their chests and rattled the tips of nerves bringing the pain of sympathetic injury. The Elder Doe darted toward the tree line only to turn back to petition her sisters to join her in seeking the Buck. His life was in peril.

But the other does refused to go. To meddle in the situation could prove fatal. It was more than self-preservation, however. The envy they carried—that murmuring devil—had set fire to their insides. Smoke was rising in their brains and choking out all rationale. New, barbarous thoughts began to form. The Buck wasn't their suitor. He wanted only the Elder Doe. Why should they care? He was a stranger. There'd never been danger on the Old Man's land until he came. They cursed the Elder Doe for luring him to the acreage. They spoke in new tongues, their limbs and heads shaking.

The scent of blood spilling on the forest floor was suddenly carried on the breeze. The Elder Doe tried reasoning with them emphasizing the threat at hand. Intruders were breaching the property, and they were sitting targets. Yet the does were blinded by devil hands.

*Why should we stain our coats with the blood of an outsider? Let him die!* they growled through clenched jaws and grinding teeth. Cruelty had grabbed even the gentlest of creatures in the Bluestone Woodland by the scruff of the neck.

The Elder Doe turned her back to the clan and dashed into the tree line. Sunlight was beginning to seep into the gaps between trees. The path before her brightened but only as much as the canopy permitted. She had no time to think of danger. The wildwood scene bled together about her peripheral sightline, a noisy, multihued roundabout. And yet the forest remained silent, fixed—a hopeful but also a desolate sign.

She heard a stirring ahead as she vaulted over a fallen tree. By the stream, a pool of blood came into view. It trickled through the drab underbrush. The Buck lay sideways shot through the right shoulder. He was struggling to breathe as he thrashed about the ground.

The breeze shifted direction and was blowing north. All she smelled was the hollow whence she had come. Caution was paramount. She crouched under a tangle of deadwood and listened with scrutinizing ears to make certain it was safe enough to draw near the Buck.

Far-off crow laughter punctuated the forest … and then nothing more. With several glances to either side of the clearing, the Elder Doe took her chance and sided up to the Buck. She bent down to her beloved and nuzzled him. His intent to return such tenderness was cut short by breath-stopping pain.

Her instinct was to clean the wound. It was just beneath the coat—a weeping lover's knot. She lapped the bullet hole. The Buck recoiled. Blood continued to pour from the wound, and the earth sopped it up like dry bread. Panic drove the Elder Doe's mind running it ragged with ideas. She searched for something constructive but was anchored in useless thoughts—how the Buck's blood tasted of iron and coated her mouth.

The Buck was immobile, and the Elder Doe refused to leave him to die alone. Danger crept along the service road with a rifle and a hacksaw, quick footed and crooked fingered. They could do nothing but lie together and wait. Soon, their combined blood would swell about them and pollute the nearby stream.

Overhead, a call to action sounded. It was the cry of the falcon. It spread its angel wings across the sun and looked to the earth. Its cigarette-cherry eyes blistered from its face. It carried with it a soul in migration from the land of man. There was no real death, only reassignment. A precious spirit swaddled in falcon feathers needed its next dwelling place. The tresses of fate had yet to be fully braided.

High sun then enveloped the Doe and Buck in healing warmth. A current, hot and damp, began to eddy about the Doe. It released her musk into the wet atmosphere. It deadened their pain and aroused their lust. For a moment, they abandoned fear of the impending shooter and obeyed their primal desire.

The Buck gathered all his strength and raised himself in a tremendous motion. The Doe stood about him readying herself to support his weight against her wide haunches. He staggered behind her rubbing alongside her flank to keep himself stable. At last, groaning, he threw himself on her hips and mounted her. He caped her back with blood as fine as mulberry silk. With a swift and powerful thrust, the Buck planted his seed in the Elder Doe. He then collapsed back to the ground gasping.

High above, the angel song spun in circles from out the falcon's beak. It dove toward the Elder Doe tucking its wings against its sides. She feared the bird would impale her, but at the last moment, it shifted course and flew directly across her. It fanned her coat with its torpedo-shaped body and rocketed back into the sky. The spiritual transaction was complete. New life stirred in the Elder Doe.

Now tree branches cracked. The Doe squinched down peeking about the undergrowth. The Buck's breathing had softened, but it still had an audible friction. It crackled like campfire. She tried to pacify him as she would a fawn. The woods rustled as if by a wind, but the air remained static. It was so quiet. All the forest concealed itself in the presence of such evil. Even the angel feared to sing.

The rifleman stampeded into the clearing, a crooked right finger about his nose as he blew a wad of snot free. The Elder Doe watched him approach the brush where they lay. By then, the forest was well lit and the scarlet glow of blood popped from beneath the undergrowth. He took a step closer and saw two deer cowering instead of one.

He locked glances with the Elder Doe. It was as if the earth's tilted spinning had stopped and they were staring at each other for an eternity. She studied his face. He smiled at her, a chipped incisor appearing beneath a thin lip. His black eyes were empty, like those of dead animals. And deeper still, she saw the thing hidden in him that covered his secrets. She knew it was the old devil feeding on his suffering and shame.

The Elder Doe wondered why creatures turned bad like apples from the same tree. Some rotted and fell while others desperately clung—to what? Perhaps to the inexpressible thing from which all life came, larger than anything and rooted in truth like a tree such that in storms of the soul, this thing like that very tree, jutted strong and pliant even as life bloomed and wilted and budded afresh all around it.

"Bet you never thought to see me," the Man with the Crooked Finger jeered. "Like a thief in the night."

Early that morning, he had driven a route that skimmed the back edge of the Old Man's acreage. It was a service road, long forgotten and overgrown with grass and brush. His intent was not to stalk the Buck. He was after the does. He wanted to send the Old Man a message. Harboring unclean animals would no longer be tolerated in the Bluestone Woodland. He figured the Old Man would stumble upon his dead does just as he had the she-coyote years earlier. It was high time the Old Man had a reckoning with his life. After all, his very existence put the Bluestone Woodland in danger.

In the subconscious of the Man with the Crooked Finger, the type of person the Old Man was had been wedded to the reason he hated deer. One of these things he actively repressed while the other he had pushed away into the shadows of memory. It was always bubbling up to the surface. He felt compelled to wipe it clean.

As he was driving south toward the woods that neighbored the Old Man's field, he glimpsed something in the trees. He grabbed his binoculars. It was a blessed sight, and he flashed a broken-toothed grin. Bedded down in the brush was the Buck that had slipped away only days earlier. This time, however, he wouldn't miss. Such a chance meeting was surely divine providence.

The Man had taken out his gun and steadied it against a rock. The Buck lifted his head and rose. It was already too late—the evil eye had latched onto his hide. The Man clenched his jaw in concentration and squeezed the trigger. The shot ripped through the woodland and hit the Buck in a kill zone. The Man watched the animal flee knowing once the adrenaline wore off, he'd drop. In the meantime, there was a well-used hacksaw he needed back in his truck—The kill may have been ordinary but such trophy antlers certainly weren't. They wouldn't be for keeping though. They would be for selling. He'd get top dollar too.

Shooting the Buck had set forth a cosmic chain reaction. The finger of God stirred the breeze. As the Buck bled out in the woods, so did the Man with the Crooked Finger's wife across the river. It was eye for an eye.

Yet now he was staring down at the Elder Doe. Her eyes had yet to avert his gaze. It made his skin crawl—he felt analyzed. "Don't stare." He lifted his rifle to his shoulder. "Last time you'll stare. Gonna shoot you right in the forehead. Then you ain't gonna have a head to see out of."

The creaky joint of the crooked finger was inaudible as he coaxed the trigger. The anticipation of killing excited him. It was the only form of arousal he didn't repress.

There came a sudden thudding by his feet. All the Man saw were two topaz eyes. The falcon, which had been below the brush, flew up in a wild flailing and took its talons to the Man's face. They hooked into his flesh and slashed across his eye. It let out a high-pitched bleating and climbed toward the sun.

The blood poured like syrup and occluded the Man with the Crooked Finger's vision. He slung his gun over his shoulder and cupped his left eye. He wiped his bloody hands on his canvas pants and began the dash back to his pickup. He bellowed like an injured animal, fighting tangles of deadwood as he scrambled. As soon as he had managed to clamber his way back to the pickup, he rigged a bandana across the eye tying it above the ear and tucking it under the opposite lobe. The engine revved, and he sped down the road in a duster.

A crimson handprint marked his driver's side door, but it was too late as the destroying angel had already passed over. It spread its falcon wings high above the acreage; its shadow streaked the apple tree. The wheel of fate spun. Sometimes, fortune favored the bold. Sometimes, favor fortuned the meek.

The Old Man sat at his desk with a strong cup of coffee. He deliberated whether to go to town. If he did, he'd be taking matters into his own hands. Of course, he'd leave Crane out of it. But what if an altercation arose with the Man with the Crooked Finger? He worried about his age and strength. As such, his conscience begged for reconsideration. Could he simply allow himself to be silent in the face of alleged murder? He shouted to the photo of Fay on the nightstand, "What should I do?"

Fay had been gone for years having succumbed to a motor neuron disease. Testing had at first proved inconclusive, but then one day, Fay couldn't lift a casserole out of the oven. Everything had all gone downhill from there. It was something the Old Man wished he could wipe away—Fay gasping for breath, unable to swallow, wasting. It shook the Old Man to his core. Though there had been nothing he could have done to save Fay, he felt such guilt as a physician and even more so shame as a partner unable to protect his beloved.

41

"I'm terribly afraid." He stared blankly down the short hallway that led to the bedroom. A box of hospice supplies was still under the bed. It was strange, but throwing it out felt like discarding another piece of Fay from his memory. "Honey, I wish you were still here."

He remembered the day he had met Fay on a blind date. Fay; an Irish descendant with a Gaelic name. Fay meant raven, and it suited him with his black, nearly blue hair. But it wasn't quite fitting to the Old Man as he equated ravens with Poe while Fay had a sunny disposition. Of an average height with a well-built frame, Fay was covered over with porcelain skin that gleamed under his dark hair. A black Irish they had called him. He had slivers for eyes—shark's eyes— with irises so dark they had married themselves to the pupils.

As the years passed, Fay and the Old Man grew together in love and companionship. When the Old Man finally retired, Fay lived a split existence spending weekends on the acreage and continuing his Monday-to-Friday schedule in the city. During that time, cataclysmic weather had devastated the nation. Global temperatures were at an all-time high. Hurricanes and coastal flooding had hammered the city until its downtown was two feet underwater. Fay endured as long as possible, but ultimately, he took an early retirement.

Once the two were together full time in the Bluestone Woodland, they received a good bit of resistance and more than enough snide comments. Community attitudes certainly changed with the coming decades, but it seemed they were regressing into superstition and a sort of puritanical intolerance.

When Fay died, there had been no funeral for him in the country graveyard, where most residents went to sleep in sugar maple caskets. It had been Fay's wish to be interred in a family plot in the city. And when the coasts rose, waters surged all around the cemetery where he rested.

When the Old Man called out to Fay from his desk, he wondered if his voice somehow reached the grave at the verge of swelling bay water.

After he became a widower, the Old Man considered leaving the Bluestone Woodland. But outside the secluded mountain community, global warming was in full effect. Seaside towns went underwater, fires in the West never stopped burning, and droughts in the South caused widespread devastation and famine. There were a record number of earthquakes, hurricanes, and tornados. Even in the Bluestone Woodland, the sugar maples migrated north for cooler climates. The Old Man could have followed suit but felt he was too old to start over. *I have every intention of dying in this house*, he thought, and the universe carefully listened.

"I ought to confront him, Fay. I owe it to him and to myself. I have to put a foot down." He rubbed his coffee mug white-thumbed. "But I'm putting myself in danger."

In a woodland teeming with whitetails, it didn't take much coercion for the Man with the Crooked Finger to turn the community against deer. It was a hometown campaign ripped from the pages of the Old Testament. Unclean animals were dangerous! An abomination to God! Crops destroyed and viruses spread! His Thin the Herd campaign meant just as it sounded; it called for the extermination of deer, and the community adopted it as dogma.

The Man with the Crooked Finger framed it as spiritual warfare, and he used his wiles to convince them that they were doing God's will. In truth, the Man wasn't religious at all; he just knew how to sell religion. Yet he was obsessed with God … Had a bone to pick with him. He kept his grudge with his maker buried in himself as he went about town pretending to be God's megaphone until Thin the Herd logos appeared everywhere. It became an emblem of protection for the community, like a *hamsa* or a cross, and it was slapped on every building, stapled on every lawn placard, and flown on every flagpole.

The Old Man had been double marked by sin. As his relationship with Fay had deemed him a degenerate, the community viewed his deer harboring as yet another sign of a fall from grace. But they didn't want to give up on him. Hate the sin but love the sinner. They sent him gentle yet persistent reminders. At first, cars pulled up only as far as his mailbox leaving chicken-scratch tirades. However, over the years, it became a stream of crank calls and leaflets bedecked with the slogan Thin the Herd and the graphic of a deer in crosshairs. They wondered when he'd turn from wickedness and purify his land.

The Old Man often wondered if God was as angry as these people believed. It was foolish to define God as one thing or the other because to the Old Man, as soon as you figured God out, God became something completely different. The community stood firm in its attachment to a vengeful God, but God was not purely angry or purely loving. God was nature just as nature was God. All things were bound in shades of grey. The Old Man wasn't sure what or who God was. That was just fine. He turned to the window and looked at the field and the trees. *Windy out.* It always surprised him how much give-and-take the tallest trees had as they swayed.

He stretched his arm out from a knotted shoulder and glanced at a canvas in the bookshelf—his painting of the buck, the doe, and the falcon in the apple tree. With a twist of the neck, he studied it. Though he was uncertain of the meaning of God, he was doubtless the divine had played a part in joining the Buck and the Elder Doe. The white-faced Yearling was the miraculous sum of their union— little Saint of the acreage. The Old Man still felt raw about the day he had painted that canvas. It had been nearly two years, but he remembered much—Never mind that he couldn't recall where he'd left his car keys only yesterday.

"Okay, Fay. To town I go."

It was once again on that hot October day that the Old Man had rolled up his sleeves to paint and grimaced. Upon his cuff was a spot of blood. He dashed back to the sink and worked a sponge into an extravagant lather to wipe and dab the spot. His friend, the Woman, had been in a terrible state. She didn't want anyone to know; she refused to go to the hospital. He had advised her weeks earlier, had even made a recommendation for discreet treatment. It was something they'd have to keep between them. Their well-being depended upon the ignorance of the Man with the Cooked Finger.

The Old Man wanted to lose himself in his work. His hands he scrubbed like a surgeon. He returned to his composition of the courtship of the buck and doe. Antlers had become a smaller duplicate of apple branches while the bodies of the doe and the buck mirrored one another. He traced the shape of the falcon in the tree with a wet brush tip.

In his abstract style, the bird had a primordial character like a petroglyph he'd seen in Utah as a youth. He could almost rub its incision in the rock wall and feel the desert sun radiating on the exposed strip of neck between his hairline and collar. *Thunderbird—bringer of rains, open the sky!* Not even the ancient ones could save humanity from itself. Now, the West with its serrated mountains burned. No doubt the wall and the petroglyph were damaged beyond recognition.

This petroglyph had chiseled itself into his subconscious. He'd sketched a similar image for a grave in the cemetery. It had been as a gift for his friend, the Woman, to honor her late grandmother Ava. Falcons had a special meaning for the Woman when she thought of her grandmother. Besides, Ava's grave plaque was woefully plain and in need of repair. An engraver transferred the Old Man's rendering onto her headstone, placing it above a line from Ava's favorite psalm, "I will lift mine eyes to the hills, from whence cometh my help." The Woman had yet to see the headstone, however, as her husband expressly forbade it. He was threatened by Ava's memory. Memories could be amulets just as much as they could be armor.

All the Old Man's renderings echoed the same thunderbird he'd seen as a youth. It gave him pause. He connected a line from petroglyph to canvas to gravestone via the living falcon in his apple tree. *Thunderbird—deliver us from evil!*

Voices reeled him back. He blinked and waggled his head to shake away the daydream of bygone times. Mozart's *The Magic Flute* was on full blast. It was the only recording of it he had, an English-language production from Covent Garden. He let the music inform his passes over the canvas as the final chorus rang out, *Thanks be given to you, Osiris! Thanks to you, Isis!*

*Isis and Osiris—now that was a love story*, he thought. He lifted one side of his mouth into a half-smile as he spoke aloud, "A bit incestuous but certainly committed!" A closed-mouth laugh forced the air out his blowhole nostrils.

He moved back around the canvas to reassess the apple branch where the falcon had rested when suddenly he jumped as the red brush leaped from his hand. A figure stood on the porch, snout and back sopped with blood. At first glance, he wondered if it might be a dog, but there were no dogs there. With five plump, hair-covered fingers pressed against his chest, he made his way to the door and opened it gripping the handle as if holding a shield. "What in God's good earth?"

It was the Elder Doe.

She didn't move while he scanned the field and tree line over the top of her head, nor did she flinch as he winced to see red on his shirt. "Paint," he whispered. He then doubled back to wipe his trembling hands and lowered the music as though turning down the volume would somehow help him see better.

Approaching the Elder Doe was crossing a threshold for the Old Man. He came nearer to her than he'd ever been to a wild animal. It set them both on edge; each was studying the other's body language. He observed her, and she remained still. He couldn't see a laceration, but he saw much blood. He drew closer, but she didn't recoil. Her behavior concerned him.

The Elder Doe smelled his fear and knew that by seeking out the Old Man's help, she'd breached the natural order of things. However, there was no time to fret about customs or conventions. She turned and leaped off the porch, and after so many steps, she turned and stared at him. A few reiterations of the pattern she thought ought to broadcast an obvious message. She needed him to follow her to the Buck.

Before long, the Old Man was tailing the Elder Doe deep into the woods fearful of what he might discover. He wondered if he had gone senile. Past the doe bower they went, and he hobbled down the path. He was anchored to one side with his physician's bag, which he had retrieved only moments earlier. The bag was heavy. He wondered if he had packed a brick in it.

At last through a split in the layers of underbrush, he saw blood and deer legs. The Buck was lying on his side kicking about the ground. The Old Man gasped as he lowered himself to the enormous deer. The Buck's eyes widened and flitted forward and back, but he was too weak to do much else. His wheezing worsened. It sounded wet.

"How could this have happened?"

The Old Man moved the Buck's body to get a look at the wound being cautious of his antlers. He braced himself as he did a quick examination clenching either free hand into the muck. He opened his fingers wide to comb through the Buck's coat, his flesh pasted with the mortar of clay and blood. He wiped his hands on his trousers and removed several items from his bag. He began to cleanse the wound and added a salve to the gash.

As he worked about the injury, he was unable to see or feel an exit point. The bullet had entered behind the right shoulder blade and was probably lodged near the lung and the vertebrae. The spine appeared intact as the Buck was able to move, but the Old Man feared the worst. *He needs an antibiotic,* he thought.

He bandaged the wound and packed up. He needed to get back to the Cape Cod for a jug and a pail. The Buck would require water soon, long before he would be able to stand. This was of course assuming he wouldn't die first. The Old Man stood, clutched his bag, and began to push homeward but turned to give the Elder Doe a glance from the shrub where she had concealed herself. He marched back to the Cape Cod lopsided with bag and arthritic knees.

The Elder Doe approached the Buck and sniffed the bandage. Blood stained it as if it were concealing crushed red fruit. She nudged him, and pain yielded a curling of his frame. She retracted and studied her beloved as he twisted in agony. Her gaze was fully on him, but her vision drifted into darkness. It started as a speck in her sightline and then dilated. It was that black gaze—All she saw was the Man with the Crooked Finger's eyes dead set on devouring them.

Early the next morning, the Old Man returned to administer a dose of penicillin. The Buck squirmed in fever. Hope was slim that he'd survive, but at least he had made it through the night. In the Old Man's imagination, the scavengers were already circling. It was a compulsive thought that he tried to clear from his mind. Thoughts were magnetic. He feared the imagery acted as some sort of cosmic homing device.

The Old Man caressed the Buck's coat. It was coarser than he had imagined; it tickled the grooves between his fingers as his hand moved along the stretch. It was surreal to be this close to such an imposing creature, a mystical being in the form of a whitetail. A tear fell down the Old Man's face. To see it had come to this, on his land, and at such an hour broke his spirit. He patted the Buck. "Sorry." The Buck listened; his eyes softened; they were fatigued, but they appeared empathetic. "They finally got you."

For some time, the Old Man stayed by the Buck's side keeping him company. He remained well through the changing light of afternoon. He administered one last injectable formulation for pain relief and started home. He saw the Elder Doe's two eyes like black-violet drupes peeking behind the viburnum. The autumnal flush was just barely percolating in their fading leaves. "Good evening, gal," the Old Man whispered.

Once he had gone, the Elder Doe came forth to tend to the Buck. For the rest of the afternoon and into twilight, she held vigil for him. Bedding next to him and caressing him, she watched suffering distort his face. His eyes rolled to the back of his head, and his tongue hung from his mouth with white paste caked at the corners. She was uncertain if he was aware of her presence. To soothe him, she sung lullabies all through the night. She guarded him into the dawn. She remained steadfast in her surveillance though she knew it was in vain. Should the Man with the Crooked Finger return with little warning, they'd be no match for his rifle.

Sprawling aside the Buck in temperate afternoon, she dozed off in spurts. Each time she awoke, panic overtook her. She envisioned the Man standing above them. She rose and walked about the brush shaking off her drowsiness. She looked at her beloved. At last, some solace. He no longer convulsed in pain. Something in her core shifted; it was indescribable, subtle, almost impossible to comprehend. Then she just knew.

By late afternoon on the second day, the Buck had pulled about some grass where he'd fallen. He was lucid and tried to stand. The Elder Doe cleared space for him, but he collapsed back to his sickbed. She dropped back down to him and nestled aside his panting flank. She licked his head and cleaned around his bandage. A black-billed cuckoo sang.

From inside the Cape Cod, the Old Man too heard the birdsong coming from the forest. He sat at his desk mulling things over, even praying. In the closet was a rifle, and out in the woods was a suffering animal. It wasn't something he wanted to do, but he had serious concerns about the Buck's ability to pull through. And while he was the protector and preserver of his deer, he considered whether a merciful death wasn't also umbrellaed beneath his stewardship.

The cuckoo recapitulated. A breeze lilted about the lovers.

Maneuvering about tines of antler, the Elder Doe positioned herself facing the Buck. They looked into each other's eyes for some time. The forest was quiet.

Then the Buck said, *As an apple tree among the trees of the forest, so is my beloved among all. With great pleasure, I sit in her shadow, and her fruit was sweet to my taste.*

The Elder Doe replied, *The voice of my beloved! Behold, he came leaping over the mountains, bounding over the hills. My beloved is a stag. He is mine and I am his.*

The Buck smelled the change in the Elder Doe. Her odor had a new character. He let the sun sink before asking to be left alone saying he'd sleep better by himself and would heal more quickly. The Elder Doe hesitated, but he insisted; he assured her that he could flee if need be. She knew he could hardly stand, but she agreed.

She moved through the clearing to the wooded wall turning back one last time before fading into the forest. He watched the white of her tail drift through the trees like a lantern. He had memorized her face and wondered if his fawn would have it too. He shut his eyes.

The following morning, the Elder Doe sought for an apple to bring to the Buck. The doe clan watched as she approached. When confronted about their behavior, they denied any wrongdoing. They had no memory. Yet they turned their backs to her. They had grown bitter and distrustful of her.

The Elder Doe grasped an apple, mushy and sweet and easy eating for the Buck, then took leave of the doe clan. She sped away from the tree passing in front of the Cape Cod. She heard the Old Man speak from the kitchen through his wide-open window. He was airing out the living room just like he aired his grievances. Eggshell-brittle words were carefully strung together so as to not break; it was a vocal quality she'd never heard him use.

"He's been shot through the front right quadrant, been down for a few days now. Gave him an injectable NSAID and penicillin. He's suffering, and I'm torn as how to proceed."

The Old Man was multitasking. While he talked to the Woman, he sorted through a box of items he had collected during his travels. The filing box was labelled Finland/Peru/Utah.

"It was only a matter of time before he, *er*, someone did it. Really worried about my does."

He scowled; couldn't find whatever it was he needed. Then his eyebrows raised crimping folds of forehead skin into a closing *sensu* fan. He lifted a brown staff that had been tucked to the side. It was a carving.

"I think I have pentobarbital. I don't know though. I've never euthanized an animal. Somehow, maybe the rifle's quicker."

The Elder Doe heard the Old Man's voice some distance into the woods. She hurried along with jaws aching from overextending around the fruit. Spit foamed at the corners of her mouth. When she arrived, the fruit dropped falling to earth a final time.

"On a much welcome side note, you'll never guess what I found."

The Old Man was holding his replica of a neolithic artifact, the Finnish shaman's staff in the form of a serpent. The near two-foot dark-brown wand, uneven and simplistic, had a special meaning to him and had brought with it its own promise of the resurrection. It had a lore: for when such a shaman died, he was reborn as a serpent. It did not matter that it was a mere reproduction. Any object could be sacred and potent with magick given the intent of belief put behind it. The carving consoled him now in this moment of decision making. More than just easing the decision at hand, it soothed his feelings about his own inevitable mortality. He'd lived more years than he had left. At this moment, he saw himself as the Buck.

The sun began to set. The Old Man had long finished his call with the Woman. He put the serpent staff on his desk to give energy to the Buck. Though it pained him, he had sworn an oath as a physician, and it was a binding spell. He grabbed the medical bag over the rifle. He looked in double-checking that he had the vial of pentobarbital. "Forgive me. Not sure what I'm doing."

By the time he'd hobbled out to the spot where he'd left the Buck, the trees were mere black cutouts of themselves. Everything stood in front of the red screen of sunset. All motion in the twilight woodland was shadow puppetry.

As he approached the clearing, his bag dropped from his hand. The Elder Doe's eyes were once again glimmering from the safety of the viburnum, her coat yet tangled with bloodstain. All that was left of the Buck was an indentation of a body in the grass and an empty pail. His blood had long since been dried brown in the sun, and the Elder Doe's apple rested some feet behind it.

Breath was near visible in the cool night air. From far off came howling that punched through the red, papier-mâché sky. In front of the Old Man's bag and imprinted in the soil between him and the fallen apple was the broad paw print of a canine. Ghost-white, he looked at the Elder Doe and then past her—through her—toward the cold, hollow coyote den that still gouged the field's flank.

Aslam of the door announced the Old Man as he hurried toward his vehicle. If he lost momentum, he'd be unable to face the Man with the Crooked Finger. His car's faux leather seats melted like taffy in the sun. He turned around swearing and made his way back up the porch. He'd forgotten his keys. *Maybe now's a good time to get into a habit of locking doors. Oh hell. Can't teach an old dog new tricks.*

High summer had overcome the land. The heat was fierce in the mountain country, and the herd spent much time bedded down. The does were splayed out in their reposes swatting ears and tails against a barrage of black flies that covered them like a shroud of cracked peppercorns.

The Yearling couldn't stop thinking about her father. She watched the waning moon in anticipation as it would soon wax toward full. At last, they'd be together as a complete herd and bound for the North Territory. Even after two days, the apple he had gifted her yet clung to her senses. When she rolled her tongue all around her long mouth, she believed she could still make out its flavor.

Seated about a mat of barren strawberry, the Yearling turned to her mother, who was settled like a brooding hen. The grass forked out beneath her mangled nest. The Elder Doe searched the horizon and saw a cloudless sky and the roll of hills. She looked to her watchful daughter and sunk her head to the ground. She couldn't bring herself to convey her suspicions to the Yearling about her father. Sheer willpower must have kept the Buck alive all that time. The horizon would remain inanimate. She looked at her daughter and shut her eyes.

The waiting was the hardest part. To know someone was dead spared one from anticipation. Much of the past two years had been an etude in marking time. Being pregnant and joyless in cold winter—at least the horizon had been clouded and teeming with snow flurry. It had kept the mind active and hopeful such that at any moment he could appear through the haze. But in oppressive summer with nothing but crystal-clear blue stretching infinitely, there was no guessing what lie beyond. He wasn't coming, and that was a fact for miles and miles.

After his brush with death, the Buck never returned and the cold arrived. The Elder Doe wondered if he had made it to the North Territory or if he'd died. She had been isolated from the others for most of the winter. A severe snowstorm hit. Even they couldn't be so coldhearted to a full-bellied doe. They let her back into the fold but only for warmth. Something had happened to the doe clan. The Elder Doe felt an unnatural chill rushing around them even in the middle of a blizzard.

There in the midst of a storm, she longed to be reunited with her beloved—to caress his neck and bed with him in the warm, green-blooded forest. To search for him would be too dangerous and too strenuous while she was pregnant. She'd have to wait until her fawns were born and strong enough to make such a journey.

Days crept with persistence, and the skies shook away the last of the snow just as the Old Man beat the dust from his Turkish rugs. A seemingly endless winter relinquished its stronghold over the land. Springtide conquered. Near a creek splattered cerulean with forget-me-nots, a newt plopped beneath the frigid water. The Elder Doe was ripe with fawn and was uncomfortable. The time approached, and she needed to ready herself.

The memory of the Man with the Crooked Finger still possessed her. His eyes watched her from every hiding place she could imagine. She feared he'd return for unfinished business. One night in a fitful sleep, she'd dreamed he stood before her with seven heads. As she birthed her fawn, he sat watching, waiting. Then he lured the newborn to him and stomped it until all that remained was a bloody froth that he gathered in his hands and lapped up.

After that night, the Elder Doe sought with urgency a hiding place. To the field's end and then north into a dense bit of growth sat a boulder. Underneath, dead roots had rotted creating a sagging in the soil. It was burrowed wide for a den. It had been abandoned as it didn't smell of any creature. It was a little grotto flocked on both sides with brush and fern. The den wasn't visible from the backside of the boulder as it appeared flush with the soil. It was perfect; the Elder Doe could fit snugly in it and spread just enough to birth her fawns.

A crack of pain stripped the sky of its covering. And it was there in the wilderness on the night of the waxing crescent moon that the Elder Doe grunted and cried out in labor. Overhead in the April sky, Virgo gleamed safely above Hydra.

The Old Man woke up and opened his bedroom window to welcome the sound into his quarters. The field was almost pitch-black, and the silhouette of the apple tree blotted out the far distance. Movement flashed behind the tree's shadow. The Old Man grabbed his glasses off the dresser and blinked his eyes. He mumbled and lowered the frames to wipe the smudges off the lenses. He lifted them and balanced them on his butternut-squash nose.

He would have dropped to his knees had it not been for the bracing window ledge; he saw at the edge of the field the Buck and his stump-crown of fresh-growing antler. He was looking toward the tree line. He limped forward, his right side unhealed. He kept his distance cutting a patrician figure on the horizon.

He had returned as Lazarus and just in time to greet his babe. Voices lifted in the night. Was it birds crying or a coyote howling? It sounded like a hymn.

In the protection of the old coyote's den, the Elder Doe birthed but one fawn—a daughter. She slipped out of her body soaking and still. After a moment, she arose with clumsiness and greeted her mother. A white patch about her head and face served as the only source illuminating the night. The Elder Doe nursed her after she had consumed all traces of placenta and blood. She cleansed the newborn with unrivaled devotion—a mother's christening.

A thud came from the living room. The Old Man could hardly tear himself away from the occasion; he reluctantly shuffled down the hallway. He saw that his Bible had fallen from the bookshelf and had landed with a page opened to Revelation.

*Now a great sign appeared in heaven: I saw a woman clothed with the brilliance of the sun, with the moon under her feet. She was wearing on her head a crown of twelve stars. She was pregnant and was crying out in the agony of giving birth.*

*And another sign appeared in heaven: behold, a great, fiery-red dragon with seven heads. He was wearing seven diadems. The dragon's massive tail swept across the sky and dragged away a third of the stars and cast them to the earth. And the dragon crouched before the woman who was about to give birth—poised to devour the baby the moment it was born.*

The Old Man trembled.

Outside the den, the falcon kept a centurion's watch from a dogwood all night. When finally the morning broke and the Buck had once again departed, it flew over the trees east into the jubilant sun.

Not too far from the den where she was born, the white-faced Yearling watched as the Old Man reappeared out of the Cape Cod, his presence denoted by keys jingling. He stumbled along the porch and to his sedan. He often stumbled, more so when a joint jutted from his mouth.

The Yearling noted his gait—still doddering but more pressing, more adamant. He slammed the car door and revved the engine. He shot down the drive nearly grazing the slanted mailbox on his way out, its rust-trimmed door bulging with ears of rain-ragged mail.

She watched his car zip around the bend to make its dirt road descent. It had distracted her from the insects until a sting redirected her concentration. Having had her fill of black flies, she took leave from her mother and scurried into the woods. There were creatures about every leaf, log, and stone for her to observe. Sometimes, she startled a brush-tailed squirrel that would swirl up a pine like the stripe on a barbershop pole. She overturned any number of bluestone fragments to expose handfuls of wood lice rolling into their little armored spheres.

For fear the fly swarm would catch up to her, she hurried deeper than normal into the woods. It was a good opportunity to stretch her legs, which were no longer the gangly limbs of a fawn but thicker and visibly ribbed with sinew. With speed, the breeze picked up all around her. It cooled her and cushioned her. She sailed through the trees buoyed on it.

The route forward became nebulous as she pushed through patches of beating sun. It blinded the Yearling. What she thought was a fern was actually a lichen-covered rock. What appeared to be a few stumps with curling bark was in fact a rafter of wild turkeys. They paused their own brisk strut to stare with wrinkled throat flesh quivering.

There was something joyful and exhilarating about being unable to see clearly, to pass through the shadows and glare of the forest at high speed. Dangerous or benign, the difference didn't exist to the Yearling. Blinded with giddiness, she sprinted through the trees, a frenzy of shapes and colors that quickened her breath.

Near a fallen tree, char-black and draped in moss velvet, an object came into focus. The tree was massive; it must have once stood as an imposing figure. A round, reddish-brown patch aside the dark wood popped. It looked as though the tree had been wounded, as if the wound had never healed and it had succumbed to its injury and fallen. The supposed wound was actually a creature. It had auburn and taupe fur and was nestling itself sidewise the bark.

It was a cottontail. Its coloring was reminiscent of her mother's summer coat. It conjured the image of the Elder Doe back on her grass bed. The Yearling stopped to take a closer look. What could she do? Maybe she could startle it. Try to outrun it. It was small, and it would be fast.

The din of water perked up her ears. Its splattering made her aware of her own thirst, and she decided to leave the cottontail but for a moment's drink. It'd been a long while since the Yearling had seen a rabbit. She worried it'd be gone by the time she returned, but her mouth burned. She rounded the fallen tree with its slumbering wound once again hidden.

Ahead was a stream where the waterway curved. At one point, its figure distended into a width large enough for bathing. The Yearling dipped her muzzle into its depths. Given the heat of day, its bitter coldness startled her, leaving her breathless. It stung only for an instant as it gave way to bliss. The dash through the trees had made her rather thirsty, and she lapped up mouthfuls.

Once she'd filled herself, she paused to catch an image reflected in the diminishing ripple. When the water's mirror was at last calm, she glanced at the visage staring at her and lunged back. She turned in circles around herself and saw nothing there but dappled forest.

She peered down again into the water and tilted her head to contemplate the image. It also tilted its head. When she grunted at it, it grunted back. She waited for its next move, but it remained as stationary as she. Its panting had become synchronized with her own. No sooner had it dawned on her who she was staring at than she groaned loudly.

Yet the water's mirror was revelatory. She was quite taken aback to see how much she had matured. She was no longer a fawn, and it had never occurred to her how much she resembled her mother. Her eyes did seem larger, and her long, lean neck had broadened. All of her was fuller in shape and breadth. Once rust-orange, her coat had mellowed to more earthen shades. Above her right eye, she observed the beginning of the white patch atop her head.

A final taste beckoned. Her tongue once again disturbed the surface. She drank herself in, and the image blurred and skewed until it ruffled away toward the pool's edges. A number of ravens passed on high as they surfed the wavelets of stream water.

She hurried back to the downed tree. The lazy rabbit was still sleeping aside the bark, and she could hardly contain her delight. Her first instinct was to stalk it and then jump at it. She hoped it would meet the charge, perhaps give her an indignant screech. Cottontails tended to be skittish. It would likely just dart off to some bit of brush rather than play. Maybe then she could race along with it to a shielding briar patch.

The Yearling inched toward the cottontail. The forest was hushed, and she crept forward holding her breath. Out of the air came the cawing of a raven. The Yearling's ears flicked, and she halted. It was a strident call, and she kept an eye on her target. But the rabbit didn't flee or cower; it slumbered away in its nook. The bird call dissolved into silence, and the Yearling's stalking resumed.

Once she had managed to get close enough, she took her chance to flush out the cottontail. She cut loose her pent-up energy and speared herself through the air. Limbs launched her upward, and her flying body stretched long. At last she landed in a patch of brushwood, her arrival giving way to a whooshing and crackling below.

Still the rabbit didn't move, didn't so much as squeeze out a pip. The breathless Yearling stood with her head cocked. She lifted her right leg and tucked it under herself. Puzzled, she abandoned her strategy and walked right up to it. When it refused to rouse, she lost her patience and let her front hooves drum down about its head pummeling up puffs of pollen and dust.

The cottontail remained still. From a hemlock, the raven cawed once more. The sun had moved since the Yearling had set out. Its light hit the rabbit from the west. Now she nuzzled it. In doing so, this released an unfamiliar scent—sweet and foul. It flooded the herbaceous summer air as it climbed from the little bulging body. She retreated snorting to evacuate the stench.

Once the initial disgust had subsided, she homed in on the russet fur. She became lost in every detail—from the rabbit's flopping tongue to its bloated belly. All the while, the landscape around her grew vague and blurry just as it had earlier when she flew about the trees.

A small motion redirected her gaze. Over the eye of the cottontail, which should have been plump and wet, crawled a fly. It easily roamed the length of the withered cornea. And when the rabbit neither blinked nor flinched, the Yearling realized something was terribly awry.

The raven increased its cawing, and it wasn't long before the woods were invaded by a faint droning. At first, the Yearling's breathing could cover it, but it grew in volume and climbed in pitch until it became a ringing. It was speeding toward her. The singular, constant noise of it split into many individual sounds like a pane of glass cracking.

She lifted her tail high ready to run. It was that unexplainable sound. It had usually terrorized her sleep, but it had found her alone in the mid-day forest. It surged until it blared. A wobbling overtook the initial ringing. It sounded like a bouncing branch. After seconds, the sound smoothed out; she thought it was the call of a human. She couldn't tell where it was coming from, and before she could even breathe, it stopped. A crack halted it as crisply as rhubarb snapping in the garden.

But it wasn't silent after the sound dissipated as the summer flies approached. They overtook her their wanton screaming filling the air. Flies had a clairvoyant ability to find dead things. They were already upon the cottontail crawling into any orifice they could access. They laid their eggs in it. It was now the maggots' creche.

The Yearling kicked about the riot tormenting her with a thousand little stabs. She thrust about in circles until she finally outmaneuvered the swarm. Into the grove she plowed until she was able to clear a good distance. The farther she sprinted, the fainter the cacophony sounded until it faded into hot air.

It was late afternoon, and the herd would soon begin grazing. The Elder Doe would be searching for her at the field's edge. Slowing her pace to a trot, the Yearling was able to take in the forest at last. What had earlier been blurred and joyful had been utterly transformed. In the changing light, the forest was stark, each detail somber in its clarity.

As she neared the field's edge, she turned back to where the rabbit's body lay deep in the trees. She had a clear view of the relative area and was startled to see the distant flies yet visible. They swarmed the creature like whirling ashes from hidden fire. But it had become apparent that what she was seeing was not a fly horde at all. The flock of ravens, which had heeded the cawing of the solitary watchman, descended on the scene. They quartered and tore away at the cottontail barely able to taste such meager fare.

The Yearling turned herself away and stopped to stare at the apple tree. For some time, she meditated upon its bowed branches with apples falling to the ground for gnashing deer mouths. And when the Elder Doe called her forward, she found she hadn't yet grasped what it had all meant. The cottontail rabbit hadn't been sleeping; that was something altogether different. And whatever it was, the mysterious sound was tied to it.

A little later, the Old Man returned from town and pulled into the drive. He killed the engine and rested his head against the steering wheel and stayed that way well past sunset—with his car doors locked.

Three weeks had passed since the Old Man had confronted the Man with the Crooked Finger in town. The days marched toward the full moon. The Bluestone Woodland was marked by summer's increasing mugginess. There'd been a thunderstorm that had brought a powerful windfall to the acreage. Apples dropped in great numbers. Aside the house, a sash of Virgin's Bower clematis had been stripped clean away.

The does took advantage of the windfall and found themselves feasting on the abundance of fruit. It was a harvest of little effort. The laziest of the does bedded about a smattering of apples had to merely stretch her neck to eat.

The Yearling longed to rip into the heart-shaped foliage of the hostas surrounding the Cape Cod and especially luscious about the north-facing wall. Bordering the house, they opened wide their arms. To approach them meant risking being too near the Old Man. This went against the Yearling's instincts. Thousands of years of evolutionary design had near-vouchsafed her survival in a human-dominated world. She knew the Old Man was harmless, but she had never been near him. Nor had the others for that matter save the Elder Doe. It was just how things had always been. No one thought to cross the threshold.

The blue hostas waved in the breeze from the white clapboard, and the Yearling salivated. The play of tender foliage in the wind created music that pulled her close to the house, closer than she'd ever been. She hadn't yet realized it, but she was beyond the raised beds facing the Cape Cod and well-nigh the porch. *Only a few more steps* they chanted, and then she'd be bathing in forbidden foliage.

When the front door unexpectedly crashed open, the Yearling lifted into the air and sprinted back to the Elder Doe to hide behind her bulwark-like flank. Out the door teetered the Old Man with a canvas tucked under his arm and his painting caddy gripped at the handle. He braced himself down the steps with his free arm and hobbled out to the field. Supplies were plopped directly in front of the apple tree. Doe heads and tails tilted and lifted at varying angles and speeds. Even the bedded doe about the apple hoard hoisted herself up. None had ever seen the Old Man so close.

He had rings of sweat about his chest and underarms as he walked back and forth from the Cape Cod to the tree. He grabbed a folding chair and his easel and made his return having a bit of struggle with his footing. He wiped his forehead with his arm, the underside of the bicep floppy with age. Beads of perspiration dotted his face. He blotted it dry, and with a pronounced sigh he planted himself in front of the tree.

"Mind if I join?" He attempted a smile, but it lost traction on his downturned face.

Some does had gone back to grazing while others still gawked. The Elder Doe had bedded herself down behind the apple tree. She kept to herself as the distance between her and the doe clan had widened. She relaxed in the shade without reservation and didn't move on his account. Her perception of the Old Man was unique; crisis had afforded her an easiness in his presence.

Of course, to her, it also seemed obvious to find him so near the tree. As wisdom had dictated to her, all things were eventually pulled toward it. She could tell he was old by the white bristles on his head, and she smelled the years ooze from his skin. In old age, he drew near the tree as he drew near the inevitable—that unseen truth that rooted the universe.

The Old Man painted but struggled. He furrowed his brow, turned his head to one side, and squinted. He turned the other way looking at the vista with narrowed eyes. He relied on his glasses, but they were little help. He removed them, puffed on the lenses until they were foggy, and wiped them spotless.

Under his foot, he had located an apple that he was rolling to and fro. It helped his concentration. He stuck his tongue out and held it at the bruised corner of his mouth maneuvering his hand via small, linear motions. He paused to dab the sweat on his face and neck with a handkerchief being careful with his swollen cheeks.

"Pretty strange to see me out here," he addressed the does over his brushwork. "All these years, I've kept my distance." He stopped painting and sat back in his chair. "Just don't see as well as I used to."

He fussed with his left arm. It wasn't the usual pain he attributed to an irritated nerve but a possible injury that deserved attention. The bruise on it alone had been dramatic; a tie-dyed spin of Tyrian purple on his bicep that had turned jasper stone brown-yellow. It'd been three weeks since. The encounter ran through his head on repeat, and he could no longer paint. He had no more visions for his canvas.

"I know what you did!" The Old Man quivered. "This has to stop! You hear me?"

He had driven to town and had found the Man with the Crooked Finger at the diner. He was lunching with his cronies, and they all spread out between a few red booths. At the diner, the Man with the

Crooked Finger received meals at concessionary prices for his service to the community.

The Man rose, clamped down on the Old Man's arm, and pulled him toward the door. The Old Man floundered, tripping over his own feet as he attempted to restore his balance while knocking over glasses on a neighboring table. "You're hurting me!"

Laughter erupted from the dining room as they watched the Old Man being shoved out the door crowned with a sign that read Senior Citizens Eat Free Thursdays.

"Let go of me!" The Old Man tugged his arm loose and cradled it. It felt rope-burned. "I've known you since you were a little boy. What happened to him?"

The Man jeered, "He died, Doc. 'Sides, what's so wrong with me? I'm a savior!" He lifted his arms and opened his hands wide. "I'm the only hope for this town, don't 'cha see?"

"Only thing I see is a delusional narcissist."

"Oh yeah, you see? You see! Ha! There's a lot you don't see—a lot you never saw. Wanna know what I see? I see you still harboring deer on your lot—just like you harbored Fay."

"Don't say his name."

"Oh, but I bet you did."

"You know what, you really are sick. We should have tried harder to help you. Do you even know what you've done?" Adrenaline toyed with the Old Man's speech cadences, which made the Man with the Crooked Finger snicker as he listened. "First the deer … and now murder? You can't just kill something and call it dangerous and expect that to do."

"But I can do whatever I want." He smacked the Old Man's bicep and grasped him by his collar. "Just like you do whatever you want, like conversing with the wife behind my back."

"She's my friend. Don't you dare hurt her."

A tow truck motor began grumbling, and the Man released his grip on the Old Man's collar. He waved to the driver hooking up a tireless, dented-can hatchback. Both men turned in its direction.

"Ah, yes. That? That's what happens to squatters. Let's just say," he smirked, "I cut him down to size. Besides, he was trespassing on Red's sugar bush late at night. He looked dangerous, too—I'd know. It was self-defense." His smile was so muscular that it pushed his cheeks high, rumpled his lids closed, and enhanced the scar stretching across his left eye. "I put him down just like a rabid animal. I can be humane."

"Humane? You're about as …"

Something then clicked into place for the Old Man, and he asked, "Just you two boys? Why were you and Red alone at the sugar bush late at night anyway?"

The Man grabbed the Old Man's face and squeezed until fingers and cheek skin nearly touched inside the Old Man's open mouth. Capillaries burst making tiny violet antlers. The Old Man knocked the pincer grip away with a blow to the Man's forearm. "I may be old, but I'm not weak!"

The Man massaged his forearm with a thumb and then shook it out railing his fist. "Don't come down here ever again and provoke me. And if you think the law is going to care, think again. What I say goes. And what I'm doing for our town—Shit, I'm a goddam hero!"

"You're not a hero. You're a psychopath. And if I were still practicing, I'd have you committed."

"Have me committed?" He straightened the Old Man's collar as he spoke. The Old Man was unflinching. "Careful. I'm not the unclean one, old man. Unclean. Dangerous. *Phew*, I may not be able to have you committed, but—"

"But?"

Gravel scuffled under the Man as he pivoted his boots leaving the Old Man. "But—my fries are gettin' cold and my soda's gettin' warm. Enjoy your deer while they're still around."

He finger-combed his dirty blond hair before he pulled the diner door open, his reflection aside a Thin the Herd decal adhered to the glass.

"And don't drive to my house no more to talk to the wife." He grinned as he slipped back inside. "Don't want you to make her unclean and dangerous too."

Light had shifted, and the Old Man was slumped in his chair. His brush resting against his pants stained them. He resumed his work. The once fluid motions of his brushstrokes had grown marked and aggressive. He kept wiping at sweat that was dripping into his eyes. Suddenly, the rolling of the apple from underneath his foot stopped. The Old Man slammed his fists on his easel. The does perked up while the Yearling, who had been mesmerized by a swallowtail dotting atop a stretch of flowering weeds, darted back to the Elder Doe.

The Old Man slung his face into his hands then looked up and took a deep breath. Well aware that he'd frightened the Yearling, he bent over. He reached down to pick up the apple he'd been rolling beneath his untied boat shoe. "Come, Saint. Got something for ya." He spoke to her as to a child.

She saw he was looking at her, gesturing. He held the apple out and beckoned with his troublesome arm. "Little doe, patron saint of my field, receive this apple as a prayer."

It was a very strange thing to do feeding the Yearling, but he felt very much outside himself. He was descending into despair, and all the while, he'd endured God's silence. He therefore sought the divine directly at its source. Though hand feeding a wild animal went completely against his principles, there was something about the Yearling that murmured of sanctity and wonder. It's why he used his injured arm, in case the act of communion somehow miraculously healed it.

"Don't be scared, Saint," the Old Man said.

The Yearling crept forward but stopped and turned back to the Elder Doe, who in turn gave a reassuring glance and nodded with her thick neck in the direction of the Old Man. With nagging reluctance, the Yearling resumed her ceremonious crawl to his chair. He lifted the apple to her mouth. Bowing her neck, her brilliant white patch on full display, she carefully received the apple from his hand and scurried back to the tree. At last she had crossed the threshold. The covenant with man was sealed.

"Amen, Saint. Amen."

The Old Man packed his materials into their case and stumbled back to the Cape Cod. He latched onto anything in reach. Once he had made it back through the door, he shut it loudly and didn't return for the chair or the easel. Facing the apple tree, he left them to their fate. The breeze blew the easel over. The canvas had nothing more than lines and red smears on it. The empty chair stood alone facing the darkening east.

In the sky, stratocumulus clouds loomed over the house. Other clouds traveled through, casting shadows on the field and blackened the green like fleeting scorch marks up and down its length. The chair, a well-worn white, turned grey in the overcast.

Finishing the last of the apple, the Yearling looked toward the house. There was no trace of the Old Man traversing his routes. She moved her tongue around her mouth; the tree's fruit tasted different. Her mother was still bedded, and the two exchanged glances. She ventured over to her where she'd sleep for the remainder of the afternoon. The summer sky was always mercurial in the Bluestone Woodland. Weather could unexpectedly turn tumultuous at any moment.

Inside, the dimming house was quiet. The Old Man stood in the kitchenette, which tied the living room to the hallway leading to his bedroom. He faced the opened door. His duvet and pillows still held his form as if an invisible man slept in his bed.

How could the little boy who used to pick apples from his tree have grown into someone so violent? A secret was written in the tree's bark, and though the boy had tried to show the Old Man, he never could see. How many hours had the Old Man spent studying the tree? He was ashamed it had taken so many years to finally figure it out. If only he'd been the child's father. Then he could've helped the boy— the boy who would grow up and around a crooked finger like a tree with an ax lodged in its side.

The roar of the boy's truck sounded in his mind just as it did the afternoon it scoured the trim line between the field and the drive.

Many years earlier, the Old Man had stood under the apple tree weighed down by an array of fruit unlike he'd ever seen. "Strange tree indeed."

He had difficulty understanding the tree, how it self-pollinated and bore such yields. Maybe it was a side effect of pollution or chemical rainout. Such sweet, red-gold orbs. More than just sweet, they were all-encompassing—earthy yet tart with a pithy but firm texture. It left an astringent aftertaste reminiscent of amaro. It could have been a Winesap variety, and like wine, it had the power to coax out the truth. The tree was rooted in the one, whole, and divine nature of the universe. To taste of its liqueur and eat of its flesh were to return to the core of one's being.

On that warm day, the does were in the timber grazing the sparse greens that thrived in shadows. It was cool and dark; the branch-veiled sun pulsated on high in its tangerine dome.

A truck roared from the hillside drive and pulled along the road that scraped the field's end. It stopped to park in the shade. The driver, a lanky teenager with blond hair, crossed the front of the pickup. Its cherry-red hood blistered, and his fingers grazed the metal. He walked slowly.

"Your dad know you're here?" the Old Man asked, wiping the sweat from his forehead with a thick, linen-sleeved forearm.

"Nah. I'm eighteen."

The sun broke free. The boy's eyes burned in the light; his pupils were but two distant birds deep in a blue stratosphere. He shielded them by cupping a hand over his brow revealing a crooked index finger. Once he saw the Old Man staring, he thrust his hand into the pocket of his denim trousers.

"Come over here. Get out of the sun before you blind yourself."

The boy approached, saying, "I'd almost rather be blind." He looked beyond the Old Man to the window where Fay stood slipping a shirt over his bare torso.

"You haven't been here since you were a little kid. Remember how much you loved picking these? Always struggling with an apple just out of reach. Your mom and I would watch and laugh …" He joined his hands in front of him. "I was sorry to hear."

The wind whistled through their silence. They heard insects sizzling as they near cooked upon hot bluestone shards. Then with a swift reach, the boy smacked hold of the Old Man's hand and squeezed. "I'm not here for apples." He tugged the Old Man's arm— the very same arm he'd come to injure years later. "I'm here to tell you something."

The Old Man felt his pulse pounding against the boy's grasp.

"There's something inside me." He shook. Tears welled up in his eyes. "It's either I become one thing or I become the other. And I won't be able to turn back."

A shimmying freed the Old Man's hand so that he could rest it on the boy's shoulder. "First of all, you can always turn back. There's gotta be a solution for—"

"There's not!" The boy shrugged him off. He paused but quickly returned to squeeze the Old Man's hand with a force that could draw blood from stone. "I came to you because I know. Okay? I know. And either I become who I am or I become who they want me to be."

"What's this about, kid?" Again, he wriggled his hand free. His smile didn't once waver—a smile that didn't betray a growing sense of dread.

The boy dropped his hands to hang heavy fists and began to pace. "All the things they have done to me. And they say I'm weak. And my old man," he scoffed, "my old man says you people are weak and dirty."

"Your dad and his friends giving you a tough time?"

The boy kept pacing but said nothing. The Old Man knew the answer well enough. He reached forward to touch the boy's hand, to draw him in and embrace him, but the boy hid his hand behind his back. His crooked finger pained him.

"Let's go inside where it's cooler and talk."

"Don't want to."

As he swiveled away from the Old Man, the boy caught sight of the boulder at the field's edge that covered the she-coyote's den. "Is that where the coyote slept?"

"Where?" The Old Man strained his eyes. "The coyote? What do you know about her?"

"Nothin'."

The Old Man now grabbed the boy's arm and shook it with soft hands. Fay knocked on the window mouthing words behind glass and casting clouds upon the pane. The Old Man asked, his voice hoarse, "Do you know what they did to that poor animal?"

But the boy didn't hear. Again he looked past the Old Man to the apple tree. His eye—his awful, powerful eye—zeroed in on a particular area in its bark. "There! You see?" The boy pointed with his crooked finger. "There's a message in the tree. That's what I am. Right there, in the bark!"

The Old Man searched the length of the tree. He touched the bark, scanning for signs and letters but became distracted by the hand he'd used to shake the boy. "Sorry, kid." The wind etched a line between them. "I don't see anything."

"Look harder!"

The Old Man scrutinized the tree, but could see only ridges in the bark. After a final, thorough pass, he realized they were getting nowhere, that it was starting to feel a bit like child's play. A good dose of reason was what they needed. He was a scientist, after all. When a patient had been distressed, he remembered HALT: hungry, angry, lonely, or tired; distressed people were almost always one of those things. So he started with H. He tugged, and then he plucked an apple, which held on for dear life. "You know I was a doctor, and I can't tell you how many times I'd seen patients affected by low blood sugar. Eat this, and let's go inside and chat."

However, an inner voice was speaking to the boy. Its steady stream of whispering deafened him. It talked of the tree's intent to sear his tongue with but one taste of its fruit and force him to speak the truth—the truth of who he was and the part of himself he kept hidden and that men wanted to kill. The voice said, *Swallow this delicious shame and quench your weakness.*

The boy pulled away from the tree's shade with a slow drag of the feet. Daylight washed him out, from his shoe straps to the crook in his peach-fuzzed chin. Tree leaves rustled as a warning as he drifted from their protective roots. The Old Man still held the fruit out, his hand just beginning to shake. "Take it. Let me help you."

Through the trees came the deer, their buttered coats frying in the sun spitting forth black eyes like hot beans. The boy feared the does, and their eyes dotted his vision until the acreage was punched full of holes. Then all he could see were deer bodies hanging with tongues skimming the ropes—all he could smell were the mildewed floorboards of his father's hunting shanty.

Fay had stepped onto the porch. He grabbed ahold of the guardrail as he leaned forward peering in their direction. The veins in his arms swelled behind his skin, and the muscles of his long neck became slicked with sunlight. The boy paused to take in the details of Fay's form with his peppery body hair spurting above his low collar until blush marks splotched the boy's chest and ran up his throat.

"No, keep away from me!"

Shame coursed through his veins in infinite circuits without a means for release. It washed through him until every last one of his cells was soaking in it. It changed the natural molecular properties of his body. The inner voice said, *Your disgust is a power. Use it.*

Again he directed his preternatural gaze to Fay—his blue eyes that whitened in the sun. And he no longer loved his eyes for what they had seen; how his visions put his soul into conflict with his brain. And thus his gaze became the evil eye and at that moment it spread itself over Fay, darkening his face and twisting his stomach in knots. A cloud passed in the sky, and the does stampeded in a horseshoe shape back into the tree line. All the while the empty porch chair rocked by itself.

Without warning, the boy approached the Old Man and knocked the fruit from his hand. "To hell with your apples, faggot!"

And with that, the boy tore free of the apple tree and ran hard until he was able to crawl up and into his pickup, slamming its door on the verge of unhinging. The Old Man walked toward the vehicle with his arms outstretched, entreating him. "Stop! Come back, kid!"

The cracked driver side window lowered in a zigzag. "I'm not coming back." The motor roared. "Not until you're dead." The boy took his hand and fashioned it as a pistol, the pointer finger a crooked barrel. He simulated firing at the Old Man, and after doing the same to Fay on the porch, he flipped the rig in a ring upturning the grass where his tire veered from the drive and sped downhill.

Fay met the Old Man in the field as he stared down the drive. They braced one another up.

"Fay, I worry for that boy."

"No," said Fay. "It's too late for that."

A half hour had passed, and the Old Man was still standing in the kitchen. The does had moved to the tree line to hunker down in the grass. And though the weather was growing volatile, it was being relatively quiet about it. He began thinking of the worst of the conversation from outside the diner—the part that he kept barred from his memory; the part that he skipped over as it repeated in his mind. He jammed his fingers into his ears just as he'd done as a child.

The Old Man was often superstitious, yet now more than ever, he wanted to be logical. But wanting and being rarely shared the same bed. Maybe the devil, like God, donned many faces and forms. If the devil could be terrible with might, perhaps the devil too could have once been slight and small. The little boy who used to pick apples just beyond the kitchen window— what was it that he had said outside the diner in a grown man's voice? Somehow the Old Man's fingers had slipped from his ears as the Man's words resurfaced tugging at his hurt arm—not to beseech him, but to throttle him making damn sure that he listened.

"I shot him and quartered him for the syrup stove. You ever watched someone being quartered, old man? Messy. I had to burn him, of course. Stood a long, long time over that stove. Do you know what a human body smells like while it burns?" He smiled. "I wouldn't worry about it. You won't be there."

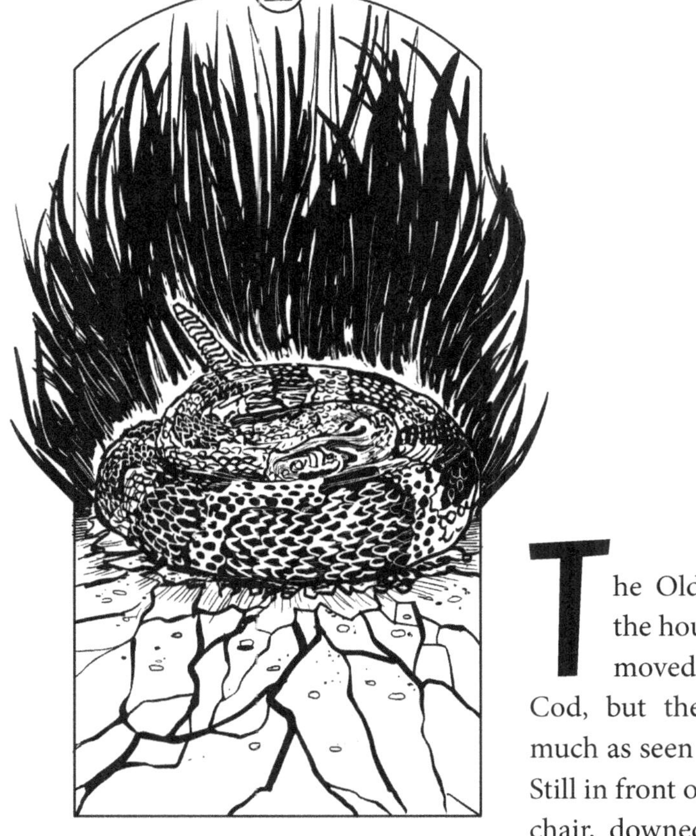


The Old Man hadn't left the house in days. Lights moved about the Cape Cod, but the does hadn't so much as seen a shadow of him. Still in front of the tree were his chair, downed easel, and canvas. The sky had since opened and dumped rain. Plastered over the canvas was a plethora of dirt and debris that had crusted under the hot sun. As for the sullen chair, a volunteer morning glory had already wound a tendril up its leg. The abandoned items were in jeopardy of being swallowed up by pasture and metamorphosed into landscape.

The grass of the field hadn't been this long in years. The Old Man had liked things to be kept neat and was diligent about trimming the spread on a riding lawnmower. He enjoyed doing the chore while savoring a joint of the mellowest cannabis his friend, the Woman, grew in her garden. After a few puffs, it gave him a buzz that was a tremendous guilty pleasure for him. Then at its finger-singeing end, he would get nice and high and coast along the field as if on a motorboat hypnotized by the waves the mower produced in the green.

Besides having an aesthetic eye, keeping the field short was his method of deterring ticks and timber rattlers. He'd encountered some fairly concerning tick-borne illnesses while doing pro bono work for the local Health and Welfare. Tick populations and illnesses had become prolific with global warming, and new species and strains popped up nearly every third summer. But he'd never once seen a snakebite.

Through the tall grass, the Yearling swam her way toward the hosta bed. Once she had passed the initial raised gardens, she drew near the siding as if approaching a temple or a mausoleum. The ivory clapboard and the white patch on her head bounced sunlight off one another in constant play. It was so bright that even the Old Man caught a glimpse as he lowered the bedroom Venetian blind midway.

The Yearling was finally in front of the house; it made her feel woozy, as though she'd suddenly been lifted in elevation or was breathing the air of another planet. She pushed forward as she no longer feared being near the Old Man. It freed her to tear away at the mounds of hosta foliage and to strip each leaf clean of its fibrous stem. At first there was a twinge of shame, but it was fleeting as the glorious flavor spread up and down her tastebuds. Eagerly, she devoured them as if it were a last supper not once pausing to raise her head for air.

A disembodied voice sounded. The Old Man appeared in the kitchen speaking on the phone. He opened the window next to the porch and sat at his desk. The Yearling paused to peer around the corner—She could barely hear him over her own chomping.

"I keep having terrible nightmares." He groaned, but it was high and light, more of an acquiescence than an aggravation. "We're in danger, you and I."

The Old Man sounded like a different person, and that alarmed the Yearling. She smelled the despair coming out the window, and it soured her long-pined-for meal.

"We have to stop him."

The Old Man faced the large living room window. His vision blurred and distorted the shape of the apple tree. He began to tap on the desk stopping only to grab his left arm. His speech was unmetered. "The deer, the man he butchered … Who's next?"

The other does had seen the Yearling about the hostas, and they became angry. They had never deigned to go near the house. *Haughty young doe!* Filled with jealousy and unable to contain themselves, they condemned her as having brought nothing but division and trouble. Even her unnatural appearance broke rank in the clan. Why was she the chosen one? They believed it should have been them receiving the Old Man's offering. They trotted up to the house and began to demolish the garden in protest. A few circled the Yearling and knocked her against the clapboard siding. The laziest one of them had somehow risen on two legs like a human and pummeled her with dirt-clad hooves.

"People are being exterminated along with the deer. My God, it's the slaughter of the innocents. The earth is burning and flooding. It's the end of days." The Old Man walked over to the bookshelf and grabbed the serpent staff. "We have to go into the city for help. We have to bring in an outsider." He noticed that his little deer carving had fallen from the bookshelf. It was resting in pieces on the floor, the headless half thrust atop a blood-red Turkish rug. "Christ. I'm afraid it's even too late for help."

Meanwhile, the Elder Doe, who had been napping under the apple tree, was roused from sleep by a gentle rattling. Once her eyes had adjusted to sunlight, she peered through mounds of reed and into the field. Nothing but sky-high grass. She arose and approached the easel and chair, searching around them before lowering her head to sniff along the heavy clay. Something then caught her eye—a glossy ring and a slim black slit. She jumped back then dashed toward the house punching through the abandoned canvas with a swift hoof.

Charging toward the others at the side of the house, the Elder Doe let loose a cry. *Danger in the grass!* The does looked up from their frenzy, but were too distracted to see the creature in the field. Its path was denoted by the swaying of high grasses where it slunk. Some of the does had taken notice but then simply brushed it off as a bit of wind. The Elder Doe, unable to convince them otherwise, collected her daughter and moved to the safety of the tree line.

The clan was possessed, and their jealousy mandated total destruction. Anything that sustained life had to be torn away. They went from one flowerbed to the next uprooting plants and stomping them. The hosta garden to the north of the Cape Cod was nothing more than snapped stems, and the remaining plots were in ruins. Every bit of garden had been defiled.

"I still have a friend in the city who works in law enforcement. Detective Robin Byrd. It's outside her jurisdiction, but I'm going to call and see if she can come out." His sweat-soaked oxford was unbuttoned. He patted his damp skin with its hem. "In the meantime, I want you to run far away. I'll come get you—Whatever it takes."

The Elder Doe and the Yearling kept their distance from the herd and far from the creature in the grass. They had at last been outcast as the doe clan wandered into the trees at the field's end to create a new bedding spot. Mother and daughter opted for a pocket nearer the house. High above, the pines kept watch as they rested—the same pines where the falcon had once perched.

"Listen to me!" With the phone tucked soundly beneath his chin, he rubbed his shoulder and worked his way down the arm. The pain was accelerating, and his hand had gone numb. "You have to get out of that house before it's too late!"

The Elder Doe felt everything rushing toward a climax; the time was upon them. She and the Yearling would wait until the full moon for the Buck's return, but she had resigned herself to the notion that the two of them would be trekking north alone. Over the treetops the clouds floated past, their underbellies stained red by the setting sun.

The Yearling watched as the creature winded about the chair and easel. It wrapped itself around a leg and spiraled upward dethroning the morning glory. She could at last see it as it rose out of the sea of grass; its head became visible for a moment like a surfacing basilisk. It had a rigid, auspicious brow. Its tongue flickered about the air as it assayed its flavor. She knew it carried things miraculous and awful on its scaled back. It then sunk back to the soil and shook its rattle about the reeds.

It called to the Old Man, but he spoke loudly and couldn't make it out. He squinted out the window but then closed his eyes and kneaded his forehead. The house was darkening. He was trying not to think, but he had a tendency toward obsessive thoughts. Pain shot along his left arm as if a fiddle bow were scraping nerves. Something was trying to overtake him.

"Damn you!" he shouted. "Get out, devil!"

The phone dropped. He fished the spinning receiver from off the floor by its curling cord. A long line of concern came through the receiver. "What do you mean I don't sound like myself? … Don't mean to scare you—" There was a pause, and he mumbled, "I'm scaring myself." The handset never quite made it back to his mouth, and he spoke at the receiver a distance from his face. He felt rummy headed, and everything began to blur. "He'll be home soon, won't he? Anyway, I need to rest. Let me make some calls, and I'll get a hold of you tomorrow … Yes, you too. Goodbye, honey."

He struggled to hang up the phone as he latched onto his burning arm. Maybe he had better make a doctor's appointment in the city though he hated to the leave the safety of his home. Besides, the city was impossible to navigate with all the flooding and devastation. There was always something to contend with when one visited the city.

It was all too much to consider and sort through at the moment. He was exhausted, felt nauseated. He needed to rest so that he could find a logical solution; otherwise, he'd just be an emotional wreck. On his way to the bedroom, he tripped over the phone cord. "Son of a bitch!"

Before setting it back on the mount, he gave the headset a swift kick. Yet he hadn't merely pulled the receiver from off the mount when he caught his foot on the cord. He had unknowingly yanked the plug out of the jack.

Cold kitchenette counters and fan-textured walls received his caress as he felt his way toward the bedroom. Once he was able to at last creep into bed, he tapped on his brow to knock the ache from his head. Out in the field, the creature called to him again from under the easel and chair. That time, he heard it distinctly. "Rattlesnake?" he whispered.

He took to bending his arm back and forth at the elbow. Fingers rolled over bands of muscle. He stretched his arm out moving it in a sort of slinking, sidewinding fashion. He grew drowsy; he felt disconnected from his body. The field was shadowed by clouds carrying the promise of rain. In the bedroom, the Venetian blinds were half-closed and the room was losing light. He took a final look at the photo of Fay on the nightstand then shut his eyes.

Hours later in the pitch of night, the Cape Cod was soundless except for a sporadic drip from the kitchen faucet. Meanwhile, over the river, the Woman was trying to reach the Old Man by phone, dialing his number and hanging up and doing so with frantic repetition. The calls would never get through to the disconnected phone, and each time the Woman tried his landline, the snake let loose its sympathetic rattle from under the dark obelisks of grass.

VIII

**N**ight smothered the land. The Yearling and her mother nestled together under the pines, but their sleep was hindered. Being separated from the herd had left them with an overwhelming sense of vulnerability that couldn't be shaken. No matter how terrible the doe clan had behaved, being split apart from the greater group felt dangerously unnatural for social animals.

The Yearling watched the Elder Doe—her mother, whom she loved so deeply—as she tried to sleep. Things would change; the moon was near full, and they needed to hold on only a little longer. They'd soon be moving north with the Buck at their side.

The Cape Cod was so radiant that the Yearling found its sheen distracting. She closed her eyes tightly, but the glow remained. As the moon was practically full swollen, it made seeing relatively easy. The other does were tucked deeper into the tree line and well obscured by brush and shadow while the Elder Doe and the Yearling sheltered themselves under a heap of honeysuckle riddled with black, bitter berries.

A mosquito swarmed the Yearling's ear buzzing as it stormed the canal. She flapped her ear to rid herself of it, but the insect droned more resolutely in response. She flung her head up and shook it about and then swatted the air once more. At last, silence. She put her head back down and rolled her body away from the house.

But the buzz started again, and she lay motionless as her irritability escalated. The stronger her aggravation grew, the higher in frequency the buzz lifted until suddenly it was all consuming, deafening, and spreading all about the acreage. At first it was a splitting noise, but then it trembled and percussed. Like the ball of a roulette wheel jumping about different outcomes, her mind spiraled with fearful imagery. Yet it didn't take long for her to arrive at a conclusion; that this sound was no longer the work of an insect.

The Yearling prodded the Elder Doe with her snout, but she was under the spell of sleep and only lifted her head drowsily to caress the Yearling along her flank before lowering herself to continue her slumber.

Dismayed, the Yearling darted her head to and fro searching through the dark timber toward the doe clan. Over at the far end of the tree line, she saw them in a heavy rest. It was apparent now; this sound—this thing—was meant for only her to hear. Mustering what courage she could, the Yearling rose and trotted to the center of the field. The area wasn't as much vibrant in the milk-light of the moon as it was pewter. The Cape Cod sat wide eyed, its phosphorescent face watching the east. The sound electrified the acreage and made it whir under her hooves causing the hairs of her coat to stand straight up. The Yearling looked in all directions, but nothing revealed the unexplainable sound's origin.

Finally, it let out a cracking noise like a snapping branch that echoed against the surround of hardwoods, and nothing more. Night returned to its habitual silence. And while it seemed to have stretched on for ages, it had lasted only seconds.

Ringing, splitting, wobbling, wailing, and then cracking—Her mind was unable to find any reason or definition for the sound. In the quiet void of the field, she was suddenly choked by fear having only just realized that she was standing there all alone. Too frightened, too breathless to walk back to the Elder Doe, she shut her eyes as if being unable to see meant she too was invisible.

Silence prevailed, and after a few minutes, it became clear that she would be incapable of standing still all night. She eased back into walking with tremulous steps. Her eyes wandered toward the pines, but she felt something in the darkness watching her. Her muscles seized and her hairs bristled. She pivoted her head carefully toward the house.

There, staring out the window of the Cape Cod, was an unearthly, pale countenance. His eyes, buried beneath puffs of baggy skin, were webbed over with the cataracts of moonlight. He stood very still and looked right through her to the black horizon. It was the Old Man, and in a dramatic wrenching, he clasped his left arm and disappeared into the lightless room.

With that, the Yearling dashed to her mother fighting her way through limbs of drooping honeysuckle to at last burrow into her. The Elder Doe roused, but she only briefly stirred before nestling into her daughter to drift off. The image of the Old Man at the window didn't sit well with the Yearling. She tried to ease herself into her mother's warm body hoping to nod off, but she couldn't find the calm to let go. She wondered if the Old Man too had heard the strange sound.

An hour had past, maybe only minutes. At last, the Yearling's eyes had closed for sleep while her anxious mind kept a steadfast watch from behind slumbering lids. A rustling in the distant trees flung her tired eyes open. The moon peered through honeysuckle branches as through a hunter's net. She waited, listened—Yet only her breath filled her ears.

Then seconds later came another sound, the quick latching of one of the Cape Cod doors. Her head jolted up, and she caught sight of a shape slipping into the trees, a dark figure running north. It looked human.

She stood and moved quietly through the intertwined honeysuckle then made her way northwest and rotated her ears. She winced; something slammed in the distance, and there came a motoring like that of the Old Man's sedan but deeper. She drew back once more behind the safety of the honeysuckle until the roaring engine had traveled a good ways and then faded.

There hadn't even been a chance to lower herself aside her mother when a sudden whooshing sped through the night air. She scanned the sky through honeysuckle branches with quick, darting jerks of her head. The stippled underwings of a bird glided toward the Cape Cod. It perched in a tree behind the house and bounced backward into the recesses of limbs. It chirped as it hid there with eyes glowing like coals in the shadows.

But then its chirping opened up carrying with it a singular, crying timbre. Rounding the honeysuckle's facade, the Yearling creeped again toward the field's edge. The bird's voice vibrated from the old-growth behind the little house. It shone brightly perched in the highest tree branches—so much so that she could hardly stare at it. It was the falcon. It spun its head in a full circle ending its rotation to gawk at the Yearling. In its foot it held a goldfinch, and it dropped its curved beak to pluck the delicate, dandelion of a head from its body.

The Yearling once again sealed her eyes. Against her better judgment, she remained fixed in place trusting that morning would shortly arrive. However, it was but the witching hour, and the first flush of dawn was still concealed beneath the hills.

Two days later, a car arrived on the property. An older gentleman, tall and lean, climbed out of his low-sitting vehicle and approached the front door. He took note of the disheveled gardens and then knocked. He turned around and would have admired the scene of mist-blurry hills, but the image of deer about the apple tree unnerved him. By proximity—and by association— he felt like fair game.

After a moment of waiting, he rapped again while referencing his wristwatch, the imitation snakeskin straps shedding at the edges. No answer. Bending his neck to peer into the living room window proved fruitless; nothing to see but an ordinary life, a desk, and spotless Formica counters in the kitchenette. Another glimpse at his watch; two minutes had passed. He pounded on the door. A howling came from the trees. *What the hell was that?* His foot he thumped, a more-anxious version of his compulsive tapping habit. Another howl, deep and limpid. Swooshing deer bodies moved through tall grass toward him, and he turned sprightly with heavy breaths denoted by the thrumming of his nostrils.

Another minute passed, and still no one came to the door. He mumbled to himself. Then he heard a croaking. *Now what?* He looked over to the end of the Cape Cod and saw piles of decaying plants. He heard a voice come from the north side of the house. It sounded like the macaw his aunt had kept back on the ranch when he was a child, which she had taught to speak. "Over here. Over here," it had parroted.

He gave a quick, disbelieving glance and made his way down the porch and sidled up to the masses of dead garden plants. What had looked like a clump of rich, black garden soil had in fact been a midsized raven. As he approached the bedroom window, it fluttered its wings and took to the sky. Crane jumped backward into the garden space—a living scarecrow. He grabbed his chest, saying, "Jesus Christ."

Once he had gotten his breath underneath him, he braced himself against the clapboard siding. Before lifting himself onto his toes to peek into the bedroom window, he noticed boot prints coming from behind the house leading into the trees. And as he had poor depth perception, he smacked his head nose first into the window to peer through the Venetian blinds. He saw the Old Man in his bed. "Doc? It's Crane!" he cried out rubbing his aquiline nose.

The Old Man didn't move. Alarmed, Crane backtracked to the lawn to wipe his loafers on the grass, taking note once more of the boot prints in the muck. *Fresh tracks.* He then marched to the front door. He hesitated only a second or two before turning the handle—the unlocked handle—and entered with a hearty push.

The Yearling had been watching all along as she'd never seen other humans in the Old Man's house. His property had been as bereft of other folk as the woodland had been of deer. Near the upended flowerbed—stalks of dead plants peeking from under dirt clods—she watched until after a brief moment the gentleman visitor appeared in the living room hollering and throwing his arms about. He had discovered the unplugged phone cord and reconnected it to the jack. Trembling hands gripped the phone as he dialed. His long face protracted in a state of alarm like a crescent moon.

Wading back through the haunch-high grasses, which seemed to carry the weight of water as she struggled against each upsurging cluster, the Yearling rejoined her mother near the apple tree. They searched the windows of the Cape Cod for signs of the Old Man, but the house had gone still. Nothing moved. No bit of warbling in the woods, not even a rustling of breeze. Hot and heavy hung the summer air over them. Somewhere near the service road, the raven called. Legs grew leaden in the atmosphere. Two more caws. A doe with eyes rolled in the back of her head grunted. Three caws. It was a warning.

A siren sounded in the distance. The whole herd convulsed in fear. And it wasn't long before two vehicles turned onto the long drive bordering the south side of the field, causing the does to run toward the trees.

Screaming the emergency call, a smaller car was followed by a larger rig. They flashed blue and red. The gravel of the drive ricocheted from under tires firing at high speeds into the grass and clipping the Yearling's right side. She let out a whimper as the white spot of her head and face undulated with the light of the flashers.

The vehicles stopped at the house. Out of the small car came a squat, square man clad in a deep-blue uniform and with hair trimmed very near his scalp. Behind him, two men exited the larger vehicle. They rushed toward the house; the little man let them fly past as he pressed his body flush against his car and then tagged along behind them.

There was quite a bit of racket coming from the house. The two men from the larger vehicle exited the Cape Cod. They opened the back of their rig and retrieved a stretcher. Into the house they hurried brushing past Crane as he was leaving. His elongated face was scrunched. He hyperventilated on the porch, finally slumping into the old rocker and staring off toward the mailbox at the corner of the field. Something scampered behind it, grey-gleaming and spry, and he gasped as it came into view but made no mention of it as he had aspirated with such a gasp and was coughing.

The sheriff's voice, a strident sort of falsetto, was heard from the living room window. "We got an ambulance crew over here now. No foul play, but the phone was disconnected according to Crane. Perhaps a trip. Old people … You know." He crouched with his tape recorder still glued to his mouth. "I see a broken deer statue, a little thing, lying on the floor. Lots of religious shit and art stuff. Definitely looks like he took a stumble."

All artifacts were in their place except one.

From out the house the two men came with a figure in a body bag atop the stretcher. They moved it down the steps of the porch and bumped along the uneven path. The larger of the two hopped into the vehicle and readied himself to hoist the front of the stretcher into the back.

A wind picked up and blew about the figure. A small section of the body bag had been left agape, and it whispered out and onto the breeze where it traveled toward the herd. The Elder Doe caught a tinge of the odor and understood immediately. The Yearling too picked up on the scent, but she couldn't grasp its meaning. Inside the body bag was a great mystery, and all she could envision therein was the little cottontail aside the fallen tree with a fly crawling across its sunken eyeball.

The sheriff, who had held the door open for the paramedics, had gone back into the house. He moved from window to window until at last he exited the Cape Cod with a slam, which caused Crane seated in the rocker to jump up. The sheriff jiggled the doorknob and pressed into the door, which towered over him. He nodded. It was well secured at last but days too late.

The sheriff tore down toward the apple tree. He was as heavy footed as he was short. Arriving at the base, he placed a hand on the trunk and leaned crossing his right foot over the left. He ogled the herd and played about his chin. Then uttering a groan—which was more of a pip in his octave—he jumped away from the tree shaking out his hand. A spot in the bark invisible to his eye had stung his palm. He gave his hand a good dusting on his slacks and marched back to his rig. "My my my! If I was one of these does, I'd be heading for the hills." He laughed. His cackle was shrill and rapid as though a ground squirrel had burrowed in his throat. The paramedics were silent, and Crane was still atop the porch twiddling his thumbs and waiting for answers. He watched as the sheriff joined the paramedics to shoot the shit.

"So we were at my pop's place the other day hunting on his pond. Lots of geese out there. Ducks too. The birds got scared and flew up, and I just fired into the bunch of them," the sheriff said scratching his chin and ignoring the deer as they watched.

The Yearling turned her sights toward the Cape Cod's two black living room windows. They looked back at her, the edging of the snapped-stem hosta border underneath resembling a mouth full of teeth. And as the Elder Doe crossed in front of her from a distance and turned, her head became perfectly centered in the image—a little nasal cavity. It held the Yearling mesmerized. She tried to blink the image away, but it stayed. The house had become a skull.

"So I downed something speckled, and it flew over the pond and dropped into the trees. Me and Pop hurried over to see what it was. And there in this beech tree was a falcon of all damned things. Its wings were stretched out and sort of impaled on the branches. Just hung there kind of struggling and squawking and bleeding all over the place."

Behind them, Crane—who had crippling social anxiety—stood waiting for the right, brave moment to interrupt.

One paramedic chimed in, "What did you do with it? Eat it?"

"*Awww*, what a wiseass. Who eats falcons? I mean, we eat almost everything, have since food started becoming scarce, but definitely not a damn falcon. Pop mentioned something about a verse in the Bible saying falcons were unclean. He wanted it gone. So I used a long stick and smacked it a bit and got it out of the tree. We were getting rid of weeds and trash that evening, so I tossed it on the burn pile—"

Crane interrupted with nervous babble. "I must go, gentleman. I assume you'll find Doc's distant relations, but I'd like to know how to inform any inquiring parties in regard to his interment and wishes—next steps and such. Also, did you happen to see the boot tracks aside the house?"

The sheriff spoke high and slow. "We'll look into it, Crane. As for next steps, well, I got my orders."

"Oh?"

The sheriff sighed. "Yes, Crane. Looks like we already know what to do with the remains."

"You already read the will?" Crane twisted up his face.

A look cracked the sheriff's face revealing a Cheshire cat grin. "No. But like I said, I already got my orders for the remains."

"Which is?"

"Incineration."

By afternoon the next day, the Yearling and her mother were gorging on apples and other fodder to bolster themselves for their departure. There were no signs of the Buck, and the full moon was lifting. Nightfall would take them into the well-lit land en route to the North Territory regardless of the Buck's return.

As it was their last day on the acreage, the Yearling pestered her mother into allowing her to go off alone into the trees. A final look at the wooded part of the acreage was all she needed—the place where she'd spent many hours at play and in awe. Danger advanced and daylight waned, but as there was yet business to tend to with the rest of the herd, the Elder Doe gave in to her daughter's pleas and consented.

The Yearling rushed into the tree line each step sending a dull stab to her full stomach. Specks of dust and pollen floated about the air like gold powder. She ambled through each cloud that covered her head and breast like gilt. Leaping over a knot of weeds, she freed her coat of the dusting and paused to scan the scene. It was a peaceful woodland. It closed in on her like a cocoon and verged upon claustrophobic, yet she succumbed to its swaddle. It was like the first moments of life in the narrow coyote's den.

It was still unclear what had happened to the Old Man. As she thought of him, her ears burned. Not because someone was speaking ill of her but because she was tied to the Old Man; for at that very moment, his body was being cremated in town.

She took in a vast breath of bluestone air, let it fill her until it lifted her from the stone-shattered earth like a balloon. Then it swept out of her tickling the boughs that dangled before her and thrusting her back onto the ground. A distant motion through the cracks of twigs and brush caught her eye. She tilted her head and lifted her leg as she did whenever she was uncertain of what she was seeing. She dropped her hoof to the ground and pivoted her weight on it, leaning in its direction. The thing was pale and liquid, and it coasted through the recesses like waterfowl on a lake.

Back on the field, the Elder Doe approached the clan. Wickedness was nearing the acreage, and it darkened their gaze. They fluttered their bristling lashes until a blackness like ink began to flood the whites of their eyes. The Elder Doe called to them as the distant apple tree jutted out from behind her like wings. They flicked their tongues at her and groaned. One doe growled like a dog.

The Elder Doe began to retreat toward the tree, but the herd encircled her. They threshed about and danced on hooves barely touching the earth. Many voices raised from out their mouths, and they issued a series of blasphemies and defamations. Foam bubbled at their lips and ran down their long necks toward their breasts. One stood on her haunches to walk like a man. At last they had corralled her against the tree; the coal-black orbs of their many eyes were the damnable inverse of the sacred apples.

Meanwhile in the trees, the Yearling was evaded by the fleeing figure. It led her through the labyrinthine woods. Where at first it had startled her, it now enthralled her. She reasoned that it must be her father making his way toward the pool of winter runoff as promised.

First, it seemed to be branches, but then, it appeared as antlers. A wind shook the limbs and shrubs that obscured her vision. One moment later, she saw his hoof, and next, it turned out to be the stub of a snapped pine pole. The silhouette lured her to the service road. When it ultimately stopped just beyond the layers of tree and fern, the wind raked the path once again muddling the view. She drew nearer, and in the clearing, she at last saw it.

As she breached the opening, a low growl rumbled guttural and constant. Instead of her father awaiting her, she was greeted by two ivory fangs bared about a snout; they protruded from pink-red gums strung with saliva. The beast's tongue lifted and flickered sympathetically with its coarse grumble; the folds of its silvery brow were crimped on two bronzed eyes. It snapped its jaws at the Yearling—a muted clunk of teeth on teeth.

The Yearling backed away with her ears held firmly against her head. She couldn't catch her breath; her ribs squeezed instead of opening which nearly cracked cartilage. The beast had lowered itself, its body building with kinetic energy such that at any second it would lunge and rive her throat to pieces.

The Yearling lifted her nose, but this animal emitted no scent. She saw its low-hanging teats swollen and red. When the beast noticed her studying it, it thrashed its mouth and growled furiously; its neck fur was standing on end like a ruffled collar.

Something else then drew near. The creature, suddenly distracted, rotated its ears; its eyes darted to and fro from the service road and back. And before the Yearling could muster a thought, the beast—the revenant she-coyote—had unexpectedly sprung at her.

With a twist of the body, the Yearling bounded through the clearing back toward the acreage. A terrible howl drew the attention of the doe clan away from the Elder Doe, dropping the walking deer back to a four-legged stance.

Self-preservation had dulled the Yearling's keener senses. In her haste to escape, a greater danger snaked its way up the service road. As she disappeared into the dense forest with the she-coyote nearing her haunches, two vehicles had crept up and pulled off to the side. Motors stopped. Car doors opened.

When at last she returned to the Old Man's field, she saw the doe clan about the apple tree. They faced the Cape Cod in a triangular formation with her mother to the back. The Yearling rushed toward the Elder Doe, who gave her daughter a troubled, knowing look. Behind her, the she-coyote was absent, and so she slowed her pace to a trot as she made her way toward safety. However, coming from the opposite direction, another beast was about to make its presence known.

There was a slam. The Yearling froze. She kept her eyes on the apple bark. Footsteps crunched on the gravel drive, and she turned slowly in their direction. Before the herd stood six men.

The one who strode from his truck—the seventh man— pushed forward with an arrogant gait. He used his crooked finger to caress a scar that embossed his face from his left brow to his nose. Clearing his throat loudly, he spit out a wad of brown saliva. "My God, fellas, this place is infested," he scoffed and sniffed the dirty, crooked finger he had used to pack chaw into his lip. "Sure as hell. Like I told the Old Man, time's up."

He took his tobacco-stained finger to his mouth and joined it with a thumb. He gave off a piercing whistle meant for the men by the service road. He smiled; his broken yellow teeth were mottled with flecks of snuff. "Boys, I told you we had our work cut out for us, didn't I?" He laughed low and slow as if he were choking. The other men joined. The noise bounced off hardwoods and shot into the red sky. Rifles with straps were in chapped hands.

Dusk smothered the land, and far away, thunder sounded and the cry of wounded birds falling through the sky was heard. Evil had come to the acreage, and it forced deer joints to bend and snap, and they bowed before the great beast, the Man with the Crooked Finger. The clan looked back to the Elder Doe and commanded, *Lower your eyes*, yet she kept herself upright, her body open and her face stoic. The hour had finally arrived, and she knew it was too late.

Thunder rolled in the distance. Tips of apple branch dipped into the sky's red pool. Thick, damp air bore down on anxious bodies while from the trees came the accordion drone of insects. The men's semicircle was nearly punctured by the herd's arrow-tip formation. Any moment, a gun could go off. The smell of fermented fruit was pronounced, and the Man with the Crooked Finger scanned all about the ground. Under a mound of grass, he found the least blemished fruit, raised it high, and studied its every angle like a diamond. "Somethin' I wanna see," he wheezed through broken teeth. "I wanna know how dumb these bitches actually are." He stretched his arm forward with the apple in hand. He flicked it and snapped his tongue as one calls to a cat. "Come get it!"

"They're not tame," said Red, smoothing his fiery whiskers.

"I know that, Red," the Man replied. "I said I wanna see."

Raising his hands with palms outward, Red acceded with an eye roll. "Whatever." The Man smiled at him and carried on making snapping sounds with his mouth. He bobbed the apple until his shoulder burned. "Dammit! Come here!"

The does were savvy interpreters of body language; they knew what he wanted. It was the moment their jealousy had longed for. It seemed as good a time as any to rid themselves of the little doe who had rushed into their world bringing with her disunion and danger. In a moment of telepathic synchronization, several does pushed the Yearling forward. Blocked by their bodies, which they had formed into a wall, the Elder Doe was unable to intervene. One doe used her snout to butt the Yearling toward the Man. She stood exposed in the center of the human semicircle. The betrayal was complete, and the raven croaked from the hemlock.

"*Ho ho ho!* Look at this freak!" The men roared with laughter. "You see the way they offered her up?"

The Yearling was fixated on the apple in the Man's hand, the crooked finger parted from the middle finger and grasping it like a curveball. In her mind, she envisioned the smiling Old Man on the empty chair with the same offering. What was there to fear anymore? This stranger and the Old Man were surely a part of the same herd.

"'Attagirl. Eat," the Man rasped. His hand trembled; it was foreplay. He shifted his gaze to Red, and Red watched reluctantly. In the presence of the Man, the Yearling could hear a faint sound. It seemed far off at first, but as she listened more intently, she realized it was near—very near in fact. A swallowed and desperate cry was coming from inside the Man. It was the voice of a child.

But it was cut short by pounding hooves. The Elder Doe, who had rammed her way through the wall her sisters had formed, now bounded headlong for her daughter, who had the Man's apple at her mouth. At the last possible second, the Elder Doe prodded the Yearling back into the fold. The Man didn't even blink. He eyed the Elder Doe with a reptilian gaze and let loose a little gasp. "*Ah!* Here's a face I recognize." He traced his scar with a finger. "How could I forget?"

There came a flash of movement from behind the keyhole of his pupils. *Ah!* She too hadn't forgotten the old devil who squatted inside him.

"Hungry?" He lowered the apple near her snout.

What else could she do? She paused but then stretched her neck toward the fruit. Her tight jaw opened. Bands of muscle creaked like an old door, and her tongue lifted in response. She readied her teeth to grasp the apple. But before she could even taste the fruit, there came a sudden, terrible pain as if her breath had been sucked from out her lungs. She watched the world spin as she was hurled through space. A throaty whimper punched out of her mouth as she crashed to the earth. The grounding of her body cracked her ribs.

The Man's steel-toed boot had come from nowhere. He had employed a kick that had sent her tumbling until she was flattened to the earth. The Yearling grunted to her mother, but she couldn't yet hear the plea. Queasy and disoriented, the Elder Doe shook her head. Her vision resumed gradually through a starburst, and her hearing returned in a roaring as if she were rising through water toward surface.

Again, the Man laughed doubling over and almost taking a tumble himself. One thing was then certain to the Yearling; he and the Old Man were most assuredly not from the same herd. The Man was a wicked, cruel breed; she too could now see the old devil in him. Even his lackeys looked to one another with discomfort. And though they'd grown to loathe deer via his fanatical hatred, the gesture was for them disarmingly inhumane. But since they were afraid of him, they were silent. One attempted a smile—the corners of his mouth forced up as if lifted by marionette strings. Even Red pulled a face.

When he realized his was the only laughter, the Man became angry. "Come on! Don't go limp-dick on me now, fellas! They're dangerous!" He gestured to the herd presenting a benign group, the majority standing solemn while the injured Elder Doe leaned on the Yearling. "This tree's a problem! It makes finding food too easy. Now we have a population issue again." He moved behind the pulpit of the abandoned folding chair. "They transmit disease. They destroy our crops. What then will we eat? And when we hit them on the highway, what will we drive to our jobs? How then will we feed our families?"

The lackeys lowered their heads. The Man then moved toward the tree. It sunk stones in his stomach. He saw the spot in the bark that revealed his secret. He then stood face-to-face with his shame—his original sin. To the east, brewing storm clouds bruised the orange sky. He turned away from the horizon back to the Cape Cod. He felt so near to the Old Man in spirit, and worst of all, he was flocked by deer. He spun on his bootheels and barked, "Red, go get your chainsaw!"

Red was a sawyer; because of the former family business with the sugar bush, he always had a chainsaw in his pickup. He headed to retrieve it but paused midway. "Doc's dead. I don't know. Doesn't seem right. Besides, I haven't sharpened the chain since you cut up—"

"Doesn't seem right?" the Man asked. He walked up to Red, cupped his groin, and squeezed. "You still got balls under there, boy?" Red slapped the Man's hand away, but the Man drew nearer. He lightly rubbed up against Red speaking very close to his face, lip almost touching lip. "When I give you an order," he whispered, "you just do it."

The others watched quizzically when the Man and Red had one of their moments. Red had the special privilege of conversing with him like an oracle or a psychic medium. The others didn't or couldn't. The Man never deigned to speak to any of them—only spoke at them. Probably didn't even remember their names. And when he bounced ideas off them, they were as good as walls or photographs in matters of participation.

The Man continued, "Nobody gives a shit about the tree, and nobody gives two shits about the old doctor. The town's relieved he's dead anyway. He was a baby killer."

"But he didn't actually kill the baby."

As soon as Red had said it, the other men tucked their heads. The Man's eyes narrowed. He could hardly open his lips curling tight with tension. "Well, fine. His wasn't the murdering hand." He swallowed hard. "Even so, the old man was a faggot."

The other men turned white and grew ill. The word *faggot* carried dark magick.

"Really? A faggot?" Red retorted.

"That's right." He walked up to Red and drove his crooked finger into his breastplate. He could feel curls of ruddied chest hair through the fabric of his shirt, and when his finger slipped, he grazed the line of a muscle-clad rib. "You got something else you want to say, Red?"

Red was silent, but his lips and hands quivered.

An abrupt fluttering of wings from behind both cut and amplified the tension. A bird had flown from out of a hemlock and into the garden. The Man half-expected to see Fay on the porch gripping the railing, his black hair shining blue. But it was a raven, and it kept watch from the raised bed outside the Old Man's window. It cawed at the Man heckling him. "Go to hell!" he cried. The raven cawed again, but that time, it was a fit of ribbing laughter. It shone indigo in the sun, and the Man's heart raced to see the familiarity of it.

He turned away from the raven with a jutted jaw underlining a forced simpering. "Fellas, let's not get off topic." He flashed a used-car salesman's smile. "I love this land, and I hate to see it ruined. The deer, the old man, the squatter in the woods, even the apple tree; all these things are—and were—abominations. They are simply not in line with my vision. Don't we all share my vision of what our community should look like? Don't ya trust me?"

The men's faces lightened to see his anger abate and because they did trust him.

"We're doing this for our cause. For our fathers' cause." He ran his hands over his hair. "And my friend, Red, you had mentioned the tree. Let me put it to you this way. If you have a rat infestation in your house, Red …" Red raised an eyebrow like a burning ridge upon his face; he'd been caught off guard studying a particular spot in the trunk of the tree. "… Red, do you leave food in the kitchen for the rats?" Red's first word was barely vocalized. "It's rhetorical. Don't speak. And the answer is no." Red's freckled face flushed. "You eliminate its resources, which is something the old man was too weak-minded to do."

At that moment, the raven, who had been supping on squirming knots of earthworms in the piles of decomposing plants, took flight. It festooned the Old Man's window with the obsidian-hued arrow-feathers that escaped its wings. And even though he had heard its departure, the Man would not turn back and give it the satisfaction of his attention.

"Who knows?" He spoke loudly, and it was unclear as to who the intended audience was, the men or the raven. "Maybe the old man is thanking us this very minute as he watches us from above." He put a finger to his chin aping contemplation. "I dunno. Maybe he's looking *up* at us." The men snickered. "So Red, get your chainsaw and let's carve out our vision for this woodland."

Red had a conviction twisting his brain. "All I'm saying is, it seems a waste to cut down a perfectly healthy tree after what happened to the sugar bush." He went to the truck and grabbed his Husqvarna. Its heft yanked upon his shoulder joint, which struck him as odd as it had normally felt light in his grip. The walk to and from the pickup gave him space to think. Meanwhile, the tree still revealed its hidden message to him with holographic effect.

"Somebody move this shit outta my way." Red struggled to maneuver around the chair and easel being overgrown with grass. A chubby, bald fellow directed to relocate the items untangled them from the pasture and waddled each item to the side of the porch.

Amid the commotion, the does started to jerk around, which caused some of the men to ready their guns. Upon seeing the barrels rise in a sequence of upthrusts, the deer froze in the midst of their squirming.

Insects continued to bow their melodies. The chainsaw cord was tugged. Nothing. Red yanked it again. The motor quickened for a moment but petered out. Insects still buzzed from brush. Red couldn't focus. The superimposed image in the tree bark was making him cross-eyed. It defied the laws of visual dimensions.

"Okay, I'm not nuts," Red said, "but I see this thing in the bark. You see it?"

The Man paled in face and tone. "I don't see nothin'."

"Yeah, it's right here." He indicated it by tracing its outline in the trunk.

Closing in on the tree, the other disciples began to scrutinize the area looking to one another. Some scratched their heads while the chubby, bald man giggled.

"It's a sequence. You guys see it? It's becoming clear."

"You wanna hurry up, Red? The boys up at the service road are probably getting antsy waiting for my signal. Besides, I don't see it." The Man blushed and twiddled the fingers of one hand along his rough blue jeans before exploding, "For Christ's sake, jackass, just get a goddam move on!"

As Red turned back toward the Man, he severed his gaze upon the bark, and as such, the message in the tree was hidden. "Don't you ever call me a jackass," Red said. He shook his head, and the other men could see his anger in the spasming of his impressive masseter muscles. He continued, "So chief, should I saw under it or atop it?"

"Just cut it down, smart-ass—I mean, may I call you smart-ass?"

Red again rolled his eyes and mouthed a few choice words before using all the force he had coordinating and tightening every muscle in his right arm. The chainsaw blared. The blade whistled as he began the notch cut. As he sawed the bark, a liquid oozed from within, a richly colored sap. The deeper he cut, the more it spewed. It splattered his face with its saccharine gore. A sight so bizarre and at the same time so captivating had brought human and deer together. They surrounded Red and the tree evenly dispersed.

He made the second notch cut. The chainsaw stopped. Nobody noticed that the chorus of insects had gone mute. In fact, the whole of twilight was quiet. Red stood back and decided where to make the felling cut—under the undecipherable symbol, where he would separate it from the nourishment of its roots. At last, it would wither and turn brittle and be burned to ash and forgotten much like the Old Man.

The Yearling braced her mother as she too teetered on the verge. It pained her to put any bearing on her injured leg that delivered a sting to her bruised ribs. The moment to escape would be narrow and imminent; she hoped her body would allow her to fly.

The chainsaw revved up once more. It railed at the tree lamenting the horrors it had seen. Red indicated with a flip of his vascular hand for everyone to clear back and took his saw to the side. The deer dared not move as the chain screamed infiltrating the bark with liquid spurting.

Suddenly, the saw was stuck. There was a bit of a struggle to push it farther. Red leaned into the trunk with his solid frame. The resistance stalled the saw. Either that or some mechanism in it had become gummed up by the sap.

The creek in the forest reversed its flow. Insects rose heavenward then fell from the sky in a lace-winged rain. All at once, a ripping and crackling sound rang out. Red stumbled backward with his saw jammed in the trunk. From the saw cut all the way up to the branches, the sacred apple tree split in two. It was a gravity-defying fissure ferocious and slivered. The two halves fell opposite each other, and it parted itself revealing the endless, darkening distance. With its mighty crash, the creek resumed its direction. Insects crawled along the soil dragging shattered wings. The roots of the apple tree released their embrace on the bluestone bedrock. Its foundation lay fractured.

"That was one hell of a show, gents!" The Man surveyed the tree wreckage with a self-congratulating look. "After we've done the duty our community has called on us to do, let's be sure to cut up some of this wood to take with."

Green wood was less than ideal, but it could be used to augment what they already had. The Man with the Crooked Finger envisioned swirls of smoke rising from his victory pyre. He slung his gun loose from his shoulder then looked to his disciples, his puffed-out chest tugging at the fabric around his shirt buttons.

Sensing the shift in the atmosphere, the does lowered themselves. The psychic energy was oppressive. While the storm traveled above, the running black line of its shadow was about to cross over them. And all the while they stood around it, the tree continued to weep.

"Well I'm pretty damn sure the boys in the trees are just chomping at the bit waiting for our signal." Thunder shook the cracked bluestone field; the old Cape Cod windows rattled. The Man licked his dry lips as he watched Red collect his chainsaw, which had toppled aside the tree. "Come on, Red! Shake a leg, boy!"

Red dragged his feet to the bed of the truck, dumped the chainsaw atop its black, ribbed liner, and grabbed his rifle. He rejoined the group unaware of the sticky dried patches of tree sap adhered to his chest and face and beard. He kept his eyes down. Thunder rolled again. The black line of the storm passed over them, and the once hot, heavy air chilled and encumbered them in a new way.

"Gents, you feel that? The power of the storm! God gives us his blessing as we cleanse this land of filth and si—"

A rumble in the black cloud stifled his words. At the same time, twin shots from the service road had underscored the thunder blast. The lackeys turned northward while the Man glared into the tree line. Men tucked near the service road hadn't waited for the agreed-upon signal. A trophy had passed before their scopes worthy of disregarding orders.

Another barrage of thunder coupled with a sharp crack of lightning, and with it, the does took their chance to flee. They scurried north into the forest. Guns went up. A bombardment of shots littered the field. The Elder Doe and the Yearling crossed into the timber. Behind, a body dropped hard to the earth. Then another. The Elder Doe diverted their escape east toward the coyote's den avoiding the service road.

They charged to the eastern edge; their clambering hooves were covered over by men's voices and the sound of doe bodies running into branch and bramble. Blood pressure soared. The Yearling saw her pulse in her vision. Rounding the large bluestone boulder of the den, the Yearling and the Elder Doe lowered themselves to their bellies before its opening. They listened as the shooting suddenly cut out. The opposing groups of men had found themselves involuntarily firing at one another; some had taken shelter behind trucks parked up the service road and were crying out for a cease-fire.

With her snout resting at the entrance of the den, the Yearling caught an odor—very faint but peculiar, enough so to recognize instantly: this was her birthplace. She was surprised that her memories sprang up with such clarity. She remembered the way the night had smelled in the den and how omnipotent the tree had appeared when she first entered the field. Now it lay split, the two ragged sides opposite a tattered, seeping trunk. All the while, doe blood soaked into the ground.

Seconds passed. Silence prevailed. The Elder Doe moved to a vantage point offering an unobstructed view of the field. The panorama was bleak: to the north, the hindquarters of a dead doe were sticking out from the grass. The men all seemed to be at the service road; she heard their rough talk bouncing through the wood all congratulatory and boisterous. When the cuckoo began its nocturne from the stream, the Elder Doe closed her eyes. She pictured the beloved who had once spoken: *As an apple tree among the trees of the forest, so is my beloved among all.*

Rain began to sprinkle the land and would soon pummel the earth and wash away the blood of fallen does. Would this blood offering appease man's vengeful deity who now controlled their destiny? Was it enough to barter for safe passage?

The Elder Doe signaled to the Yearling, and the two crossed the field making little sound. They could escape into the west-facing woods where they'd later curve north and bypass the service road. South would be too dangerous as it followed the hillside drive, and besides, it would lead them opposite the North Territory.

All remained hushed except for the fluid swishing of grass about their sides and the rumble of men's voices near the service road. When at last they traversed its length and approached the apple tree, another crack of thunder discharged. It was breathtaking in its sheer volume. Aside them, they saw the tree sap that was drawing flies. A soft fruit lay hidden underneath, and the Yearling stamped her hoof through it; its pulp splattered up her right leg and then down warm and thick. The dying tree doled out portents yet.

A subdued but coarse voice called out, "Leaving without saying goodbye?"

They halted and turned. Planted in a wide stance was the Man with rifle to his shoulder. Behind him, a gunless Red watched with arms crossed. Immovable, he posed aside the propped-up chair and easel, his white skin the marble of garden statuary.

"We've unfinished business, old girl. Saved my bullets for you and your little freak. She's young—She your baby?" He closed his left eye; the full length of the scar's disparate halves finally connected via the eyelid. "Must be nice to have a baby."

The seconds were slow. Behind the men, a rattle shook with persistence. Tunnel vision had overtaken the Man, who didn't hear the sound—only the devil whispering in his ear. Red could however. His pose somewhat loosened as he scanned the gardens and the porch.

The Man dispatched his evil eye. It went straight to guaranteed kill zones, and with a black magick, he could transport himself very near his target and latch onto them and infiltrate them. All it would take now was one shot, a slight twist of the body, a cocking of the bolt action, and then another shot and both does would be dead. Again, the rattling sounded. It had drawn nearer, but the Man heard only the inner voice entreating him to kill the white-faced doe with haste.

The crooked finger began to squeeze; the Elder Doe and the Yearling had no chance to run. The Yearling closed her eyes hoping the inevitable wouldn't hurt. The evil eye bound them where they stood, and they heard the whispering in the man's soul as it swept against them. The Man let his breath out through gapped teeth and pressed his hooked finger against the trigger. He saw in the white-dappled face of the Yearling the reflection of a child he longed to forget— longed to destroy—and centered the crosshairs on that spot.

When Red suddenly began screaming, the hooked finger let up off the trigger and the sharpshooter jumped and turned in rage. His wicked gaze had been foiled thus breaking its command over the does. Freed from its constraint, they dashed behind the house and into the cover of the western woods.

"Dammit! Look what you did!"

Red clutched his leg. He patted his calf and inspected his hand. He touched it again dabbing the muscle with his palm. Red raised up and moaned, "I got bit!"

The Man looked at Red as if he were growing a horn out his head. "What do you mean you got bit?"

Red replied, "There! Underneath the chair. It was a big rattlesnake. It was sliding between the easel and the chair. I looked down. All I saw was its eyes. Then it struck." His face and hair were a monochromatic hue.

The Man looked west behind the house. He signaled to Red to get in the truck. "Let's go to the goddam clinic then."

Insect choruses had once again enveloped the acreage. The sky opened and dumped drops onto the field; its grass, long like tousled hair, was hanging upside down toward heaven. From the driver's seat, the Man studied the chair and easel. Nothing stirred or slinked. He cast his powerful eye into the forest dripping with diamond rain. He'd collect his bounty. And as Red began to moan with panic, he started the engine and sped down the gravel drive.

Watching from the raised flowerbed, the serpent coiled itself around an oriental lily, where its bloom was spent upon a spiring stem. It was centered directly in front of the Old Man's bedroom window, skirted with black-blue feathers. The snake ebbed and danced in the pouring rain, rattling in victory for a while and then slipped away. Even the raven seemed to be singing from the hemlock, *Let it be known: The mighty evil eye has been thwarted by the meek!*

**T**he forest was dark, and the journey was unfamiliar. Rain hammered down in sheets. The Elder Doe and the Yearling kept a feverish pace up deadwood slopes and down to clearings. Without game trails to guide their noses, their race to the river would be touch and go. The Yearling strained to see her mother, the white-washed timber turned black by nightfall. Yet their flight had a saving grace—the beacon of the Elder Doe's large, downy tail lifted and glowing. With a swift glance backward, the Elder Doe likewise could track the Yearling by the beaming white patch of her head.

The farther north they went, the more they heard vehicles. Distant motors roared as they came and went around a bend. As the does passed a skein of shrubbery, the Yearling keyed into a pattering of feet. She turned back, and the sound ceased. She wondered if it had been a trick of acoustics—perhaps the sound of their own running as it echoed off forest surfaces. Another engine sounded, that time much closer. Its rumble tapered away as it rounded the bend. They'd have to pass over the road to reach the river. Once across, they'd be free to make the ascent to the North Territory, but they feared they'd stray without the Buck.

The terrain leading to the mountain highway was deceiving. It had all the qualities of the Old Man's woods—familiar trees and plants and lichen-green stones—yet it was still foreign. It had a dulling effect imbuing a false sense of comfort. However, if they looked closely behind each one of those recognizable features, there was a furtive danger tightly wound. In the true wilds of the forest, it was an unrelenting dance between life and death, and they'd have to learn quickly.

The last of the sun had faded, and the scuttling of hidden feet returned. A panting then chugged from the rear. It tailed the does causing the Yearling to cry out to her mother. She did not turn back. The deluge was deafening, and the thunder still boomed through the rolling hill valley.

Ahead, the Elder Doe had dashed under a canopy that muffled the downpour and slowed its torrent. Deciding it a suitable area to slow the pace and take advantage of refuge, she turned to the path behind and saw the Yearling lowered into the brush, her mewling masked by rainfall.

She lifted her nose in the air. The wind was against them; nothing behind could be discerned. Forest floor crackled as something closed in on them. It was hard to decipher what was stalker and what was cloudburst. A light began to shine from ahead. Their orientation was now parallel to the highway. A passing car's headlights traveled along the wood. Just before the lights drifted as the car rounded the hill, its glare caught two small orbs. As the beams disappeared, so did the pair of eyes.

The Yearling scurried to the Elder Doe. They stood side by side and heard the low, guttural roar. A figure began to appear. It was shapeless, just suggestive at first, but then it materialized detail by detail—nails, paws, and then a silvery-brown breast and long snout. It snapped its jaws strung with silken threads and spun a velveteen growl. It backed them out from the coverage of trees, and rain began to pelt their bodies once again. It joined them under the open canopy but remained as dry and white as bone. Leaning forward, the thing was at last clear. It was the ivory-fanged coyote in all its terrible glory.

It lunged at the Yearling, and the Yearling retracted in return. But instead of fleeing, the Yearling stopped and stared brow dripping at her pursuer. The she-coyote pounced forward that time snapping low toward the Yearling's leg. Yet after backing away only a little, the Yearling found herself unable to move. This went on for a short while until the Elder Doe wedged herself between them and pushed the Yearling along, freeing her to make a run for it.

Upon her hindquarters, the Elder Doe rose to knock down the she-coyote, but a stabbing pain in her side brought her right back down. The gesture of it however was enough to make the she-coyote yowl and slip back into cover. Hurling herself in a wide arc, the Elder Doe searched for the creature in hiding. Nothing could be seen in a forest obliterated by shadows. She turned toward the road and rushed to catch up with the Yearling, who had already gained quite a bit of distance ahead of her. She braced herself—At any moment, the jagged bite of the she-coyote could be upon her.

Breaking through the tree line, the Yearling found herself on a clear-cut strip of land. No longer the moss and mulch-padded surface of forest, the floor was wet and rippling yet hard as bluestone. Inches of water covered it. Farther ahead, it was washed out in a cascade. She questioned whether the flooded mountain highway was a shallow stream-bed. Had they made it to the river so soon?

She looked back to the trees searching for movement. No Elder Doe in sight. At first, only sheets of rain ran thick in the distance, but something soon caught her eye. It was coming up the dark causeway. From around the corner, two beams emerged and grew larger in her eyes. They had a sedating effect—flaming, constant, halogenic—and she could not move.

Appearing at the road's edge, the Elder Doe charged forward with the she-coyote low at her hooves. She watched the vehicle ripping down the highway and headed straight toward her daughter. Without slowing, she flung her body and shoved the Yearling once more out of harm's way. It sent the young doe gliding on the flooded road as she skittered over the northern embankment. Her hooves at last dug into the slope with enough force to bring her body to a full stop.

A grinding of truck brakes crisscrossed with the cry of the Elder Doe. The consequent screeching cut through like a blade running along the belly of night. The truck skidded with unstoppable tires bouncing as they hydroplaned. The driver screamed; his window accidentally lowered as he grasped onto the side of the door. Try as they might, the brakes were no match for the water-covered road. The driver shielded his face as the vehicle rushed straight into the Elder Doe.

Everything had become silent in the slowing of action. A steadily building siren engulfed the muted scene and it escalated as it converted into a wobbling noise. A sensation overtook the Yearling; she felt as though she were falling—or perhaps spinning. Its arrival had taken her by surprise. She could run from a coyote, be pushed clear of a speeding truck, and slip past the Man with the Crooked Finger unscathed, but at this moment, she could not elude that mysterious sound.

It repeated in a loop as if it wanted her to study its details—as if it were sentient. First, the high, ear-ringing ping of splintering. Next, the teetering, bouncing sound of wood. And then a tremendous howling. She quieted her mind enough to allow the sound to show her what it was—what purpose it served. Its image then manifested and became clearer—in much the same way the tree had revealed its secret to Red—but as soon as she drew her attention to it, it blurred again. The harder she tried to see it, the farther it drew away from her until at last the split second had passed and a terrible, sharp cracking had stifled it bringing her back to the present.

The truck hit the Elder Doe with such lethal force. The Yearling watched as her mother flew through the air lit by headlights like a passing nightbird. Down the side of the slope the Elder Doe vanished, and the Yearling sped through the cloak of rain following her mother's scent. From up at the road, the driver appeared. He was a brown silhouette superimposed in front of the yellow glare. There was blood on a headlight. He searched for the doe pacing up and down the length of the strip.

The truck radio blared with a plinky, one-note speaker: "Stay safe out there, folks. Here at home, we've got every sort of storm and calamity imaginable. It's doomsday! The people are afraid and are running for the hills. Get to high ground, brothers and sisters! Get to high ground! Lord, give us the wings of a bird so we may fly into the wilderness!"

At last, the door slammed and the truck flipped around and journeyed away from the washed-out highway and crept back around the slick bend whence it had come.

The Elder Doe was standing when the Yearling found her in flat, low ground, but she wasn't mentally tracking or communicating. Her empty gaze was fixed northward, and the Yearling shepherded her toward cover. The Elder Doe's head drooped and lifted in a breakneck repetition. Buckling legs stumbled in a rock-ribbed line. The Elder Doe's hooves were scuffling heavily with legs extending back in smooth, arch-like motions like a *media luna* figure. Sometimes, they balanced weight forehead to forehead or cheek to cheek. They moved like lovers tangoing.

A thicket stood before them, a family of tall paper birch insulated by surrounding stones and brush. They wound and stretched around each other toward an opening in the forest ceiling. They weaved and knotted themselves, and their spindly trunks somehow ballooned outward at the base then twisted together toward the top in a teardrop shape. It was a thicket of tears.

The Yearling went ahead and inspected the entrance. Inside was a domed ceiling with ample space for the two does. She pushed her mother in and struggled to get her through, scraping her head and back on the narrow aperture. Breathlessly, they collapsed. The Yearling did her best to blanket her mother with her body. The night ahead would be long and dark, and she worried that the she-coyote might find them, that she'd awaken to see jaws on her leg or her mother's body being dragged into the woods.

She began to lick her mother's head just as her mother had done for her. Above them, the domed ceiling so tightly braided kept the water from infiltrating. It felt holy inside the thicket somehow. The Elder Doe wanted to speak but couldn't. She had lost the faculty. She kept her eye bound to the woven canopy. At last, she was experiencing firsthand what happened to all old does who wandered off alone into the depths of the Bluestone Woodland.

Through the stormy night, the Elder Doe somehow heard the snake rattling all the way from the acreage. It had gone inside the Cape Cod and slithered to the haunted bedroom. It rose from the Turkish rug aside the nightstand with the beloved's photo on it. With one ferocious strike, the snake had taken fear and grief in its mouth and swallowed them whole. In a day or so, it would slither back out to the field and wrap its long body around the trunk of the felled apple tree, taking its tail in its mouth. It would then defecate all that pain, digested and transmuted, to nourish the sacred tree. For deep in its core, there was yet a molecule of hope—a bud waiting to swell and throb with the green blood of life. Then the rattlesnake would dance through the wilds, slink over the highway, and enter the thicket so that it may at last carry the Elder Doe's spirit back home.

ight creeping through slits where birch poles failed to overlap grew dimmer toward the bottom. The Elder Doe was calm. She hadn't yet opened her eyes, and her breathing was quiet. The pause between intakes was elongating; it had been since early morning. Her coat slightly adhered to the ground where she lay as blood was thickening and gelling beneath her.

The Yearling couldn't see the extent of the bleeding or understand the gravity of the situation. Morning brightened her face. To see her mother at last so peaceful after the nightmarish flight encouraged her. She had spent long evening hours forcing herself awake. She nursed her mother, kept her warm, groomed her just as her mother had done for her that first night in the coyote's den.

Soon, the Elder Doe would need nourishment and water. Wary of their pursuers, the Yearling slowly poked her head out of the thicket. Once she had deemed it safe enough, she wriggled through the lopsided opening.

Purple clouds—the residue of the storm—meandered above. The woods were brilliantly hued. Rain always made forest colors richer. A gust of fresh, cool air enwrapped her, and it elicited a deep breath within sweeping and cleansing her lungs and filling her with optimism. It slingshotted her upon her way.

Finding water proved simple; there were ample collections of rainwater in every pocket and crevice of the forest floor. The difficulty would be transporting it to the thicket. This area of woodland was brighter than that of the acreage. It was less dense and freckled with bundles of birch and pines. The puddles shone in the morning sun embellishing the land with countless little mirrors. Each pool housed a tiny image of passing clouds. Every step gave the illusion of walking in the sky.

The land began to slope as it would ultimately meet the river. The Yearling wasn't ready to wander that far, yet the river called to her. The farther she foraged, the louder the roaring grew. It was a turbulent whirring. She'd never before heard anything of such force. Not even the mysterious sound compared to the river's might, a power that had brought the land to its knees. The deep valley had once been an ancient plateau. Hilltops now contemplated one another divided by the gorge—distant, broken selves dreaming of oneness.

Farther into the woods, the Yearling kept her nose about the ground. Everything had become mush after the warm sopping of rainwater. Stubborn dried leaves from the previous autumn finally succumbed to fate and disintegrated. Out of them came a proliferation of new life. Little green things were pushing up everywhere.

She rounded back to the thicket fearful of wandering too far. Underneath a black cherry that faced the entrance, the Yearling noticed little nubs, very white and osseous in appearance like the sun-bleached tips of a ribcage. Her mouth watered. It was a patch of mushrooms. She plucked one. It squeaked between her rubbing teeth. She plucked another. Such bland, creamy flesh. It felt good to put food in her stomach. She collected more grasping at them hurriedly with her mouth. Cradling them with her bowing tongue, she made her way back. The tender little caps would be easy for her mother to swallow.

Into the thicket she squirmed; the Elder Doe was still splayed out on her side. Her breathing had become full-blown gasps; the silence between each inhalation was longer than before. Her abdomen and ribs shook as the air—once a companion but now an intruder—forced its way into her.

The Yearling laid the mushrooms beside the Elder Doe's foamy, soil-caked mouth. She nudged them very near, but her mother was unresponsive. She cleaned the Elder Doe's mouth and licked her head with her long tongue. Each of the Elder Doe's labored breaths carried with it a puff of mushroom spores.

The Yearling ventured back out for water. A small pool was near. She gathered it in her mouth, bloating her cheeks with the warm liquid, then squeezed back into the thicket. She dripped the water over her mother's parted mouth, a small crack revealing hints of teeth. The water seemed to drain into her mouth and nothing more. She gasped again; her snout soaked in the puddling fluid that had escaped through her unclenched molars.

Once again, the Yearling went back to the puddle, lapped up more, and fought her reflex to swallow. A quick and dotted chirping came from the treetops. She paused to look but saw only vacant limbs. She squeezed back through the thicket gap. The sun raged through the birches; its brilliance gave the two does a golden-orange sheen as if the thicket had been set aflame.

Hoping for a different result, she dumped the water over her mother's mouth, but the Elder Doe wouldn't drink—wouldn't so much as speak or even open her eyes. Panic was setting in, and all the while, the bird kept on chirruping, which nettled the Yearling.

But it was a fleeting irritability as a strange sensation overcame her. The birch thicket began to pulsate. It swelled and squeezed; it was breathing. Beyond the heaving thorax of tree limbs, a shadow stirred. Coyote or man she knew not. It glissaded past the entrance with many thousands of trailing images behind it denoting its movement through space like a time-lapse photo.

Against her better judgment, she poked her head out of the thicket wanting to follow. Along the forest floor, she watched it scurry. It was a pudgy, little cottontail. It went from one end of the wood to the other pushing its way through undergrowth, its path a quivering sequence of plant tips. But when it stampeded back toward her on mighty little feet, it morphed and then melted into the forest floor.

The Yearling jumped and hit her head on the thicket opening. The form of the liquified rabbit appeared round and black like an oil spill until it suddenly sprouted coal-colored wings and spread them wide. Along the ground, it moved in long figure-eight patterns. But it was not actually on the ground—rather, it was the shadow of something in the air. It called to the Yearling from on high as it circled the thicket.

She walked out, carefully assessing the scene. She depressed her ears and lifted her leg up toward her body but staggered sideways. Then she splashed and zigzagged along the puddled ground trying to stabilize herself. Her head felt as though it had doubled in size, and she struggled to keep it aloft.

She then caught sight of the bird's shadow sliding toward her. It immediately stopped and hovered in place without so much as flapping a wing. The whole of the forest floor surged and swelled like the tides; the bird's silhouette rode the waves rolling toward the thicket like a sea comber.

It covered the Yearling over, taking her under the earth as under the sea. Folding her into its dusk, she sunk down uncertain if through dirt or water. Air bubbles swirled to the surface and popped around a ring of pale flame. Breaking through the surface, she suddenly found herself dumped up and onto solid ground. It was night, and she lay beneath an enormous moon.

Smoke inundated her nose. She heard men's voices blustering in the moonlight. Behind her, the thicket still stood, but the edges of the woods were frayed. She stumbled back inside to find her mother barely breathing with her tongue hanging from her mouth. The chirping had returned, and she saw the bird through the paper birch entrance. It was in the black cherry tree and covered in red light. The glimmer danced about it like molten copper. She slipped through the birch gap and approached. Above her perched the falcon. It penetrated her with citrine gaze.

Smoke scent was now strong. It was acrid and sulfurous and smelled of charred fat and burned hair. The Yearling retched. A screaming ascended. It was an animal in unbearable pain. Ripples of ember-orange light danced in the falcon's eyes.

All at once, the black cherry tree caught fire. The Yearling watched as the blaze shot up and blossomed over the bird. Despite this, it sang. Fire seared its feathers and burned its body until black ash fell to the ground. The fire was a flaring lily bud, and the Yearling glimpsed herself in its mirror-like flames. She stared at herself as ash passed overhead. Suddenly, her mirror image was transformed in the rippling fire. It was a horrific sight, but she couldn't tear herself away from it. Her reflection had become that of the little cottontail aside the fallen tree covered over with feasting birds and flies. All the while, the falcon's singing whispered in segments from its ashes.

Using all her strength and gritting her teeth until she feared they'd break, the Yearling dug her hooves into the sod and dashed from the cherry tree. When she turned back, however, only dark forest appeared. Silence save the sounds of the distant river pervaded the land. The smell of smoke was heavy in the air. To the north, she saw a glow beyond the river, and smoke rose like a toadstool. Her mouth was dry, so dry that her tongue stuck dead and limp to the roof of her mouth. She drank from a small pocket in the forest floor and staggered back into the thicket.

The Yearling felt unwell as she bedded aside her mother. The Elder Doe was terribly warm; when she nestled her from behind, the heat soothed her stomach. Her eyes slipped shut until everything faded into a smoke-scented slumber.

In the middle of sleep, she heard her mother's voice. The Yearling opened her eyes. The birch wood ceiling was iridescent—peeling white bark slashed with black streaks. She lifted outside herself and turned to the Elder Doe. From the opening of the thicket slinked the rattlesnake. The Yearling, levitating high above their sleeping bodies, watched as it crawled up her mother and coiled itself around her leg. It slithered up the Elder Doe's body until it reached her mouth. With its diamond head, it coaxed her jaws open and glided past her lips until the whole of it rattle tail and all was inside her. The smell of wood fire permeated the thicket, and the Yearling again lost consciousness.

In the morning, she awakened to the sun pouring through the gaps of birch pole. It imbued the thicket with an overwhelming feverishness. She had cotton mouth, and her body baked in the rising light. Her mother lay still, and despite the heat, her body was stiff and cold.

A burning surged in the Yearling's stomach. It wasn't a hunger pang but a sickness. There too was a throbbing that plagued her leaden head as blood labored to rush through swollen vessels. Despite such afflictions, her dreams replayed unhindered. She nudged her mother and tried to rouse her. She inspected her mouth and only her tongue peeked through; no rattlesnake found moving in her throat. But the air did still smell of fire. Outside the thicket over a northern ridge, smoke curls were dissipating in the orange, apocalyptic sky.

The Yearling ventured out for water. The warmth of day had evaporated the little pools of rain. She would have to go farther for a drink, which would make bringing water back to her mother considerably more difficult.

Before her stood the black cherry on which the falcon had perched. It was untouched by fire. Two main roots of the tree protruded from the earth and flopped on the ground. It gave the impression of sitting cross-legged in perpetual meditation. The white-capped fungi were yet harbored in its small root basin. Going forward, she felt it would be prudent to steer clear of those mushrooms.

She wandered past patches of mire, now just cracked gapes of sunbaked turf. How quickly the forest floor had changed as the sun went about its course. Overhead, a giant, bare-branched sugar maple lurched toward collapse. A strong wind would surely topple it. Nearby hardwoods were in a similar state. This was the first sign of a pervasive sickness throughout the Bluestone Woodland from which the acreage had sheltered her. Trees were the architecture of the forest, and it pained her to imagine the walls tumbling down.

Over a hump of land and down into a shallow gulch, the river, which had been just background whirring, thundered in her ears. A flash of light panned over her eyes. Sun played upon a creek as it sped toward the river cutting a path through the impenetrable bluestone. She forced her tongue into it barely skimming her mouth—It was abrasive. At first glance, it appeared to flow ordinarily, but its speed was unyielding; she had to be quick to get a mouthful as it was in such a hurry. Creeks were living things with feelings and memories. She wondered what it had seen as it escaped the woods.

She took a final, mouth-ballooning gulp and journeyed back to the thicket. Her jaws burned with a mouthful of creek that trickled out in drips and drabs. As she approached the thicket, she heard scurrying. Joy stretched her bulging face forcing water to spurt out a foot in front of her. She was certain the Elder Doe was at last stirring.

Yet once she neared the opening, she saw shadows inside. Black bodies angular and strong swayed about and covered the Elder Doe over; they soaked up the intense sunlight. And when she at last broke through the small opening of the thicket, she saw three turkey vultures. Their dark, silky plumage hung about them like robes. The thicket was crepuscular as the blockage of light had noticeably chilled it. They were mumbling and chanting over the Elder's Doe's body and offering up her spirit. They bowed and bobbed their heads in an act of consecration.

When the Yearling's whimpering interrupted their communion, they turned their bald, red, and rumpled Franciscan heads. The largest bird, in the center, had something hanging from its beak;

its cavernous nostrils were flared. It was a little bundle like a satin purse—it was the Elder Doe's eye. And after a slight pause, they were down on her again with one pecking away at her discolored, dried tongue and another scraping into the hollowed eye socket.

The Yearling was filled with rage and anguish. She wanted to charge at them, tear into them, and send them off in a fit of terror. However, she had an epiphany. All the things she had seen were now assembled in their ultimate form—images of the motionless cottontail, the Old Man in the body bag, and now her mother. Their silhouettes merged until a larger figure was wrought. It greeted her. It was Death. At last it had shown her the meaning of mortality. It felt stark and cold, and she turned to the morning sun.

She stepped slowly away from the thicket and began trekking toward the river. There would be no stopping, no turning back. Not yet. Perhaps not ever. She walked through the woods and returned to the creek. Off to one side, a shoulder formed where water slowed and cast quiet reflections. There, the Yearling contemplated herself just as she had the day she had encountered the dead cottontail. And like that day, she saw her mother ashen faced and strong on the water's surface. The warmth of her body still enveloped her, warmth that had insulated the Yearling during all those nights in the tall grass. How would she ever get on without her mother?

However, the pain was transformational; it was every doe's rite of passage. The sun swirled around her bouncing off the water and spotlighting her white-patched face. Crossing the highway of man had been a crossing of a threshold; the transition was complete. She was no longer the Yearling. At that moment, she had taken her mother's place in the Bluestone Woodland, a place of great honor. She renamed herself the Doe, and the ripples of pool-gleam baptized her.

She pressed on looking for something to soothe her belly. A velvet sumac came into view, and she went about it picking off its leaves. After filling her burning gut, she followed her ears to the crashing of the river. Over the furious waterway lay the North Territory, and if she managed to ford it, she'd surely face other tests. For one, she'd need to locate a reliable scent trail to take her up into the hills.

But she suddenly sighed as the thought had only just gone through her head. Through all the commotion, she had put her father out of mind. Had he survived the massacre? It was unclear if he had even returned as promised. She needed to locate him hoping against hope that he was safe and that they'd soon reunite. But how could she find a ghost? As she had thought of him the morning after their first meeting, it was truth. He had passed through the woodland as swiftly and secretly as the dead.

Coming to the center of a meadow with fountains of spraying grass, the Doe found the heat constant as it hadn't relented since dawn. Her upset stomach churned and gurgled. She felt her bowels shift at the wooded edge. She dashed behind one of the tall clumps and crouched to relieve herself. A metered panting eased the cramping but not the odor, which was markedly more pungent under the sun.

When at last she had successfully evacuated the last of the mushrooms, she steadied her strenuous panting. In a minute, her breath slowed and relaxed, yet she wondered why it still sounded so effortful. Her clairvoyant tail lifted itself before she could even form a thought—She held her breath, and the gasping continued. It was coming from the wooded edge. She was still lowered in a crouch, her legs trembling and stiffening. Stems of grass snapped as something closed in on her, and she tried to keep herself still. Flies swarmed buzzing riotously like a visible tracking signal, and the panting quickened.

Keeping herself at ground level, the Doe looked back toward the meadow's opening. One grassy spray shook as it was parted at its center. Each clump was then parted as the thing got progressively closer. The nearer it drew, the more animated its panting became until she felt its breath all but dampen her muzzle. At last, the partition of grasses right in front of her face shook. From out the thick clump slowly poked a snout unveiling teeth gleaming white and two frightful yellow orbs glinting. It sputtered a low rumble from the back of its throat and lowered itself in anticipation. Its pose it held with an unusual stillness—It would never reveal the moment of attack. It was the she-coyote with a stomach that had doubled since last the Doe had seen it.

Everything was quiet in the heat, and the two animals didn't blink or so much as twitch a nostril. It seemed nothing could break their stare-down until a fly landed on the Doe's face and crawled about her brow down toward her wiry eyelashes. She knew if she so much as blinked, the she-coyote was guaranteed to strike. And when the fly passed the lashes to crawl onto her cornea, the far-off screeching of turkey vultures sounded, drawing the attention of both animals, no longer snout to snout.

With that, the Doe cleared out. She whirled her body in on itself and turned to tear through the meadow river-bound. All the while, the she-coyote stayed fast behind gnashing jaws. What little strength the Doe had left was being burned up like wildfire as she barreled toward the river. If the she-coyote couldn't swim, she might be saved if fatigue did not overcome her and she herself drowned.

Out the corner of her eye, the Doe saw the she-coyote at her side and nipping at her flank. It gripped flesh and slightly threw the Doe off course, causing her to whelp with pain. The metallic smell of living blood seemed only to drive the she-coyote more rabid. With outstretched tongue it tried to lick the drops from the Doe's heaving side but then prodded her to the right, herded her into a pine grove, and corralled her near an outcropping of stone.

The Doe's leg gave out on uneven tread. She stumbled unable to catch herself. She skidded tracks in the soil and crashed to the ground. At last at a standstill, she'd landed face to face with the she-coyote, who looked particularly pleased with itself. The Doe stood slowly and inched rearward as the she-coyote pursued at a crawl. The she-coyote kept backing her with a calm persistence, and since the Doe was too afraid to look away, she didn't see the gulch she was being pushed toward—a narrow but deep bluestone pit practically invisible in the landscape. The Doe heard rocks tumble and felt the wind sweep up and over the ledge from the depths. She was on the edge of the dive.

She lost balance when she could no longer sense her foothold. There was no time to think. Her hindquarters were slipping backward; her leg was dangling off the precipice. It was impossible to remount her stance. She searched for a secure landing. Sunlight blinded her as suddenly a chirping came from the sky. A shadow covered her shading her eyes from the glare of the sun, allowing her to see.

She followed the gliding shadow of the falcon and with a twist of the body pivoted herself from the bluestone ledge. Airborne, she propelled herself forward moving in a strange unison with its silhouette. The gesture was so swift that she had no idea what she was doing. She leaped from one side of the slim gorge to the other and landed with ease.

Behind the Doe was the little bluestone pit, a rift resulting in a large hole deeper than it was wide. The she-coyote had an access point into the hole, a flaking in the stratigraphy down one wall that had formed a natural stairwell. If she would have fallen, she likely would have been gravely injured if not killed and an easy meal for the coyote. She stamped her foot and wheezed sharply through her nose as she contemplated the cunning of the she-coyote.

The schemer cut a menacing figure on the opposing trench rim. It dropped its head, squinting mischievously. With a quick toss of its feathered neck, it howled into the river valley. It was an odd sound high and hollow, practically seraphic. It grinned again. With pulsing tongue and panting breast, the she-coyote darted off into the brush, and the Doe raced to the river.

The river had been much closer than the Doe had thought. A high wall of knotweed guarded its banks except for a little sprawl of stone-covered shore where nothing could grow. High global temperatures had spawned storms that in turn had produced record rainfall. The water's height was at its uppermost limit. The previous storm induced dramatic runoffs somewhere upstream. The normally glassy water was muddied and rich in sediment. The churning and swift flow was concern enough. The Doe couldn't tell the shallow areas from where the water plummeted into deep pockets.

She searched the shoreline for the shallowest area she could find, difficult to see through mud and debris. Areas with stony protrusions likely had less depth than areas where water surged unobstructed. She would have to swim to a boulder and somehow anchor herself for a rest. The river was wide. She hesitated and thought to turn back, but the she-coyote immediately howled. She heard its slippered paws scrambling down the ridge line; that spurred the Doe into the rushing waters.

Hooves slipped on algae-lacquered river rock. Even the force of the shallow water was considerable. She treaded forward with muscles tightened against the pull. A large rocky cap about a quarter of the way across would be a suitable bracing point. Behind, the she-coyote danced flamboyantly on the bare shore. Above the drum of water, the Doe heard its lilting steps and turned briefly to watch its macabre riverside jig.

Every fiber burned as the Doe struggled her way to the boulder. Panic overcame when she paddled her legs stretching them deep into the water but unable to scrape bottom. Her hind started to turn with the flow. She was losing course. She flailed every limb in a last-ditch effort. The water surging around the boulder created a whirlpool. In mere seconds she was overcome, caught up in the vortex. It spun her under and pushed her downstream.

Her head broke the surface. Breath filled her lungs before the ripping current sucked her under again. She opened her eyes underwater, and it stung. Swirls of peaty water wreathed about her. She rose again for another quick breath. The river hurled her downstream with bone-breaking force. Something large loomed ahead. A boulder came into sight past a white-capped stretch. There was nothing to do but collide with it. And when she was at last thrown against the boulder, her body cracked. The excruciating pain had caused her to draw water into her airway. She tried to breathe deeply but coughed out half the air, and as she went under, she knew the incomplete breath would not sustain her.

Her willowy body elegantly whirled down the river. Kicking and thrashing were futile, and then, her hooves were bound to the river bottom lodged in between rocks. She no longer had any air left. The river roared in her ears and then grew silent. In the weightless depths, a calm overtook her. She closed her eyes, was so tired. She embraced death.

Electricity. Her eyes shot open. In the murky depths, something began manifesting. It was bright like feldspar but velvety. It led her, pulled her toward it. The river stones released her. She felt something come beneath and raise her toward the light. She burst through the surface gasping for breath. Her dying serenity had given way to a frantic clinging to life. Her head dipped under again and bobbed for some time. Between dunks, she caught a quick glimpse of the thing carrying her. Branches. She gasped and went under. She rose back up. No, antlers. Then down again.

Just before losing consciousness, she saw her father. He was ferrying her across on antlers like sailless masts. It was impossible to feel anymore, but the brief warmth of joy washed over her and consumed her like the drowning river water.

Everything was calm, hushed. Sand abraded her face and crusted her over where she lay. She was in pain. She realized she was sprawled over a washed-up log. Before her towered its two remaining branches—They looked familiar. The rest of its dark-brown, slippery bark had been smoothed away from a life in water.

It was late afternoon. She wondered how long she had been unconscious. Once she was able to orient herself, it became clear that she had crossed the river. The shore opposing her now seemed lifeless in its southern repose. She'd been saved having been carried through the torrent. The beach was mere ripples of sand and pebble from heavy rainfall. She scanned everywhere for traces of her father. No tracks. No scent. Her searching eyes then led her to the splendor.

The beach was aglow with hues she had never seen. It bathed her in its colored light as though framing her in a pane of stained glass. Light refracted off objects green and clear, gold and silver. She rose to greet the northern beach as a hallowed pilgrim site, and her hooves made fresh prints along the shore.

At shore's center was a blackened circle with coals and burnt wood, and it housed a translucent box. This box was filled to the brim with a creamy, stodgy substance. Starved, she bowed before it. It smelled unusual. She licked it, spat it out, and then cleansed her tongue by scraping it with her teeth. This was new food, perhaps exalted fare, and she would have to acclimate herself to its flavor. She raised her aching body and passed outside the circle.

A breeze picked up. Her nostrils dilated. At last came the scent. Thoughts raced; scenarios began playing over and over. It was the fragrance of deer—a game trail. It would lead her to the North Territory. She wondered if her father was already ahead having been caught up farther downstream. Perhaps some of the doe clan too had managed to escape.

She looked a last time to the dark southern shore; her white-splashed face was tinted in the prismatic light. She formed the Elder Doe in her thoughts and apologized for having left her body behind never to return. She dispatched all her love to the birch thicket on the ridge. It skimmed the river's surface untroubled. She would have to put aside her physical pain, voyage into this strange, new world, and find her way north. It had been her promise to her mother.

Shooting above the pine grove, a turkey vulture spread its magnificent wings and flapped against the wind. It was the vulture that had eaten the Elder Doe's eyes. It had absorbed her gift of vision. With it, the Elder Doe sent the vulture upward to give her daughter a protective glance.

Not far behind, another bird lifted itself above the tree line. It was the vulture that had eaten her tongue. She squeezed its throat to coax out a croak, a blessing and a farewell to her precious fawn. With that, the two enormous figures soared to the south and then west behind a hill.

The Doe scaled up the grade and onto the little, crooked path in the dark forest. Behind her, the shore strobed and gleamed ostentatiously its translucent vessel shimmering in the center of the black ring. All these things belonged to the animals of the northern woods. It was their ornate beach strewn with bottles and beer cans and trash, the impression of a campfire littered with a plastic container of picnic salad left to rot in the sun.

This was the land of man.

XII

As she made her way through the northern woods, the scent of deer came and went. The one constant thing was litter. Trash and rusted scraps bulged from the soil. The closer to houses she went, the more distracting it became. Sunlit garbage glistened like fool's gold wedged in bedrock.

Her path had the typical vacillating elevation of the region. She meandered the sharp face of a slope where the roar of vehicles sounded. She got as close as she felt comfortable to the road and followed it. Her nose guided her on a scent trail that hadn't yet crossed the path of cars. It had been a lesson hard learned. Unless it was absolutely crucial, she would have no further interaction with the highway.

Her thoughts wandered, and loneliness made itself known to her. Everything reminded her that she was now a solitary wayfarer. The spaces beside and ahead of her—places her mother used to occupy—felt undeniably empty. Little light poured over the Doe under the tatters of late-summer hardwoods. Not even her shadow kept her company.

After some time, it became apparent that the highway had diverged from the scent trail. Once more, the flat terrain rose toward the hump of another hill. The surround was still quotidian: ferns and mossy greens starkly contrasted by their hosting bluestone and poles of trees erupting through detritus. Litter began to abate, and nature seemed to shake the chokehold of man's careless disregard.

Now at the summit, the view was much akin to that of the acreage's eastern face—rolling hills fading away into blue haze. However, this landscape had a more cultivated look of sweet corn fields—which induced a belly-twisting hunger—and a dirt road bordered by primitive stone walls. Congregations of trees claiming little parcels along the route concealed the roadway here and there. To the far left and right, the dirt road penetrated the all-encompassing forest, and the vista once again succumbed to woodland.

She grazed relieved to have at last found an unsullied bit of forest, but she immediately drew back. The absence of garbage only amplified a malignancy in the soil. It smelled one-dimensional; the vibrancy that had impregnated the acreage's earth was muted. The flavor was synthetic, chemical. Not even a fly or a woodlouse scurried across it.

It was unprotected atop the hill that was stuck through with leafless poles, so the Doe cut downward back into coverage. She needed to seek safety, needed to find her father. Before long, it would be sundown. She hurried along the old dirt road staying as best she could in the cloaking of trees.

It wasn't long before the wind changed course. The smell of char blew in and saturated the Doe's coat. With another gust, the odor of deer passed all about her, creating a fragrance that was animalistic, smoky. She was trying to draw a complete picture from what her nose was telling her. Everything seemed to be coming from the north. She hastily veered away from the meandering dirt road and bounded along the scent trail.

At first, it was dark. However, just ahead, she saw the woods begin to lighten. It was a parcel of open land filled with numerous stumps of long-felled maples. Dying saplings starkly apposed grey skeletons of tree. A building slouched in the distance. Up into the air her snout shot; her head pivoted about fluidly as if to sing. There was no fresh presence of man or any other living thing. There was no birdsong, not even a crow's bleak oration, only the gentle screeching of dead trees waving in the breeze.

The windows of the building were girdled with layers of dirt and debris. She searched around the structure's perimeter and discovered a few rugged pathways leading to the lower terrain. All around was abandoned machinery corroding from wet summers and the ever-diminishing snowpacks of temperate winters. Signage was scattered about along with traces of sawdust in harboring nooks. She understood that the splintered stumps had once been sawed—a fate they had shared with the apple tree.

All around her a sadness floated—very calm like oil on water coating everything that waded through it. The faint suggestion of maple sap still lingered in the air. Given the bleak surroundings, the sweetness was inappropriate. She began to pick up her pace. The sun was falling like the trees.

The ground was cluttered with sap-transporting tubes some braided, some coiled, and others innervating the numb soil. They ran down the slope in a substantial network, a web of plastic arteries that had once carried lifeblood to the heart of the property, the old sugar shack.

The bottom area held a large lot overgrown with invasive plants. At its center, the bleak sugar shack stood with a huge pile of firewood to one side; it was topped with an impressive steam stack. It was encircled by dead and sapless maples like bones plunged into the earth, their shadows lacerating its weathered exterior. Men lived in such buildings, but all its inhabitants had gone. And while the Old Man's Cape Cod had always given off its own radiance, no amount of interior lighting would brighten this haunt in the deadwood.

A fluttering arose. A flash of motion that streaked from behind a grimy windowpane was painfully reminiscent of the Old Man traveling the length of the Cape Cod. The Doe scurried along the side of the building to the entrance. She paused quietly near the door's thin crack with her black-tipped ears pointing backward. Rodent droppings speckled the threshold. Deer fragrance blew over her once more beckoning for her to keep pushing on, but the impulse of curiosity that held her spellbound was augmented by a nostalgia for home. A cracked door was a tempting invitation.

She carefully pressed the door with her snout. It brushed off bits of flaking brown paint that snowed down over the rodent droppings. It was banal, but the little shower drew in her focus. Perhaps the exhaustion was getting to her, but there was something beautiful about it—tumbling brown on brown, unified, invisible. But it was all obliterated when mid-push, an alarming creak squeezed from the orange hinges, causing her to jump and retreat. She sighed to find it had been only the old hinges.

She again approached the door. Her aching, dry eyes caught no motion. Perhaps it would be safe enough to rest a moment inside. Her body felt unwieldy, and she used that heaviness to push all the way indoors, letting the rusty hinges squeal like a wounded rabbit. She had not seen it as the facade was so darkly hued, but to the side of the door was a smeared, red handprint long dried and well hidden.

The scene was quiet and barren except for toppled buckets and a large steel vat pockmarked with crystallized syrup. The firebox smelled of ash and must have been used recently. A film of dust covered some areas of rugged flooring with pearls of rodent feet dotting here and there. The rest of the dusty floor was smeared and scuffed. Toward the door, she saw a wide swath as if something had been dragged to the firebox. On closer inspection, the Doe saw that the rodent tracks weren't rodent tracks but something much more sinister. What at first had smelled of minerals—which she'd attributed to dust—was in fact the odor of blood. The scope of splattering was pronounced. Blood was everywhere.

The Doe was almost too frightened to walk through its mottling. She wondered what she'd carry with her if she were to sully her hooves in it. The sun was sinking, and the room was growing dim. It was so hushed outside the open door that she would have been able to hear even a weightless bird's foot flitting along a dead branch. Instead, she heard its voice: *I saw it all here. I've seen terrible things.*

Scuttling hooves slipped as upon ice under the startled Doe. A sparrow had made its nest atop a beam running along the ceiling. Its fluffed-up body was hidden beneath the weavings of dried vegetation. A tiny, brown-slashed head peeked out; its voice was the specter of the sugar shack. *A man dwelled here, like me, seeking shelter from the storm. He lost his home in a flooded city and came north as he had nothing left. He was gentle, and he spoke to me and sometimes sang lullabies to me at night. He became my friend.*

The Doe moved her head in all directions as the little bird chattered on.

*He went out looking for something to eat. We starved as food was scarce and the corn poisoned. I was grateful he never tried to eat me. While he was gone, the two wretched beings came. I shook all over afraid I'd give myself away.*

The sparrow kept its voice restrained as if its song would lure evil back through the door. *They were here, the beast and the man with fiery hair. I watched them as they succumbed. When my friend returned and caught them in the act, the beast shot him with a gun. Dead things sing no songs.*

The little sparrow fussed with something in its nest while the sun, slipping fast beneath the horizon, cast shadows like a kaleidoscope. The Doe looked over her shoulder toward the door and then returned her attention to the fidgeting bird. Having reorganized the nest and having made itself comfortable, the sparrow continued its chirping.

*It was horrible. Outside, the beast tore my friend's body apart and then dragged him in piece by piece on a sheet, cloth wrapped around his misshapen finger. I hid in my nest barely letting my eyes rise higher than its rim. For hours upon hours they burned him in that box.*

Something stirred behind the Doe, and she quickly backed herself toward the beam. It whished across the old floorboards begging to make her acquaintance. From the firebox, it spewed a string of odor as fine as thread and then vanished. It was sweet and charred but also musty—It was human.

*That night was windy. As they cooked my friend's head, his hair melted off his scalp and blew from out the firebox. When they had gone, I gathered it all in my beak, and now, I sleep on it as it lines my nest.*

The Doe slowly walked to the firebox and inspected its contents—only ash and rubble. Her back then arched sending a wave of chills over her body. Under her hoof, she saw something dark and fine like cracking in the floorboards. Upon closer inspection, it appeared to be more like a clump of dried moss. She swiftly withdrew her hoof. It was a curl of singed hair.

*Leave this place before you, too, die!* the sparrow cried. *They'll burn you just like the others! Can't you smell it? It perfumes the air, and I won't fly! Run, young doe, run!*

The Doe erupted out the shack's creaking door crazed with fear. Far ahead, a whip-poor-will was sending the sundown alarm. The direction of light had shifted. The odor of deer was strong in the dusk's breeze. She drove her tired body onward without turning to look at the sugar shack. Sun slipped past its firebox. The sparrow's nest grew colorless, and its memories were pushed back into darkness.

Her course remained flat as she raced the setting sun. The roots of fallen pines exploded from the soil in a hundred wriggling tentacles. Ahead appeared a long wall of more writhing protuberances, but as she neared it, she saw that it was a florid fence. Its intricate wrought-iron design was old and tarnished. Beyond its curves and flourishes was a field smaller than the acreage but with an orderly arrangement of stones. It was the country cemetery.

Through a corrosive gap in the fence she squeezed careful not to abrade her lengthy back. The lot was dark yet tranquil and as comforting as it was sterile. The many markers were mostly bluestone; a few creamy were marble, and most were covered in moss and smoothed and weathered. Each had writing that was fading if not faded beyond recognition. She passed through rows of these little monoliths noticing some with images carved into them. One tall, rectangular stone featured a powerful and stern bird; its uncomplicated figure had been gouged deep into the rock. Words chiseled into its facade read: I WILL LIFT MINE EYES TO THE HILLS, FROM WHENCE COMETH MY HELP. Situated as if to usher in nightfall, it was the first stone to be colored by flagrant sunset. She traced its outline with her eyes—It was a falcon bird.

She crossed through the peaceful little henge to where the turned earth was still fresh. She lowered her snout to it; her white-spotted face nearly kissed the plot. Stale dirt again, but there were traces of something sharp like saltwater—like tears. There was no stone erected, just an inexpensive placard laid across the head. She examined it, but it was more human scribbling. This little turn of earth somehow felt like home to her, and she rested over it a moment. The whip-poor-will then called her forward into the woodland. She exited through another gap in the fence and resumed her flight on the scent trail.

It was a grave without a body but rather a heap of ashes dumped in a simple sugar maple box. A temporary placard by dint of Mr. Crane listed a name, a date of birth and death, and a modest epitaph: Beloved Physician, Artist, and Friend of Nature.

The Doe had sped by a number of cornfields where chemicals combed through silky tassels. Pesticides blew through the trees and crept inside the sleepy houses where lived the nameless, faceless victims of those who ate the poison. And when she had passed through the stretch of woodland farms, she found herself once more in dense forest. The scent trail had diminished to such an extent that the Doe was uncertain in which direction to proceed. It was dark under the treetops. She hadn't yet considered what it would be like to spend an evening alone in the land of man. As the trees dimmed from green to navy and the bluestone greyed, she began to feel eyes on her. Even the billows of hardwood leaves seemed to conceal some unimaginable horror.

And when the feeling of watchful eyes accelerated, she turned her neck northward; that's when she saw them. Far in the distance and glowing from behind the layers of shrubs, the Doe caught sight of many white lights. At first, she feared they may be those of men. They flickered and bobbed as they drifted in the pine grove. She took cover behind a stump and peeked wide-eyed, studying them. They weren't fireflies—too late in the season. They were much larger and more constant.

On the breeze came the odor of firewood, of fruits and of rotting. Each one of the strange lights revealed a lifting head. They turned back and eyed her from the pine grove where they stood, their tails like candles in twilight windows. Each unscathed head was accounted for as if nothing had ever happened—as if the apple tree had never been felled. It was impossible; she vividly remembered the sight of dead does in the tree line. How could this be the complete doe clan?

She gasped, wheezed, and grew hungry for air. And when she had at last caught her breath, she pushed it deep down connecting to the root of herself and cried out to them. It echoed from the foothill where they stood and back. They remained very still and stared—it was all so photographic, as if she were seeing something suspended in time. They had no color, but it was sundown and everything was fading. They continued to feed, but what was there to eat under the high pines? Nothing but dead needles that mulched over any chance of growth. The does were just as they had been under the apple tree— languid, masticating, swatting. She cried out again, and they kept going about their grazing milling up food from a floor barren of fodder.

The breeze rustled the treetops, and the many layers of shrubs blew together and obscured her view of the herd. Then a popping came. And another until it was a full-on barrage. Guns were firing somewhere ahead, and the shots were muffled. The wind stopped, and the shrubs eased up and parted. Up the forthcoming hill she watched as the doe clan raced. They did not mewl or make a single sound upon their flight.

The Doe went full tilt after the herd careless of her footing. She stumbled over tangles of underbrush and twigs with no thought given to the position of the shooters. Branches snapped underneath as she tamped the earth, barreling toward the hilltop. She watched as some does fell on the leeward side of the slope. The windward side provided safety—at least, that's what she assumed their noses were showing them. As she neared the foot of the hill, the sound of firing neither faded nor grew in volume; there was no ringing in her ears. The gunshots had no discernible origin and seemed to be coming from another place altogether.

She drove her body up the hill. Each breath thrusted out of her with motorized heaving. The hill seemed rather untraveled as if it had been years since a herd pushed through its tangles and shrubbery. They certainly would have left signs in broken twigs and upturned soil. No dropped bodies anywhere. She could no longer track them by scent. For a moment, she questioned whether this was in fact the correct hill.

Near the summit, the firing had stopped. Her lungs burned from the hard run, and she could taste metal. She cowered under some fern to wait for a signal. The absence of gunshots—of her own scuttling and gasping—had made it easy to hear in a wide radius. It was quiet as the minutes passed, and she wondered if she hadn't better shelter there for the night. But then came a sound—hushed singing, words coming in and out of intelligibility—slack enunciation closing down into easy humming. It had the fresh and sweet timbre of a young throat.

Beyond the top of the hunched hill, the source was revealed. A grand curtain of vines and boughs parted as the Doe slipped surreptitiously past. Sunset offered a surreal glow, and she could see down the slope into a small bit of flat land. A mob of colors was thrown violently one on top of the other; their nectars and pollens were spilling about in perfumed carnage.

The wind picked up speed and shifted, bringing with it the traces of fire. Everything was lost in the ambling of shape and tint until from under a mass of tomatoes the Doe saw something move. It was tan and long backed; the shape of wide-set hips showed through a minaret of purple coneflower. It looked as though one of the does was foraging for food.

She stepped down the slope for a better view. In the center of the clearing was a garden divided into four huge sections, one for each cardinal direction. To one side was a gleaming house—another Cape Cod— with scrimshaw-white paint and green trim, and aside the garden was a large-windowed shed. Far off in all directions, the plot was surrounded by pine. The garden was separated from the house by a picket fence, while the trees and the fence trussed and protected the space. The Doe had no question that this was the threshold of the North Territory. It felt mystical—a veritable *hortus conclusus;* it was the acreage reborn. And so she tramped down the hill with abandon and easily hurdled the low fence.

The murmuring continued from under the surging herbs, the blond outline toiling underneath a mass of ox-heart tomatoes. To the east was rosemary and corn, while young carrots and chamomile lilted their feathery greens to the south. A colossal sunflower transcending the leafy swell drooped under its enormous head—the all-seeing eye of the garden. There were other cultivars among the dense plantings. They knotted stems and stamens with their crowded neighbors making hybrids of love children. Numerous pollinators and late-season hummingbirds made the garden sound of sizzling oil. Many were swarming in the center of the plot where a rudimentary A-frame trellis was coiled over with nasturtium and moonflower just beginning to open in the evening air.

With head held high and ears turned outward, she crept up to the foraging doe. A golden coat pushed through the holes of overlapping foliage as if it'd been ensnared by the garden. The Doe grunted to the mass of tomatoes. From under its green tangle, the hidden figure let out a gasp, her head jolting upward causing the Doe to stumble backward. This humming deer was no deer at all.

"It's you," the Woman whispered.

The Doe and the Woman studied each other for some time. The Doe had never seen a young woman. She was beautiful with long flaxen hair. She was much like a doe with elegant limbs and large, inquisitive eyes the color of amber. Her clothing was unfussy—simple khakis and a tan button-down. Her sleeves she had rolled up as they were too short for her gangling arms. She smelled of the earth and iron and of all the rampant fruit and flowers that proliferated in this square of forest.

The Woman immediately recognized the piebald feature of the young doe. "Saint?" Her eyes grew bleary and she squinted. With a dirty sleeve, she brushed her face rosy from working in the sun. "We haven't much time. My husband will be home soon."

The Woman put her hands to work and began collecting a small bouquet of things. The Doe took it all in, her tail amicably flapping to and fro.

"You've traveled far. You must be starving."

At first, the Woman dug and struggled and labored until something sprang from the black soil. Next, she went about snipping and twisting bunches of greens. She bundled them together and offered them to the Doe. "Here, eat. There's a parsnip, sweet and earthy like a potato and carrot if they had a baby. There's parsley for your gut, mint for your lungs and breath. I added some rosemary to revive you and clear your mind and thyme to give you courage."

The Woman gently pushed the bundle toward the Doe. Below was a puddle created by her leaking hose. She saw the Doe's reflection on its surface. The Doe looked down to meet her eyes in the puddle. They stared into the reflection where for a brief moment neither could tell one from the other.

"Please, eat. You can trust me."

The Doe was leery of taking any more food from humans, but something about the Woman put her mind at ease. She sensed the

Woman was good and firm all the way to her core like a ripe, branch-bound apple. And as she was so hungry, she accepted the offering stretching her neck forward with trepidation as if anticipating the butcher's block. Once again the Doe was bound to a covenant, this time with womankind.

She took a bite and lowered the mass to the ground. The parsnip crunched and snapped in her mouth; it tasted of cool earth, and it refreshed her. She went down for more—a mouthful of things medicinal, and fibrous, and sugary. It raised the blood sugar, which sped through her veins, soothed her gut, cleared her vision, and honed her scent. Her muscles grew warm and pliant, the way they felt after a good night's sleep. This was strong medicine.

Tansy flower perfume flared up as did a metallic and peppery plump fruit. It was the Woman who was ripe; she was bleeding between her legs as she did every month. Smoke stench knotted the air too. The Doe's eyes were led to an area outside the garden that was flat and smooth with black ground studded with scores of ash and rubble. Just beyond the garden shed was something white and arborescent. She elongated her neck in its direction.

"You guzzled that right down."

She turned back to the Woman, whose forehead was marked with compost like a Lenten blessing.

"It's a miracle you're alive. Some of the men were over this morning loading the remnants into truck beds. The sight and smell were just awful. Fresh wood didn't do the job. So much smoke." She referenced the black rubbled spot by pointing. "It's eerie—almost like it never happened."

Her soiled forehead itched, and she scratched it, flaking dried dirt onto her breasts. Her tall frame then caved in on itself—sternum tucking into backbone—as she let her shoulders slope. She whispered, "I didn't sleep. The noise…If ever I imagined hell, it would have been what those men did." Her eyes dove. "I was powerless, you understand?" The impulse to cry out was suppressed, making her voice high like a child's. "One was still alive, and it screamed like an old boar. And when they threw the poor thing into the fire, head open and bleeding—"

A vehicle roared into the drive, and the Woman flipped around. The engine no sooner was killed and the truck door slammed when her quiet demeanor gave way to panic. She swatted at the Doe air-punching around her head and neck. "Shoo! Go!" She jabbed toward the Doe her eyes afire. "Get the hell out of here! Run, Saint!"

As the Doe cleared away from the Woman, she heard the sound of familiar bootheels trudging up the graveled drive. Like a wild animal, the Woman then swung full force at the Doe, sending her flying over the fence and scrambling into the woods. The Doe sped halfway up the slope, bypassing a curving footpath to an area with dense coverage. She was well obscured except for a gap in the timber that offered a view into the garden. The Woman stood beneath the giant sunflower, whose mournful head bent toward her. It was a hapless witness bound by deep roots.

From around the house at last came the figure. Nightfall followed him as if he were sucking up all the remaining daylight. Of all the dangers she'd escaped and of all the places she'd been led, the Doe could hardly believe that she'd somehow managed to barrel straight toward the Man with the Crooked Finger.

He made his way up to the picket fence and called to the Woman. Her blond hair gleamed in the dusk—Her whole being did—and reflected on him giving him a counterfeit glow. The scar over his eye eroded his face like a red river. He tried luring her out of the garden; he wouldn't step a foot inside it. He began to wave his arms and to curse the Woman. Mirroring the sunflower, the Woman let her head droop, and she reluctantly crossed out of the garden gate.

With a thrust of his strong arm, he drove his fist into the Woman's shoulder. It knocked her backward into the fence; her hair trailed behind like hay in a squall. For a few long seconds, he merely towered over her while she grimaced and rubbed her shoulder, keeping her eyes to the ground. The downcast sunflower, having had its fill of brutality, was at last broken. It began to weep black seeds that bounced on the ground and landed at the Woman's feet.

"You think I'll ever forgive you?" he grumbled, kicking her to the ground. He flashed his broken smile, grabbed her hair, and twisted it around his crooked finger like many golden rings. The Woman let out a whimper. "Is that the best you can do, sweetheart?" He throttled her head until she screamed out eliciting from him a bestial fit of laughter.

Overcome, the Doe scrambled farther up the slope. Snapping branches, whooshing of leaves, tumbling of stones—all of it was soundless as the high-pitch ringing from the Woman's throat covered all. Her screaming began to oscillate and waver as the Man roared with a spiteful sort of pleasure, but the sound kept on even after they'd stopped.

As the Doe staggered on loose rock, she suddenly knew this was more than what was merely taking place in front of the house. The terrible clamor smoothed out into unison with the Woman's pain and the Man's delight. He dragged the Woman onto the porch by her hair and into the house, where at last the slamming of the screen door cut all.

The ringing, the wobbling, the wailing, the slamming— it was that mysterious sound again and it had merged with their confrontation in the yard. The Doe then felt that she was very close to the sound, as if she'd stumbled upon its epicenter. It was becoming clearer in her mind what it was trying to show her. She breathed deeply. The garden was especially fragrant. The scent sharpening her vision.

Atop the hill was a dark, broken-down shanty she could use as a refuge for the night. As she approached its crooked door that hung loose from its hinges, she sensed a strange and powerful energy emanating from it. It pulsated outward into the blackening forest. Every last one of her instincts barred her from crossing its threshold. She opted to shelter herself away from it; she bedded down beneath a rhododendron. As her eyes slipped closed, she heard a voice neither human nor animal whisper, *Come inside, friend. Offer yourself up. Let me line my dwelling place with your exquisite hide.*

A child's voice then beckoned the Doe to enter the shanty. She cocked her head and sniffed the air but kept herself positioned underneath the refuge of the rhododendron. The shanty was evil; she feared what lay hidden in it—things undoubtedly worse than the ghosts of the sugar shack.

A power compelled her forward. It pulled her along with an unseen rope halter. Inside, she saw the child seated on his father's throne. All around stood other figures—five men who huddled about, two opposite three. They were the heads of forebears who had groomed one to be as the other. Together with the child and the father, they created a seven-headed beast.

The Doe somehow knew the child had done something wrong but wasn't certain what. All the faces were turned toward him casting judgment. They were posed and placed like one of the Old Man's still lifes. Behind the huddle of seven, she saw two grey-brown silhouettes of deer—An angel pair hung upside down. They were strung high above by old rope and were rocking and swaying, the scales of justice unable to strike a balance.

The child wept. He cried, "I'm forever trapped here. Help me!" Pain overtook the Doe. It was a twisting and a breaking. The father used the rope halter to string her up aside the other deer—their sacred black tongues ejected, eyes white and sunken. The halter had become the killing rope, and she began to squirm. The lopsided door labored shut as the father sealed them in darkness, in silence. Only the creaking of rope bound to swaying carcasses remained.

The Doe's breath was heavy, and she shook herself to dispel her grogginess. She had awakened to find herself at the foot of the old shanty, far from the safety of the rhododendron. She scurried away from it and sank down behind a heap of dead branches. With her head once more on the ground, she retraced the visions that had played through her dreaming mind. The door of the shanty hung loosely off the hinges. Inside, she saw a solitary chair heavy and splintered posing severely against the shaded back wall.

Her stomach grumbled. The little bundle of roots and herbs the Woman had offered her had lasted just long enough to get her through the night. It was early morning, and she'd slept surprisingly long. She would have to slip out of cover for food and face a blinding sun and another day in an uncertain land.

The area was thick with pines; little greenery thrived. A space in the dovetailing of boughs allowed for a ray of sun to shoot straight onto the shanty as if to say *Here*. Bare ground encircled the edifice, and an old trail grew out of it like an umbilicus. It led somewhere back over the northern slope. Water was certainly close by, but her nose detected something foul and stagnant.

Too afraid to risk going down the slope toward the little white Cape Cod, the Doe followed the trail north. Walking along the well-worn path felt surprisingly comforting; it gave a sense of order. However, she had yet to latch onto the traces of her father or the doe clan, who had eluded her by escaping over the hill as they fled from strange gunfire. Now only smoke scent remained; it clung to the wind like a parasite.

She surveyed her surroundings. West and east were but serried pine forest. To the south was the slope that monitored the little house. North, however, she saw trees clearing. She turned her ears inward to listen as if for a soft, welcoming voice—or a warning. The wind gushed toward her, and she heard a thud in the rough grass. She crept toward it with her head low on a rigid neck.

She flicked her tail once maybe twice. After a while, it had become the mindless swatting of flies. Fizzing began to crackle and bubble in the near distance. At the end of the forest, a vision of the acreage manifested in the open land.

Here dwelled a quaint apple orchard, very small with a cloud of flies and other little things working busily about its fallen fruit. Starved, she hurried to one mass of warm, soft apples. They foamed through their deteriorating flesh making the soil drunk with their fermentation. The Doe milled an apple between her teeth. It was spongy and bloated, and it burst in her mouth with its warm, yeasty liquor. It was drink and feed.

Farther ahead, past the trees, she saw the hilltop sloped downward and the land opening up into something like a meadow or field. She brushed past the other trees whose rough bark slightly hooked into her coat as if trying to stop her. Before she could catch a glimpse of whatever lay beyond the little orchard, the sound of footwork came from behind, a quick and dampened pattering speeding straight toward her. She lifted her tail at the same time as she lifted her head, and her snout shot up into the air. She then scanned the tree line, darting her eyes to the woods at the back of her and then to the northern clearing.

Under the sprawling boughs, it shot toward the Doe. It was low to the ground as it bowled down the brittle reeds of yellow grass. She could then see those unmistakable gold eyes—two ducats on a dead man's eyes. The creature smiled with triumph at her; its sharp-toothed mouth was impossibly more menacing in a grin. The river had been a dangerous, turbulent obstacle. It was unimaginable how the she-coyote could have crossed.

Even more so, its belly looked as though it would give birth at any moment. Flapping milk-swollen teats nearly dragged on the ground as the she-coyote readied itself to lunge at the Doe, to grasp her thick neck in its clamp-like jaws, to sever her throat and tear open her arteries. All the Doe could do was stare; her brain faltered. This wasn't truly the she-coyote in the flesh. This was a mirage, a ghost.

But when the coyote snapped its mouth on the Doe's slim leg, it drew blood and wheedled out a whimper from its victim. Thus the Doe began to retreat, and the she-coyote pushed toward her. Behind, the trees gave way to the unending blue horizon as if the Doe were being led to drown in it. A uvular, low rumble shook from deep within the she-coyote's breast. It sent a shock through the Doe's body, each of her muscles tautening and clenching like a hanging bridge with a foot upon it.

It only took one or two steps for the Doe to realize that this was more of the coyote's scheming, just like the day when it had backed her toward the gorge. Where was the pitfall this time? The coyote must have scouted the area as it appeared to be well acquainted with the land. The Doe watched as the strategy unfolded in its eyes. She was nearing its trap, but she refused to play a fool to old tricks.

The Doe turned right to career toward the tree line sure to be mindful of any sinkholes along the way. But as soon as she'd pivoted herself to escape, more footwork arose from the northern slope. It was the stomping of boots. The Doe slowed and turned to the coyote, who was once again smiling with a glint of light in its eyes, its panting tongue streaked red with a swatch of blood. Straight away, it let out a howl high and florid. For the second time, it'd managed to back the Doe into a quagmire. With a tip of the head, it thanked the Doe for a taste of her life-giving blood then dashed through the orchard and into the forest making no sound and leaving no tracks.

A voice belonging to the stamping feet yelled, "I just heard it!"

The Doe's eyes began to pool; her mouth flooded. She batted away tears and swallowed spit down her dry throat. Her head swiveled back and forth, but she could not find a place to take shelter—nor could she reach a decision as to which way to run.

The voice shouted back down the slope, "It was a female coyote! I seen its teats. Had to be at least sixty pounds!"

The Man with the Crooked Finger appeared armed with rifle; his disfigured finger stood slightly erect from where he gripped the stock. His voice trailed off as he reached the ridge top. The footwork softened into a hushed stalking as his chest pumped like silent bellows. The Doe had yet to escape but was unwittingly well camouflaged against the backdrop of bark and dried grasses. Yet when she jerked her head, the little motion of it made her pop out from the scenery. At last, she and the Man met eyes. For a moment, they stood opposite one another in a stare-down. The hot, maddening winds of summer blew unencumbered.

"I'll be damned," he muttered. His left eye twitched, sending a tremor through the fault line of his scar. A cloud wisp passed over the sun, dimming his face. His unforgiving, almighty eye was dilating and closing. It gleamed as it drew in the ethereal intensity ready to refract its power onto the Doe by way of the rifle's front sight. High noon was shooting through the apple branches and spreading an unnatural shadow beneath the Man. To the left and right of his boots, six dark silhouettes were cast with his own face at center. The trick of light and shadow unclothed a subtle, hidden realm. The beast growled with seven heads.

The Doe trembled. She was on his turf, where he dug his heels into the soil and could wield his power without hindrance or hesitancy. The faint presence of other men drifted up from beyond the slope, where the land fell and opened into a field. The owners of the neighboring property were longtime family friends of the Man, and they awaited news of the she-coyote. Yet he and the Doe had already forgotten about it at that point slipping deep into wooded darkness like quicksilver having used such cunning to join the two of them for an unknown purpose.

"Where's Momma?" The Man rotated his head toward all pockets of timber and to the shaded area where the old, broken-down shanty slumped. He stared beyond the Doe as if he were seeing something behind her. Beads of sweat percolated through his skin. After a moment, the Doe turned her head backward to glance at what he was seeing, which broke his concentration and reignited his rage.

"Sorry, girl." His voice erupted with a quiet, mournful indignation. "But you're no better than vermin."

He readied the rifle to his shoulder, and the Doe wasted no time turning in on herself and springing up off her hindquarters. Through the small cluster of apples she flew, her body snapping branches and disturbing the low-hung foliage.

The gun's blast sent sound waves out in concentric rings. The bullet missed the Doe and seemed to dematerialize at the wooded edge. A raven fluttered up trailing black feathers that tarred the blue horizon. Into the dark recesses and along the old shanty the Doe darted, passing its rickety form in a streamlined fashion. The Man pursued only as far as the line of the sun; he stopped his steel-toed boot right at the precipice of the forest shadow. It was too dangerous for him though he knew not why.

*No closer*, the inner voice whispered.

To the verge of the hillside she ran, crying out to her father in a bleating. As she was about to sprint down in the hopes of finding safety near the garden, she caught a hoof in a crevice. When she went to lift it mid-sprint, she discovered that it had been lodged. Instead of releasing, the hoof stayed fixed in place, causing her to twist her leg in a volatile motion. The pain soared into her joints. A loud snap burst from within her leg as her body bounced backward on it.

The Man heard the Doe groaning in pain but would go no farther. She saw him through the cracks of trees beyond the shanty. He looked like a scorned, hunch-postured, and sullen child. "Trust me!" he screamed; his face was beet-red, and veins like roots in his neck pushed outward. "I'll bury you for good!" He tore back through the orchard and down the hill, and as he roared, it echoed seven times.

The Doe managed to at last free her hoof from the crevice. She saw she'd gotten stuck between boards beneath some dried leaves and branches. All around her lay a rectangular area covered by old, warped, and soft slats. She peered between the cracks of the boards where a wood knot had rotted away. Below in the faint gleam of high sun she saw the reflection of sky in still, black water. It was the entrance to an underground root cellar long covered over and forgotten.

It was a simple root cellar once used to store dry goods, bushels of apples, and winter game. Carved out by a local grave digger, it was about fifteen feet deep and twelve feet long. It was roofed with wood and rebar, then covered by a slab of concrete that sat flush with the earth. Much of its outline had been concealed by the stratum of plant matter and wind-snapped wood. Atop a concrete footer, the storage area was lined with cinderblocks, and there was a crude underground drainage system that had become plugged. The cellar retained a foot of water; its bottom steps were submerged. A five-foot rectangular hole served as an opening where steps lowered to meet the main area at a steep incline. As it sat unused for over a generation, the entrance gap had been boarded over with slats and boards as a safety precaution. But such measures worked only if they hadn't been forgotten.

The Doe hobbled to the nearest bit of bluestone where she could conceal herself between rock and brush. The pain was unlike anything she had ever felt. Part of her lower leg began to grow numb, and she collapsed. Voices of men below in the field were amplified through the shanty. A ringing then began to go off in her ears.

It intensified, and when it turned into a wobbling noise, which was always second in succession, she knew the mysterious sound had come back. That time, as it played out, it didn't employ its usual effect by which it muted every natural thing while it shot from another universe. It sounded as if it were happening somewhere atop the hill. It seemed to ruffle the dry leaves as though it were walking nearby. She listened carefully. It was coming from aside the root cellar and shanty, where the men's voices continued to resound and grow louder and more present as if they too were right there.

All noise lapsed into a sudden silence with the brisk pop of her settling leg joint. She was lame and thus unable to get back down the hill. She had no access to water or food save the bit of greenery on which she lay. How would she find her father and the others now? She could almost see herself outside her own body as if on a vulture's wings. She was curled beneath the doming of brush and stone just as the Elder Doe had sprawled out in the birch thicket. If she fell asleep, would she awaken to a fate similar to her mother's? Somewhere in the hidden sky, she thought she heard the circling birds hissing.

The Doe lay there for hours upon hours as the sunlight drifted; her pain now inseparable from the Man and the shadows of his origins. She had nothing to do but to wait—to lie still and keep her eyes open as long as she could. Her mind was weakening, and she was fearful of nightmares. She kept her eyes on the shanty, anticipating the voice of the child.

When the Man with the Crooked Finger was born, he had come to live in a little white Cape Cod below a small hill, the only house in which he'd ever live. At the top of the hill was a shanty accessible by footpath from the house or by dirt road that ran along the field of the neighboring farm just behind the hill. The men used to gather there to drink, play gin rummy, and dress game. They'd spend all day hunting and then drive to the farm following one another along the bumpy path. Within the shanty, they'd take nips of whiskey and cavort and then go outside to pull water if they needed it for cleaning carcasses or washing their red, calloused hands. At that time, the root cellar and its ground-level stairwell had already been boarded up for many years.

Before the Man was obsessed with pain and started reviling deer with abnormal disgust, he was but a boy. Like all children, he was whimsical and playful. The world about him held his curiosity, and he was relatively untroubled. His father was mean and hurtful just as his father had been. It was a long, painful line like the future scar over his eye, which traced a history of familial dysfunction. Yet up until a certain point, this cruelty didn't seem to extinguish the boy's light.

During deer season one year, the men gathered on the hill to gut and hang their harvests and drink bourbon and share crass stories about wives and girlfriends. Below, the rural schoolhouse was emptying of children who all darted into the autumn afternoon and shielded their laughing faces from the sun.

On his way home, the boy witnessed two girls sitting atop the breaching root of a great sugar maple and making gestures to one another—kissing their index fingers and planting kisses on each other's cheeks, a roundabout way of kissing a friend. The little boy practiced the gesture as he stomped along the dirt road that cut through the trees and onto the family property.

He searched about the house for his father, and his mother pointed up the hill. The boy kissed his pointer finger and then gently touched his mother's cheek, blushing purple with a fist bruise. She at first flinched but then broke out into a sad smile and caressed his slick, blond hair. Returning to the sink to wash the stack of mismatched and scuffed dishes, she stared out the window. All the joy had been wrung from her like an old dish towel; she was an automaton of herself in an apron and a tie-down.

The boy sprung through the garden space overgrown with weeds and yellowing things and ran up the footpath, which made numerous S shapes up the slope. He was careful of his footing as the path was littered with shingles of bluestone, making it easy to sprain an ankle or worse. His father, an inebriate, preferred driving around the hill and through the neighbor's field to reach the shanty rather than risk the trail by foot.

The men had gathered in the shanty with their kills strung behind them like a fine old tapestry. They congregated and passionately discussed their beliefs. They felt insulated in that shanty and safe from the prying ears of the greater world, which they feared. But they were never truly sheltered from scrutiny as strung behind them were the ears of freshly killed deer surveilling their every word. And upon reaching the top of the hill, the boy saw the low-lying lip of a tin tub splashed with water and blood and heard the men's brash voices shouting and singing drunken songs and tumbling around as they roughhoused.

Into the shanty the boy went; his tiny body slipped between large frames that staggered drunkenly. Without any notice, he crawled straight onto the lap of his father, who was seated in a large, timeworn chair at the back center of the space. His whiskered and creviced face emerged from the background of tawny deer carcasses.

The boy put his little finger on his lips as if silencing the crowd. The men grew hushed. With his captive audience now staring at him, he kissed his peach fingertip delicately and landed it on his father's wiry cheek. He ended the whole gesture with a loud mouth pucker of his lips.

The man didn't approve of affection from his son, and the boy believed this was the perfect way to circumvent his desire to be loved by his father without having to do it so forthrightly.

When the boy grew older, he began to show signs of a tender-hearted nature that made his father ashamed. The man saw it as effeminate and perhaps indicative of an underlying filthiness. To break the boy of the sickness, he took extreme measures. Sometimes in the middle of the night—and usually for no reason other than booze and rumination—he awakened the boy and forced him from his bed; he pulled him out of his room by his pajama collar and yanked him to the kitchen screen door. His mother watched on from her bedroom doorframe, unable to protect her child as he implored, "Momma! Please help me!"

The boy was dragged up the hill—one of the few times the old man walked the footpath—wriggling and fighting while he was punched in the head and tugged along by his hair. He would be pushed into the cold shanty where the field-dressed game was still hanging keeping fresh in the chill of the night.

"It's for your own good," the father growled as he shut the shanty door, fastened it with a padlock, and forced the boy to spend the night in the freezing darkness while the deer carcasses held vigil.

And there were other times when the father's abuse took a severe turn; like when he caught the boy putting on his mother's makeup as a bit of play. After boxing the boy's ears till the canals wept blood-tears, he took him to the shanty and made him dig a long, wide trench and forced him to crawl in it to lie aside severed deer limbs and waste parts. With the shovel, the father began to cover them half-over with the soil while the boy lay side by side with a doe's head that had been lopped off its body.

"Better start acting right or next time I'll bury you for good."

As the boy neared his teens, the shanty became a secret place where one of the men behind the back of his father touched and hurt him all for the sake of satisfying his desires. The boy was lured with lies, but promises were broken. In the end, it never replaced his desperate need for his father's love. All the while, the deer carcasses looked on.

When the boy was near eighteen, he came home from school one day and heard the men on the hillside. They swarmed on the slope, and he saw a silvery figure flash beneath the brush. His father yelled for him to come, and when he arrived, he saw it was a coyote who'd been completely violated by the men. They had shot it and kicked it, and it was bloody and barely clinging to life, trying to hold on for the sake of its newborn pups.

Days earlier while driving along the service road near the Old Man's acreage, a few of the men had spotted it. The coyote had made its home near the apple tree where a bluestone den had been prepared for its young. The men shot at it and chased it through woods, push-ing it far over the river, forcing it to give birth in a foreign land atop the hill by the shanty.

The boy watched as one pup was launched into the sky and land-ed on a large boulder, cracking its skull. The men threw its litter like clay pigeons, shooting while shouting, "Pull!" Another man simply smacked the runt twice against a rock. The coyote tried to fight, but its life was near spent.

The father gave the boy a knife. This was his rite of passage into manhood. "Finish it." The boy swallowed. His hands trembled, his grip slipping on the sweat-slicked hilt. And when he tried to protest, his father grasped the back of his neck and shook him. "Coyote's dangerous, boy. Do it and don't argue, dammit!" He said it in such a way that the many inhumane forms of punishment that awaited the boy ran through his broken mind.

Under the watchful eye of all his abusers, the boy took the blade and lowered himself toward the coyote. He took a deep, uneven breath and then set upon it crying while plunging the knife into its body over and over until it began to rain blood backward.

From behind, the men discarded the pups by slipping them under the boards of the old cellar entranceway and dropping them into the shallow water at the foot of its steps. After, the father ordered them to return the coyote's carcass to the Old Man's land.

"If he finds it, he'll know it's a warning."


Yet the beginning of the end for the Man with the Crooked Finger was the moment he had climbed onto his father's lap and touched his cheek with a tiny fingertip—to kiss the father from whom he simply wanted love.

The father's face went blank but soon began to redden. He grabbed the little boy's pointer finger and began to squeeze and throttle it. And over the little boy's screaming, the father managed to yell, "Why don't you go put on a dress too while you're at it?"

The boy was then cast down from his father and fell to the dark, splintered floorboards reeking of iron and mildew. The five men looked at him with steely, lifeless faces; his father's was still flushed with emotion beneath his whiskers.

"This is what happens when that bitch takes my son to pick a faggot's apples." He rattled his finger in the boy's face. "You want to pick apples, you'll pick 'em right up here!"

It was there that the Man with the Crooked Finger sat as a little boy crying while the cold faces looked on creating a feedback loop that would play over and over in his mind—images he would spend his life trying to destroy and exorcize. The picture of dead deer hanging in the back, blood spilling from their mouths, and the terrible pain and rejection he felt while holding his little right finger, the finger that would never heal.

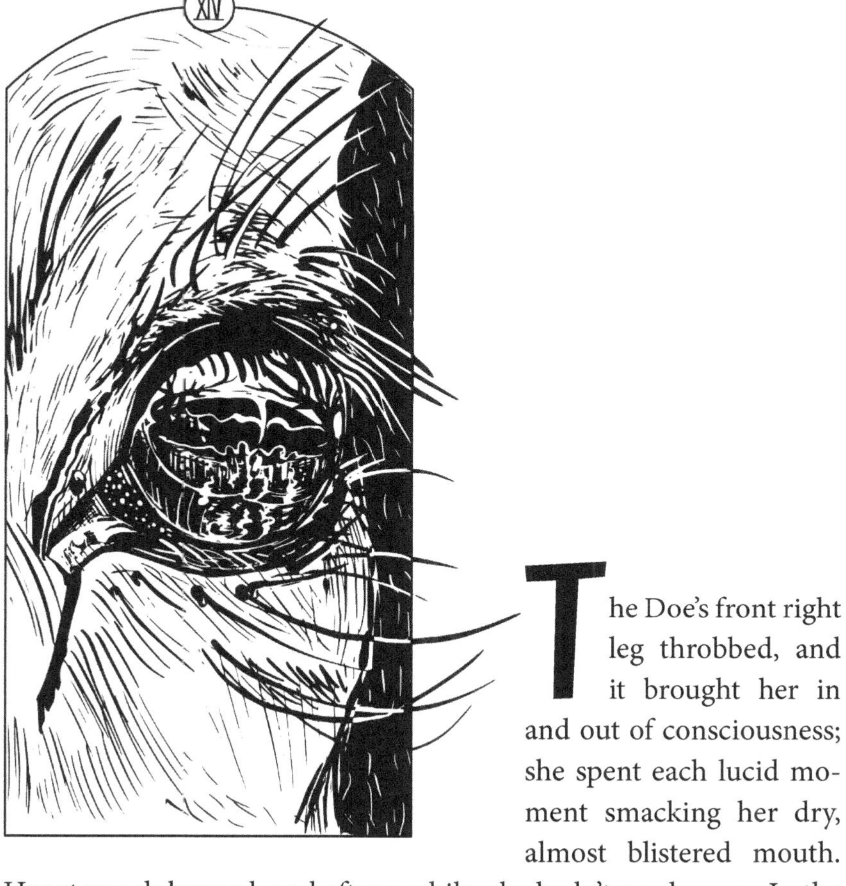

The Doe's front right leg throbbed, and it brought her in and out of consciousness; she spent each lucid moment smacking her dry, almost blistered mouth. Her stomach burned, and after a while, she hadn't any hunger. In the heat of the afternoon, she felt a terrible chill and was so weak that she could barely support the weight of her head. Brumes of darkness, coils of dawn; each visited her in cycles. Blackness, then radiance like a supernova. Blackness, and then a purple sky. Blackness, and overcast with morning light like Russian olive branches.

In her delirium, she came to realize three days had come and gone. She stared at her leg, and it scuffled in response. Thankfully, it hadn't been broken, but it was heavy and aching—All of her was. She'd have to lug her body from one place to the next in search of water. After everything she'd endured, she just wanted to sink into sleep, but that she knew would be a sleep from which there'd be no waking. There was a choice to be made: to live or to just let go.

Letting go felt good. It was similar to bedding down exhausted after a day of hard play and finally being at peace and letting the darkness wrap you up, to close your eyes on a complicated world and yield your body to the warm and welcoming swaddle of nothingness. It was to slip away into oblivion until the very notion of self became meaningless. And then at last, nothing.

The odor of deer came lifting from below in the garden. She smelled their essence only briefly but clearly. It quickened her pulse, but her eyes grew heavy again. It felt good to let them close. The scent could have been that of the doe clan—maybe other deer—but such cares were losing significance. She was even beginning to forget the burning and blistering of her parched mouth. Then a voice came: *Sleep, friend*, it cooed. *Free yourself from this troubled world.*

As soon as she heard it speak, she squirmed, but she hadn't mustered the energy to raise her head. Its voice she recognized from the first night near the shanty, where she had drifted to sleep concealed beneath the rhododendron—the voice that had called for and coveted the drapery of her hide. She questioned it, asking if it was the evil one that dwelled in the Man.

*What is evil and what is good?* it asked in a tone that denoted a twinkling in its unseen eye. *I am the angel that dwells in all creatures.*

The Doe did not respond. Her tail flicked, sweeping up the earth behind her.

*I am here to tell you it is okay to let go. I bring the promise of new life. If you only just sleep, I will make sure you awaken to the lushest garden you have ever seen. Here atop the hill will there be hostas larger than any man, supple grasses, sour berries, rich nuts—all for your consumption. It will rise around you in a veritable miracle only I can conjure.*

She murmured.

Then her mind lit up. The neurons rippled across the surface of her dark brain. She was a discerning soul, and as she had now been acquainted with death, she was able to reason with the angel. No, she mustn't sleep. The sickly soil on which she lay would grow such a garden only if she were to die on it. Yes, perhaps the angel could conjure such a bounty, but it would take her rotting body feeding the earth to allow such things to rise.

*Death is a gift. After all, what do you have to live for?* Its voice was pacifying, melodic.

Her brain felt cold and dark until a thought shot through it like a blazing arrow—a reminder of the love of her parents, a father who had carried her over the river and had crossed back from death into life to greet her on the acreage with the offering of an apple. He awaited her. And had she come all this way to forget her mother's sacrifice? It was the Elder Doe through whom she had passed into this world as one enters a doorway who had laid down her life for her. She owed it all to her mother. She would not sleep.

The angel was quiet for a moment. *You are wise, Doe, but yet a fool. You put so much trust and weight in your mother and father. Do you think they are more powerful than I?*

The Doe was silent as she began hoisting herself up, gritting her teeth as she bore down on her injured leg, her body shaking and shuddering. She panted under the grueling duress; the dead, gummy flesh in her mouth began to shed loose. She needed water urgently, and there was only one place where she'd find it: down the *S*-shaped footpath to the Woman's garden. It was an awful risk, and she could hardly keep herself stable as her body heaved over and over from an icy chill. After a while, her leg began to feel like something outside her body, as if she were walking around on a stick.

The angel had been reading her thoughts all along. *Doe, let us wager. I will lead you to water as you are so weak and worn. And while I watch you drown, we shall see if your father and mother are strong enough to save you from death. If so, I will leave this land vanquished and humbled.*

Against a tree, the Doe braced her body. Such a wager needed no deliberation. She may have been simpleminded, but she was no fool. Her mother was dead, and her father, like her, had a wounded leg.

Even she knew two injured limbs do not make a useful one. She would lead herself to drink, not drown.

*What a sharp mind! You are much wiser than the man I possess. He has limitations as all men do, but not you. You are the divine feminine. Hail, Eve! You have tasted the sacred apple and are the better for it.*

The Doe grew faint and began to slip downward the tree, scraping her flank against the sawtooth bark until she ultimately bent against her injured leg unnaturally hyperextending it. Once again, she cried out slumping on the earth defeated.

*Poor creature! So pitiful to be but an animal. The body is weak and born to rot. Sleep, my beloved. I know you want it. I see it in your eyes. You are overcome.*

She intuited that the angel could see in her the personification of all life and of all nature. It defied logic, but in her black eyes it caught a glimpse of fragility, a reflection of the inevitable mortality of all living beings. She was a mirror for all the world's suffering waiting to be broken.

*After you sleep, you will awaken all powerful and transformed. Worship me, and all the lands will bow down to you. I will place you atop the awful temple. I will conjure your parents to your side. You will rule all as the queen of Earth.*

Sovereign of all things and with her mother and father at her side? She saw its magnificent breadth, and it seduced her. Then she heard a rattling and a hissing inside herself. It slithered up from her bowels and quickly choked her as it slid through her throat, split her skull, and burrowed into her brain. *Saint*, the snake sibilated.

A vision was shown to her spanning many generations and realities on the undefined world. Of greed and power, of bloodshed and cruelty, all things that had belonged to the kings and queens of Earth; of burning bodies and red-spattered gold, of famine and corpulent tyrants, of people in chains and in prisons, of the dying forests and the slaughter of innocents. She tasted the chemicals leaching into soils and waterways, could name the few with all the riches and the countless others left scraping for barely enough. The screams blared from battles waged in the dry countries for water as precious as diamonds. From below came the perfume of a thousand flowers, of deer and of life, and it triggered an otherness in her, and an old wisdom sprang forth. Her higher self spoke through her as into a loud hailer. *Get behind me, devil! I know you well.*

The devil roared, and the land quaked upon its broken spine. The Doe once again stood with renewed vigor. At the head of the footpath, she braced herself to descend its steep grade, but as soon as she placed a hoof forward, the shingles of bluestone shards caused her to slide. She drove her hooves into the ground until the small avalanche of stone and dirt clods subsided. Halting had brought a searing pain that shot up her leg straight into her eye. She groaned but quickly sealed her leathery mouth. She took deep breaths to compose herself and began to make the first curve of the descending footpath.

*You are a fool, Doe! Go ahead and descend, but be warned! The ashes await you. The uprooted tree calls to you from outside the garden. Behold the terrible offerings men have given to me!*

High above, the circling scavengers called to one another. Their tiny shadows passed the footpath like rabbits running across the trail. At the bend, she saw the patch of garden where the colossal sunflower stood. It had somehow turned itself completely around and now stared directly at her. Its all-seeing eye devoid of its rows of black seeds was white and scabbed over with a blinding cataract.

At the steepest part of the bend, she heard rock tumbling. The stones underneath began to slide and roll away and pull her hooves along in a loamy tidal wave. The earth gave way, and her body jerked until she felt herself free-falling. The last plunking of stones diminished into a rattling sound, and all the noise of the world around her was reduced to a tapering hiss. Then all grew dark, and she was swallowed up as into night, the last thing she heard being the voice of the devil.

*Can you see it? Can't you smell it, Doe? The fragrant offering to god? I am their god! And soon, you will find yourself being split into seven for the beast's terrible, hungry mouths.*

"Come on, Saint. Wake up. Come on, baby."

Light poured in, and a face slowly became visible—a spotted face crowned by a halo. It looked like the Old Man's painting of the Doe, of Saint under the apple tree. For a moment, the Doe believed she was looking at her own image. However, this spotted face grew richer and deeper until it was purple and vermillion like the dawn on the second day of her delirium.

Then everything came into focus: it was a ministering angel crouching over her with a wet cloth. She wiped and wetted the Doe's mouth, which choked her as soon as the liquid hit her dry throat. The Woman's face was blotched and puffy in an array of bruises framed by the aura of her ashy-blond hair. "I know you can't understand, but please don't panic," the Woman said.

The Doe looked up to a high wood ceiling. At first glance, it appeared to be the birch thicket, but then she noticed other items all around—seedlings in long trays and tools, the sort of implements she'd seen the Old Man use in his flowerbeds. This was the Woman's work area, her gardening shed with large, cloudy windows. She had a sturdy table pushed up against the wall. Atop its battered surface were bottles of various liquids, dried herb bundles, and a photograph or two. High above and off center of the table was a watercolor of lilies in bloom. Aside the painting was a holy card of Our Lady of Perpetual Help tacked to the wall. A white candle sat below it; it was low to the table after many burnings.

"I heard my friend call to me from the hill. Damn. Grief does strange things." She shook her head and put her face in her hands and squeezed out a sad sort of chuckle. "But strange things happen around here anymore."

The Doe's instincts urged her to rise and run even though she was far too weak. The small domiciles of men had given her little comfort since fleeing the acreage, but there was a feeling about this shed; it was peaceful and warm. She permitted herself to lie still and rest. She stared up into the eyes of the Woman, each iris like the amber glass of the apothecary jars on the worktable.

"I went outside. The vultures were making a fuss. Went to look and saw you lying on the hillside. Dragged you down the hill. Was worried I might have hurt you."

She plunged the cloth into a bowl of warm water that had herbs brewing in it. She gently placed it into the Doe's mouth, and the Doe bit down reflexively.

"Welcome to my sanctuary. Gets decent light. I use it for starting seeds and drying herbs. Well insulated, too. I store vegetables and overwinter plants in here. I also make tinctures and other things."

She dipped the cloth back into the bowl and began to wipe the Doe's brow. Then she bathed her dirty hooves. The Doe's gaze shifted to her beaten face.

"We look the same, you and I. Spot-faced twins." She smiled revealing a crack in her lip. "It's certainly not the first time. But don't you worry, Saint. He doesn't ever step foot in here. Hates sheds—" She paused and looked through the wall to the west, to the burnt and rubbled patch on the property. "Hates deer even more. But as long as you're here and quiet, you'll be safe."

The Woman touched the Doe's injured leg. The Doe jerked. "Ooh. That's the spot, huh?" She grabbed a different earthenware bowl covered with a heavily stained linen tea towel. Steam swirled up as the linen was lifted. A sour and vegetal smell filled the room. The Woman put the towel into the liquid and shook her hand to cool scalded fingertips. "Hot hot hot!" She blew on her fingers and wiped them on her slacks. "This is an old remedy my grandma taught me. Her grandma probably taught her." She pursed her lips and shook her head. "Don't think your leg is broken, but I do think you damaged a tendon. Maybe a sprain." She spoke under her breath while examining it more closely. "How did you do it?"

The Woman turned back to the hot bowl feeling along the earthenware sides. She shook her head again. "Still too damn hot."

The Doe watched as the Woman rose and retrieved a book from the worktable. There was no title on the cover, just an old, brown fabric binding. She got back down on her knees and fanned the scalding liquid with the book.

"My grandma and her family all worked the land. Scandinavian farm people. Used homemade remedies and did a lot of canning and pickling. I think the herbal part, making tinctures and what not, came from my great-great-great-great-grandmother." She looked up as she visualized her family tree and tapped the air in a succession to denote each generation. "She was an American Indian. Never can remember which tribe. Wasn't something people spoke openly about in those days."

The Woman then touched the bowl for a longer duration. She nodded then smiled at the Doe. It was quiet except for the distant wheezing of the vultures. The Woman tried covering them over with the sound of her voice. "So I grew up not far from here.

Momma had me young and didn't want me. But I had a mother—my grandma Ava.

It took only one impulsive, passionate act under an old dogwood tree. The Woman's mother had been but a teenager when she got pregnant, her father two years older. No sooner than she'd missed her period had he been drafted to the dry nation, where war was being waged for water.

A year prior, abortion had been criminalized—Even so, the Bluestone Woodland was so remote that finding access to reproductive care was like traveling abroad. The seas rose. The deserts burned. The crops failed. God Will Provide became the slogan of the apocalypse. And the babies rained down from heaven like locusts.

The girl begged her mother, Ava, to help her terminate the pregnancy. And though Ava had refused it on many occasions, she reluctantly gave in for the sake of her daughter's future and for that of the fetus, who would be birthed into such an uncertain world. Ava expressly forbade any coat hanger, knitting hook, or back-alley doctor. As she was well educated in plants and herbs through her own mother and grandmother, she decided to give her daughter a potent tea of tansy, which had been known to encourage miscarriage. It made a pungent, hot liquid as deep yellow as lemon curd.

When the tea made the pregnant girl only sick and the pregnancy remained intact, Ava told her it was a sign that the child should live. The girl begged for more, but Ava refused any further attempts deeming it too dangerous. And as soon as she had given birth to a towheaded girl, she abandoned the infant at Ava's home and made her way west never to be heard from again, save for a postcard of ancient rock art from Moab, Utah with I'M ALIVE AND FINE scrawled on it.

As for the father, he returned two years later from the war stripped of his humanity. He was unable to face his toddler daughter and deemed his hands too soiled to hold her. So he pulled into the garage and shut the door and fell asleep with his car running.

As such, Grandma Ava, nearing her seventies then, became her granddaughter's sole caretaker. Raising her granddaughter in her sunset years was what she had called the best years of her life. She and the girl spent time in the garden, where Ava taught her all about cultivation and the properties of different plants. They read stories aloud to one another sometimes while they were in the kitchen canning venison stew or making jam. The girl liked to hug the old woman tightly and breathe her in, always smelling of line-dried linens. Some nights, she would snuggle up to her in her twin bed wedging her little body between her grandmother and the cold, firm wall. On summer days, they'd go down to a lake and fish for bluegill with a stick and line or sit on the front porch and eat salted watermelon and watch the night sky. They were free together and safe in their little parcel of land.

She'd sit aside the old woman on the velvet-like blue davenport and ask, "Are we best buds forever, Grandma?" putting her hand in the old woman's.

"Best buds forever," Ava said while squeezing her. "And I won't ever let go of this chubby, little hand either!"

The house they shared was not without spirits. Ava had described the conception of her daughter as resulting from an encounter with a divine being. A transient man had sought shelter on her land and was all the while a wandering angel in disguise. In the night, in an ecstasy not unlike St. Teresa's, the angel unsheathed his fiery sword that he had used to guard Eden and pierced her with it.

And then there were times when Grandma Ava had episodes that scared the girl. It was what the woodland folks had called *being touched*. Every so often, Ava would sleep for hours on end, and other times, she would hallucinate and speak to invisible entities. While crocheting in the living room, Ava said she saw a knot of blue and white light in the hallway and told the girl it was the Virgin Mary. On another occasion, she had awoken to find the devil walking up to her bed but then saw herself outside her body and seated in God's protecting hand. She warned her granddaughter that the devil could appear as anything, even as a shadow on the wall.

Ghosts could be found anywhere, but the most powerful specter of all was the one reflected in her granddaughter's face. Ava saw the image of her daughter, which sometimes softened the pain and other times sharpened it. She too found her in the medicine cabinet mirror somewhere beyond the wrinkles in her cheeks or the deep lines at the corner of her gold-hazel eyes.

The Woman empathized with the terrible burden Grandma Ava carried never hearing again from her daughter. Even on her deathbed while she clung to life until the early morning hours, Ava had waited for a knock at the door or a ringing phone. The granddaughter, then a young woman, had said, "Gramma, she's not coming home. It's okay. Just let go."

In that final moment, the Woman held onto her grandmother until she had at last passed. And while she held onto her, a memory cropped up—one she had often revisited. It was of a day when the Woman was still a girl. At the edge of the lake, she sat between the old woman's legs while she sang "I will lift mine eyes to the hills, from whence cometh my help" and braided the child's white-blond hair. The water was calm like glass, and never once looking to the sky, they watched upon the surface what appeared to be an angel landing in a shoreward pine.

"Look! It's a falcon," Ava whispered. The child sat quietly with mouth agape. "You know what they say about the falcon?" The girl shrugged. "That it represents the shedding of one's old self. A spiritual rebirth, like Christ had in dying. I remember my grandmother singing 'lully, lullay, the falcon has borne my beloved away.' Old folk used to believe that the falcon stood for those who'd killed Christ so's he could get to heaven."

"What's a Christ?" the girl asked.

"Someone who gives everything, even their life, because they love you more than anything in the world."

From the tree, the falcon watched, breaking only to preen itself. Ava's eyes were directed at the pine, but her gaze then grew sorrowful and she looked just above the tree. She was in that hazy place between watching and remembering. "Grandma," said the girl smiling, "then you're a Christ."

"Shame on you, child!" Ava snapped her tongue. She placed her hands firmly on the girl's shoulders, her plump, milk-glass skin puffing around tight gingham dress straps. "That's blasphemy and a sin. We cannot compare ourselves to Christ."

There was a disgust in Ava's tone that had made the girl cry. Too embarrassed to show her tears, the girl ducked her face and hands into her lap. Ava softened her voice and continued, "I'm sorry. I know what you meant, and you're sure sweet for sayin' it." She pet the crying child's head. "But we shouldn't say such things. We don't want to offend God like Lucifer did."

The girl kept her head down and tilted her feet to tap her toes. It was getting dark, and lusty frogs were singing their belching songs. Ava lifted a finger. "But I suppose as a state of mind, we are all the Christs of our own lives—as are the people we meet. 'For I was a stranger and you housed me.'" Ava leaned over and gently turned and lifted the girl's face to hers. "Yes—You're right, sister. God made all of us in his image. That's something we share with Christ. So I suppose we are like him." She shook the same finger and smiled with a proud chin. "You're absolutely right."

The girl wiped her nose with her arm then looked out to the lake. After a moment, Ava said, "But I think I'm more of a falcon myself. Sharp and keen eyed and faster than lightning. When you're not looking, I jump up and startle you!" She ran her fingers along the girl's ribs, which made her roar with laughter. The girl soon after grasped hold of the old woman's arms, and they remained in an embrace.

Insects fizzed on the muddy bank as something had washed up dead. Over the looking-glass lake, they watched as a goldfinch shot across the water. The falcon flew to greet it, its reflection a gliding cross against the pines. After snagging the little bird and killing it with a clenched foot, the falcon sailed around the bend of the lake and disappeared. Only three golden feathers remained on the dusky water while the old woman and child clasped one another.

The Woman stared blankly over the Doe's head. The fanning book over the earthenware crock was at a standstill. "Christ." The Woman's eyes widened. She let the book fall. "Telling my life story to a deer." She laughed, but her eyes glistened, and she feigned shooting herself in the temple. "I'm losing my mind."

A tear traced her purple cheek. The Doe lifted her head off the floor. She couldn't be sure whether the Woman was crying or laughing. Her slight belly heaved over strong thighs. A rolled-up sleeve passed over her face, wiping it clean—as clean as a beaten face could look. The Woman took a deep breath and steadied herself. "You know, she's been gone five years. Now when I think of Grandma, it feels like I knew her in a dream. Did it really happen?" She plucked a loose thread from her beige linen shirt and held it out. "If time were linear like this string, and all moments past and future are happening at some point on the line, that means that even still, I can trace my finger back to a spot on the thread and be with Grandma somewhere in my childhood. All things unfold simultaneously. It's a kind of time magic that keeps me sane."

The Woman looked to the wall above the worktable. She stared at the lily watercolor and the holy card of Our Lady of Perpetual Help. "But am I sane? Because I swear to you, Saint, she came back to me."

The Doe listened with eyes closed ignorant of the words' meanings. Feeling the warmth of the Woman's body aside her and smelling her particular odor gave the illusion she craved. Or perhaps if she imagined it, then somewhere in the universe it was truly happening. For the first time since the birch thicket, she felt close to her mother's spirit. And for a moment, she allowed herself to believe that she and the Elder Doe were bedded together in the old grass bower back home.

The Woman shifted off her knees and onto her backside to sit next to the Doe. Then she looked up to the hill and dark pines through the calcified windowpane. She said, "I've seen the dead walk in treetops."

"Okay, Saint. I think the liquid is hot enough. It may sting, but it has to be hot." Just self-aware enough to remember that she was speaking to a wild animal as she would a human, she continued. "This lunatic," she pointed to herself, "is going to wrap up your leg with a soaked towel to get you walking faster." She raised an index finger. "A word of warning … It's a little pungent." She illustrated her point by scowling and waving a hand over her nose while pinching it with the other. "It's wormwood steeped in apple cider vinegar. Grandma's special recipe. Pee-*ewww!*"

A bleary-eyed Doe monitored the Woman at work. Tea towel linen began to shroud her leg. Wet tufts of hair appeared beneath the thin fabric's veneer adding more dappling to an already spot-stained rag. Again, the Doe winced.

"Stay calm. I know it hurts."

Rising to the worktable, the Woman grabbed twine and cut long strings with an old Swiss Army knife. She tied each end of the towel binding it up the leg in the way a butcher loop-ties a cut of meat. It had to be tight, but it needed a bit of give. She wriggled it to make certain blood would circulate.

"It won't hold, but it's worth a shot." She rolled herself off her knees and sat cross-legged before the Doe. "My friend would have known what to do. He was a doctor." She looked to his lily watercolor mounted off center of the worktable. "His herd meant so much to him right up until he …" Unrelenting vultures were still crying. Everything made her think of death in that place. "Can't shake this terrible guilt I feel, as if I had a part to play. Losing him is like losing my grandma all over again."

Some time passed in the quiet shed; the Woman did not speak as she looked out the window. The Doe wondered if she was calmer than perhaps she should be. Maybe it was the Woman, or maybe the herbal treatment she used to soak her leg and wet her mouth, but she was content to lie very still.

"I can sit with you for a few more minutes. Husband won't be home just yet. I'll just keep talking at you." She looked at nothing in particular; her eyebrows lifted then sank. "No one left for me to talk to."

There was another long stretch of silence. The vultures had at last gone. The Doe opened her eyes and stared drowsily at the Woman and then moved her tongue around her mouth, which made a flickering sound as if it were coated in drying syrup.

"Thirsty, Saint?" The Woman poured some of the warm, herbal water into her palm and offered it to the Doe. Having shrugged off all shreds of distrust and wariness, the Doe lapped it up swiftly tickling the Woman's hand along a remindful branching of blue veins—a tree growing underneath the flesh of her wrist and palm or her father's antlers warm as blood wrapped in summer sky.

"I'm good at serving, eh, girl? Had a short stint as a waitress." She wiped her hands, and they found their way to her lap and folded themselves politely. "Grandma had died, and I was working at a cafe an hour from here. It's how I met my husband. I came to realize that he needed a wife who had no prior knowledge of who he was because no woman around here would dare marry him. I mean, shit, he drove an hour away and found the most vulnerable prey. I was chin-high in grief and had been raised in seclusion—I never knew men, never had a father. Thought I was strong then and doing what I was supposed to do, but he's taken everything. I've lost my antlers, Saint."

"Aren't you gonna sit with me while I eat?" the Man asked the Woman. She stood over him in her polyester server's uniform, ash-blond hair pulled back except for a few strands that had grazed the platter of fat-slicked fries avalanching onto a chicken club.

"I haven't been working here long. Don't want to get fired," the Woman responded looking over her shoulder to her senior coworker, an old, round woman with a helmet of tight curls. She was eyeing her like a hawk as she flitted around the dining room with two carafes of coffee, one orange-lidded for decaf.

"You want to be a waitress all your life? I thought you liked living off the land." The Man cracked his smile; though lined with crooked, chipped teeth, it still oozed a charm that made a warmth pass along the Woman's body.

"No, but I gotta support myself. Don't have anyone no more. Can't live like a wild animal."

"I could tame you or let you run wild at my place. I have a big house to myself. You could live with me. I could take care of you." He began to finger comb his dirty dishwater hair, looking at himself in a butter knife still smiling widely. "Maybe I'd like that," she retorted reddening all over. She took her leave to hurry back to the impatient short-order cook who was dinging the service bell like a fire alarm.

After the Man had finished his meal and he and the Woman had said their goodbyes, he left the cafe, turning back once through the glass door to wink and make a kissing mouth to her. She giggled and went to clear his lunch plate. On the booth seat was a pamphlet with bold, red writing. She quickly snatched it and rushed to the lot where the Man was sitting in his running truck. "Wait! You forgot this!" she waved the pamphlet high like a standard-bearer in battle.

The Man nodded and rolled down his window. "Hustle! Gotta get back to work."

She jogged toward him kicking up a blitz of pebbles in her grandmother's barely used orthopedic sneakers. As she handed the sheet to him, she gave it a once-over scrunching her forehead. "What's Thin the Herd?"

He grabbed it out of her hand and then grinned, but the charm of his smile had warped into something else. For the first time, the Woman's hot blood felt a chill.

"Didn't know wild animals could read." His blue eyes turned clear in the shade of his pickup. "Guess you'll just have to see, huh?"

"Yeah, guess so." She tried to laugh politely, but she had a conspicuous sense of uneasiness about her.

And as he backed up and flipped his car onto the road, he turned to the Woman shrinking in the gravel lot and looking like a child in a woman's uniform. From his window, he howled with a savage sort of laughter and shot at her with the air pistol of his crooked-fingered hand.

"I should have run right then and there." Something called from the hills—a bird or an insect—and she stared up at the window. "Can I still run?" She looked down to her bare feet, calloused underneath but clean on top with nails cut short. "I remember seeing the last deer I would ever see before coming here. Men had chased a buck out of the woods, and it was running down Main. It crashed into a storefront window and severed its neck. It bled to death in the back. That was probably an omen."

The Doe watched as the Woman picked up the book she'd used to fan the scalding wormwood treatment. Now an anxious thumb riffled the old, stiff pages like a deck of cards. "This is *Aesop's Fables*. My grandma used to read it to me." Her eyes veered left, and her fair-fleshed ears, large like a doe's, turned scarlet. "When you're a kid, fresh and new, these are just stories about animals. But then you live, and it hurts like hell, and suddenly the meaning of the tales rings true."

The balmy room lulled the Doe, seedlings stretched from their rows in starter trays, and the Woman was ready to combust. "He was perfectly fine at first." She spoke while examining the cracked flesh at the tips of her thumbs. "I was blinded by grief and loneliness, or I didn't know any better. We moved fast. We got married. Sold Grandma's house. He convinced me to put the money into an account under his name. What was I thinking?"

At any moment, she thought her brain could catch fire. In fact, she really hoped it would. She knocked loudly on the book's coarse cover, scraping a knuckle; the scuff mark raised like a little red fruit over the joint.

"After that, he began to change. Forbade me to leave the house. Kept my grandma's money from me. I had lost all freedom. Then I caught word that he'd married me only because of a rumor in town. I brought it up. He raped me. That's how I lost my virginity."

She took to thumbing the worn spine of the book. The pressure of it threatened to coax open the cracks in her thumbs. She kept her voice very even. "Then he started hurting me. It was just like they all say—little things at first. He'd lose his patience with me and slap my back. Then he got into a fight and came home drunk to take it out on me. Left me so bruised I couldn't see out of my eye for days."

She breathed heavily, and it stirred the Doe from her stupor. "He's hurt me so badly—He's gonna kill me just like he killed them all." She covered her mouth. She had never admitted it aloud before. "When do I burn?"

The Woman had thought of running away, simply taking off into the woods and pushing north with only a satchel on her back. If not north, where would she run? Would she cut west like her mother? She had heard that the West never stopped burning. The woodland was filled with people displaced by coastal flooding. It could be dangerous—but it would be freedom. After all, staying in the little Cape

Cod at the base of the winding footpath was a dead end for anyone who lived there.

"I'm so scared. But I want to be free. I want to be like you, Saint. I want to be a wild animal far away from this terrible place." Her face darkened in patches as light shifted in the shed. She looked masked, like a sad *commedia* character. "That's why Grandma came back to me. To take me with her into the hills. But how? Even wild animals are trapped here."

She wrestled with the notion of merely dashing into the wilderness in search of freedom. Perhaps it wasn't all hopeless. It made her believe if only subconsciously that the timing was not quite right for an escape, that there was yet work to be done. She was always holding out for another tomorrow. *I'll leave tomorrow*, she often thought, and suddenly a year had passed—then two years.

"Red is my husband's close friend. His family had a sugar bush over near the town cemetery. Called it Sugar Rock. Syrup was a big industry here until the heat pushed the sugar maples farther north."

The Woman was quiet for a moment. She seemed to be running her words through her mind, mouthing them ever so slightly with lips sort of twitching and rounding in an array of silent words. The truth was that these extended silences had become a part of how she communicated after years of being alone in the house. She got tired speaking too long, and she often lapsed into thought without realizing it. Then suddenly she'd continue as if she'd never stopped to think.

"If maple trees have the damn sense to go, why don't I?"

Sunlight no longer flooded in with intensity. Something about the fading light of afternoon made her want to read. It probably stemmed from childhood with her grandma, all those bedtime stories of tragedy clothed in whimsy.

"I wish I could leave this all behind. Wish I could just run. But you see, I can't." She opened the book to the exact spot. "Have you heard the fable of the stag and the fawn?" A shivering hand caressed a page with a dog-eared corner. "The fawn asked the stag, who had such impressive antlers, why he ran each time he heard the hounds coming. He could obviously use those antlers to defend himself. The stag told the fawn that he had wondered that too. But no matter how many times he told himself he was strong enough, when he heard the hounds coming, he gave away his power to fear."

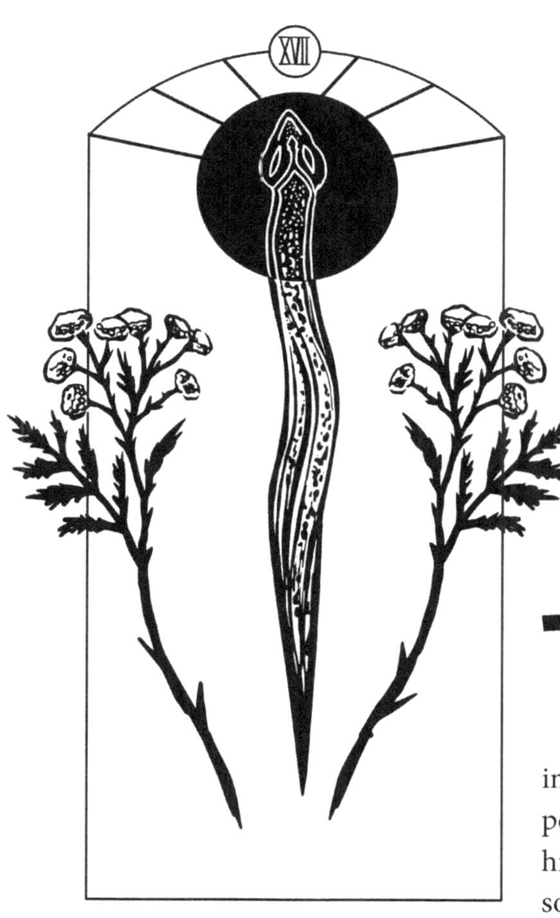


T he Woman had taken her leave long ago, but there was someone now in the nighttime room. The person turned to the Doe. In his thick hands he presented something of carved wood, a small staff. He held one end in his left hand and the other in his right. She saw it was a snake smoothed with age and primitive in design. He smiled and lifted the staff high.

He drew the snake staff toward his head. With his right hand, he raised it in front of his left eye, now just a yellow round devoid of pupil. He parted his eyelids with two fingers. Using the fine point of the staff, he punctured his delicate lens and dragged it across the cornea slicing a black slit into a golden serpent's eye.

The Doe had kicked and flailed until she freed herself from the dream. Upon waking, she had forgotten where she was and scanned the room until she could place herself in the shed. The first red slash of morning had already given way to full-fledged daylight. It was noticeably cooler and more damp. Light filtered through swirling, soot-grey clouds. An earlier shower had lined tracks of rain all down the filmy windows.

She stretched out little by little in the crammed corner of her emergency bower. Upon making the discovery, she groaned; during the night she urinated, soaking the underside of her coat. It made her cold and uncomfortable, and though she didn't like soiling where she slept, she was still too exhausted to care.

After a while, the Woman came into the shed with her two bowls—one for the Doe to drink and one to resoak her leg wrap. She did not take notice of the deer's damp underside, how the fur of her thick coat had mopped up the small pool of dark urine. The Doe again stretched her long body, but the injured leg lagged in resistance. It was out of sync with the other three limbs, though the pain was subsiding.

"You barely moved all night. Guess the herbal tea did the trick."

The Woman smiled. She plunged a turkey baster into the smaller bowl and sucked up the green- and brown-flecked broth. She gently coaxed it between the Doe's teeth and into her mouth, where the peeling, dead tissue was finally sloughing clear. The Doe closed her eyes. She remembered trying to get her mother to drink in the final hours. This felt well rehearsed.

"This is good stuff. I added more cannabis to keep you relaxed. You're not quite ready to run on that leg. Cannabis should keep you down." The baster made another wet slurp as it sucked the broth up. To the Woman, it sounded unappetizingly like the gutting of the rabbits her husband had brought home to fry for the evening's supper. "The cannabis I grow in the north of the garden. My friend loved to smoke it. I'd give him a baggie full. He'd bring me something in return, like this." She referenced the lily watercolor above the worktable. "Beautiful. He even designed my grandma's headstone." The Woman smiled, but it favored a frown. "Never seen it, only a photo. Husband won't take me."

Wind blew through the tall pines. They heard rain sprinkle off damp boughs. The tip went back into the Doe's mouth. The tube feeding became robotic. "Well, besides cannabis, what else is in here? This is another one of Grandma's brews. First, I steeped it in broth to give you extra vitamins and minerals. That's not in the normal recipe. There's basil, catnip, daisy—" The Doe watched as she plunged the baster back into the broth but clutched the bulb without releasing it. "—hops, skullcap, bee balm, and a tiny bit of tansy." *Tansy* was almost whispered as she let up on the baster's bulb, coaxing the liquid up the tube while it made another gutting noise.

The gash on the Woman's mouth shined with a generous shellacking of ointment. She repositioned herself on the floor and began to unwrap the Doe's leg. A curling vapor slipped from out of the uncovered earthenware bowl. The room was thick with the stench of hot vinegar and wormwood, which made the Woman breathe hard and erratically. "There's something I gotta confess, Saint. It's destroying me." Her voice box jounced in her throat. "My friend is dead because of me." The Woman cradled the dried tea towel in her arms; a rural *pietà*. "I need to tell someone so it doesn't replay forever. I need to release it."

She carefully submerged the tea towel in the piping-hot bowl and lifted her burning hands, shaking them out into the damp air while mouthing profanities. The Doe was slipping into a state of wooziness again. Her leg bared to the fresh air was tingly and cool. It kept her only slightly alert.

"Took us three years to get pregnant. Not that anything was wrong health wise." She scrunched up her face. "It was just that we never had sex unless he was angry." She used the turkey baster to stir the tea towel in the hot liquid. "Honestly, I was okay with that, but I started to wonder if the rumors had been true. Then one night after a fight with Red, he came home drunk, and, well …" She rubbed her hands over her mouth. "… he forced himself on me. That happened two years ago. Before a hot October. I was in the bathroom getting ready. Had the shower running. Steam was fogging up the mirror.

Took off my clothes to inspect myself for ticks. I wanted to check my ass, so I wiped the mirror. That's when I saw it."

The room started to close in on the Doe. The cannabis was making her high. Through her slitted, drooping eyes, the Woman's features blurred. A dark border rounded out her vision like a tunnel.

"My nipples had darkened into this chocolatey color. I just knew. I touched my belly and cried. It was mixed emotions."

The Woman kept it a secret for almost two weeks. At first, she was over the moon because she was terribly lonesome. Finally, she had thought, someone to love and to love her in return. Someone to care for and teach and nurture. It was this little protected bit of bliss that she entertained until at last reality sank in.

"Selfish woman! I couldn't have a baby in this home with that beast!" She rose to fetch the binding twine for the Doe's leg and then unraveled it. "I couldn't protect my baby here." She snipped the twine. It felt very final.

She lowered herself to the floor and began to wrap the Doe's leg. The liquid was hot on the Doe's skin. Maybe it would have been too hot had the cannabis not so sweetly luxated her senses from her awareness.

"I called my friend. Asked him for advice. It's a small town. You gotta be careful."

She tied off the end of the tea towel on the Doe's leg.

"It's no longer legal, you see. So my friend wrote a note to a colleague who could have helped me. She had this secret room in the back of her house. I told him I couldn't bring myself to call. He said he'd drive me. That was impossible. He inscribed word for word what I needed on a note addressed to this woman. He even signed it. He *signed* it." She hesitated. "I tucked it into my underwear drawer. Seemed safe there."

She checked the tea towel, adjusted it, and sat back and monitored the Doe. For a short while, she didn't say anything. She messed about with her hair, twisted it into a rope, strung it playfully about her neck, and then tossed it over one shoulder. "I'll keep talking. Quietly," she said. "Maybe that'll help you sleep."

The Doe closed her eyes. She soaked in the warmth of the sunspot that had found its way upon her white-tufted breast.

"Tansy tea is very toxic. Women used it in the old days. I knew I had to make it strong."

The Woman moved the earthenware bowl off to the side. She placed the smaller bowl abut it. She sat with her back against the worktable in an easy, languid recline, which was completely incongruous with her feelings. "When my husband went to work that morning, I harvested all my tansy. Spent most of the day boiling it down and concentrating it. I even used the flowers. The liquid turned this incredible gold color, but it smelled so bitter. I poured it into a jar and let it cool. For a while, I stared at my reflection on the jar."

The worktable dug into the Woman's back. She turned onto her side to lie and propped her head on her hand with elbow to the floor like a kickstand. The sunspot crept toward her belly. "When the jar of the tansy brew was cool enough to drink, I lifted it and walked to the sink. I looked out the window to the hills and cleared my mind. I felt unlike myself. Didn't know what to expect, but I was sure it would hurt. I thought to drink it down and wander up the hill. Seemed like a fitting place to lie down and die. At least no one would find me and try to resuscitate me."

The sun on her hips and belly warmed her causing her veins to open and the blood to rush madly. "Then when I lifted the jar, I saw an animal move outside the garden. Just over there at the foot of the hill." She pointed out the window arching her free arm over her head. "It was large and bright. I saw fur. It lowered itself. Through the red zinnias, I saw its belly moving fast."

Dust on the floor became faintly visible in the light. The Woman traced her fingers through it drawing lines invisible without sun. "So I put the glass down and went outside. I thought to pick up a shovel to defend myself, but I didn't care anymore. I made my way along the fence. When I came around the corner, I saw a large coyote lying in a heap of goldenrod."

The Woman drew the hill that led to the shanty on the dusty floor. She wriggled a line to the top denoting the serpentine footpath. "I was scared. Its lips were raised, baring its teeth. But then it was so obvious to me. It was fat. I saw it was engorged with milk. And it just stared, and I knew it was in labor"

An alarm went off. It was the Woman's wristwatch. She put her finger to the side and poked a tiny metal disk. "Husband'll be home soon."

As she stood, the Woman stretched her willowy arms, which were more of a weeping willow as they fell. She put her hands to her lower back and pressed her chin to her chest. It was as if she were warming up for some gladiatorial task.

"Weird, 'cause coyotes don't give birth in the fall. Anyway, I had gone into the house to get water. I looked at the tansy tea on the counter and lost my nerve. So, I dumped it down the drain and went back out with a pie plate. But the coyote had already gone. Told my husband about it, and he looked as if he'd seen a ghost. He said there weren't coyotes in the region. They had migrated."

A flush of redness appeared just under the Woman's hairline like a crown of thorns. She rolled her shoulders back forcefully and shook them. On the worktable was an object wrapped in a hand towel. "I have something." She carefully grabbed it from the table and freed it from its covering. When the Doe saw what the object was, she snorted and shuffled back toward the wall. She tried to lift her body to flee, scratching at the slick floorboards with her slender hooves.

"Easy, girl, easy!" The Woman set the object on the table and went down to the Doe; she restrained her by pressing her hands into her flank. "*Shh!* It's not real."

The Doe slunk back to the floor, subdued under the Woman's hot hands. She lay still except for the rising and falling of her ribcage. Her mouth had gone dry again.

"Didn't mean to frighten you." The Woman returned to the table and rewrapped the object. "I pulled it out so's to finish my confession." The object wriggled under its covering—a trick of the stiff cloth settling.

"I had been cleaning my chest of drawers. About two weeks ago. Got to my pantry drawer. I'd forgotten. Well, my husband was standing in the hallway when he saw the note drop. Of all the moments for him to actually notice anything, it was that exact moment. And he picked it up and looked it over. And he turned red."

The moving sunspot had found her, and she backed away from it as though it were about to cast some damning verdict onto her. "I told him that I had not had an abortion, but he wouldn't believe me—began to shake me and put his hands on my throat and squeezed. But he stopped. Told me he couldn't kill me. He then saw the signature on the note. He left and didn't come until early morning. I called my friend to warn him. Over and over. Two days later, I found out he had died."

She crossed her arms over her belly and let her head hang a little, then bent down to wipe away the finger-drawn outline of the looming hill with her hand. "My husband didn't bring it up again until the other night. Told me over dinner that the Old Man had died of a stroke. What a shit-eating grin! And for a moment, I felt relief from my guilt. But his smile. I had this horrible, ominous feeling. Then I heard they had him cremated and dumped into a hole. Just like the others."

She returned to the table once more, lifted the object, and cushioned it upon the altar of her hands. It had become both a relic of love and culpability. "I discovered this hidden in the pocket of his rifle case. If he hadn't killed him, why did he have it? I know it belonged to my friend because he had told me about it. It was important."

She set the object down upon the pockmarked tabletop. With a hand on her hip and the other on her chin, the Woman was once again staring toward the dark pines. She needed a clear view to some form of solace, but the rising hill and its lacing footpath always obstructed her sightline. Moments passed, and she had lost track of the time. The Man with the Crooked Finger was due home. She needed to return the object to the rifle case and start supper.

"Gotta go, Saint. I'll come back tonight. Don't leave the shed. And don't you dare make a sound."

She flew out the door again, bolting the Doe inside. The afternoon sun was strobing red. Rain clouds had passed long ago, but something about the light still had the subtle shading of rough weather.

The Doe shut her eyes to relocate that comfort she had felt earlier—the sleep-inducing intoxication of the Woman's tea. But the only thing she saw when she closed her eyes was the image of the Woman unveiling the object under an off-white hand towel. The object of a snake whittled from such strong wood. The serpent staff the Old Man had used to cut a slash in his eye—his serpent eye—while she was deep in a dream.

XVIII

The Doe never found her way back to sleep in the late afternoon and especially so when the Man's truck pulled in, engine dying and door slamming. Heels pulverized the gravel that lined the drive. Boots trudged up the stairs of the wood deck until they rounded the corner. At the back entrance, which faced the garden, the screen door squealed and then shut stridently.

The smells of supper started to waft into the shed—things like slow-simmered green beans in broth with drizzles of maple syrup and splashes of vinegar. Onions were sliced for a cold cucumber salad, and a crowded jar of pickled Brussels sprouts was popped open after long months on the pantry shelf. A scent unfamiliar to the Doe was that of pan-fried rabbit with animal fat caramelizing in currant jelly and wine.

There was beer too. When supper had finished, the Man returned to the deck while the Woman tidied up. The Doe heard his crooked finger rubbing alongside a wet, cold bottle and stripping its label off by inserting his thumb underneath a peeling corner. She heard the frightening timbre of his voice without his uttering a word as it creeped into each coughing fit induced by the joint he sucked with dry lips. She heard him pacing like a caged animal just outside the bordering fence so near to her hiding spot. It forced her to cower in the back of the garden shed with only a thin wood wall standing between her and death.

Her head she laid flat, keeping her eyes toward the door. She could only watch helplessly—those large, expressive eyes that hadn't changed much since she was a fawn. Perhaps she could at last latch onto the doe clan or somehow locate her father. If only she could cry out to him, sprout wings like a bird and fly to him. She could almost see him as real as anything else in the room walking through the door with antlers scratching the frame. Then time would stop so that she might scramble her broken body through the woods and lean against his until they at last reached the North Territory.

A suppressing blackness had enveloped the Cape Cod and garden. It was a suffocating humidity like a long, drawn-out asphyxiation—the windows of the shed plastered over with thin, weeping sheets of condensation.

The almost inaudible crackling of another smoking joint sounded as did the clinking of ice against a tumbler of bourbon. The Man could barely find the requisite amount of oxygen to keep himself sustained between puffs of weed and swallows of liquor. He was hot and air hungry, but he mustered enough breath pressure to mutter his beloved's name several times.

Washing up and the bright din of sorting flatware drifted from the kitchen window, as did the clinking of browned bone dropping into the waste bin and the banging of dishes being stacked in the sink. The Woman rinsed and dried, breathlessly eyeing the shed. The line of her simple bra was doused with sweat.

The Doe inhibited her own panting until her head began to feel punchy. Save for the nighttime accident, she'd been so dehydrated that she hadn't once thought about relieving herself. But now her bladder was stretched full. She tried desperately to restrain the urge at least until the Man had gone back into the house. Then she might be able to drag herself to another corner of the room and eliminate away from where she slept. But after the minutes passed to an hour, she found herself unable to hold any longer. She eased up and relieved herself and then lay in a puddle of lukewarm urine.

At last the Man's feet scuffled up the decking and the screen door slammed shut. The house grew quiet for a long while until again the screen door opened and closed with much more finesse. Footsteps quick and purposeful headed for the garden shed. The Doe's head shot up from the flooring, and her triangulating ears lifted high and spread wide.

The Woman was preceded into the room by her ash-blond locks. The small overhead fixture flipping on revealed streaks of light all over the surface of her hair like tiger's eye. Beneath her sweeping bangs she smiled, but it had an edge. She brought with her the ritual bowls. She doubled back for the earthenware crock that she had set outside on the ground before placing the first bowl on the worktable. All the while, the door behind was left cracked as a precautionary measure. She made her way across the boards with the potent tea as whips of steam circled out.

"Can't tell you how relieved I was you kept so still. I was ready for a problem. Kept an eye on my steak knife all through dinner. Not sure how you managed …" Her eyes tripped her words up when she noticed the dark puddle beneath the Doe.

"Oh, no. That's my fault for not putting down any bedding. Saint, I'm sorry." She grabbed an old, cut-up men's undershirt she used for work rags and began to wipe up the urine. She cleaned the mess with a civility that reminded the Doe of the Old Man. This act of service that somehow surprised the Doe; its simple but grand empathetic gesture drew her closer to the Woman.

A terracotta pot from the garden was filled with water. The Woman crept back in with the wrung-out rag. Fishing for something in a tote on her worktable, she withdrew a parchment-wrapped square.

She lowered herself onto her knees and freed it from the bland paper. Working the bar into the rag released its perfume. She used it to give the Doe a sponge bath, caressing her soiled underside.

"The finest soap I make right here. I use lye and a mixture of nice oils and essences of plants from my garden. This one is lavender. Got bushes of it like puffs of spun sugar when it blooms." She was very careful with her hands; she massaged the Doe's coat with a certain reverence. "I can smell the rosewater too. It's there. Just subtle—It hides." Her hands stopped, and her face remained fixed. "Like God."

She patted the Doe as dry as she could with the other half of the torn shirt. Then she went to the worktable, opened a large box, and retrieved a small jar of jadeite. She dipped three fingers into the jar and swirled them purposefully. "This is my prized perfume balm. It was harvested during a miracle. It's for special things." A yellowing in her battered cheek gave esprit to her smile. "You're the most special thing that's ever come here."

The Woman raised her balm-slicked fingers outward like a salute. She then kneaded it into the Doe's breast before anointing her white-spotted head. The Doe could see that she had goose bumps on her arms. "Grandma Ava came back to me, Saint. And when she did, the herbs and flowers in the garden became pungent. When everything spilled out of me, so too did all things in my garden."

The nightly brew with chamomile infused in it was offered to the Doe. Cannabis levels had been lowered to begin readying the Doe for life outside the shed. After the Doe had lapped it up, the Woman began to tend to the wrapping. The empty bowl she swapped for the earthenware crock and plunged the loosened tea towel into the hot vinegar and wormwood for the leg treatment. "I wanted to finish my story. I can be here with you for a while tonight. Husband's high and drunk on bourbon. Won't be waking up anytime soon."

While the towel steeped in the crock, she caressed the Doe's sides. It was out of keeping with natural laws, yet both indulged themselves. The Woman moved her hand up the Doe's neck through fur like plush carpet and ended at the white patch of her crown.

"This splash on your head. It looks like cooked egg white without a yolk. Seems important; you must've been touched by God's hand."

She fished the tea towel out of the bowl and draped it over the rim. The heat of the liquid didn't seem to affect her fingertips anymore. She moved the Doe's injured leg, gently bending it slightly at the joint. There was pain, normal aching that nighttime brings to any malaise, but the Doe felt it lining up again.

"I read once that people believed birthmarks were things you carried from other lives. Say you have a spot on your side … Maybe you were stabbed there in a past life. Was it ancient people who believed that? Don't remember. But you do look like an animal ancient people would have worshipped."

The hot towel once again wound up the Doe's leg and was retied. Breathing became less effortful as the humidity lifted. The Doe's head nodded—The tea was working expeditiously.

"You know, ancient cultures sacrificed people. I read about all those Chimú children in Peru who'd been sacrificed during a time of catastrophic weather. They really believed that those children would become sort of elevated in the next life, that they were making the world better for those left behind. Sounds barbaric. Sounds a bit like Christ."

She moved the crock and stretched out alongside the Doe. Their parallel bodies formed an equals symbol on the floor. She walked her fingers along the boards. "I'm sort of drawn to ideas of the afterlife. Stuff like this would be what my friend and I would talk about—what Grandma and I would talk about."

She rolled to her back with her yellow hair flowing all around her as if she stood before a sun. "They were both special like you—important beings, miraculous beings." Her hair she gathered in a bun to tuck beneath her as a pillow. "When I found my friend's snake carving, I knew he was calling to me. He said it was a model of a shaman's carving. And when that shaman died, he became a snake." She wiggled on the floor. "But don't you dare tell me he's a snake now up in those hills. I hate a damn snake!"

The Doe's eyes slipped closed; the fading view of the ceiling was a dark strip. Her muscles melted to the floor pliant and allayed of any stress or strain. She no longer listened to the Woman, who spoke as if her own words were lulling her to sleep—They flowed simply, easily.

"Do you believe in divine intervention, Saint?" she asked. Their breathing had become deep; the breathing of sleeping bodies. "You do. You're a saint, after all."

After she'd been unable to drink the tansy tea or risk the trip for an abortion, the Woman felt she had reached an impasse. Thus, she called upon a higher power. She had been raised Catholic by her grandmother, but it wasn't a strict observance of the faith; the spiritual world perceived by the Woman was through a coalescence of beliefs much like the Old Man. As had the Old Man, the Woman believed in the communion of saints but outside the concept of one distinct, mystical, Christian body. All energies and souls through all time were intertwined. They helped or hindered one another. Sometimes, they echoed one another; other times, they were discordant. There were planes of existence, and the Catholic experience was just one layer of countless dimensions.

In her bedroom, the Woman kept her grandmother's prayer book. It was a small but heavy, red-bound collection of meditations and devotions for holy days and feast days. On the cover was Botticelli's *Madonna of the Book*. In the painting, Mary held Jesus as she read to him from an illuminated manuscript. He listened somberly, donning the crown of thorns as a bracelet. They seemed to be in an act of collaboration. Behind them, ripe fruit had been piled in a bowl while dim cypresses appeared in a window corner.

The Woman had searched for prayers. She spoke to God, begged for his intercession. But deep inside, she felt afraid of God. If it was true what they all said, that God was a man, perhaps he wouldn't understand. Maybe he too would side with her husband and force her to bring this baby into a world fraught with pain. She couldn't risk her child's well-being. This wasn't the binding of Isaac.

The broken-backed book then flipped to a page. There in black and red ink was a prayer, a novena to Our Lady of Perpetual Help. In this guise, it was comforting to the Woman to see the Holy Mother larger than the deity and holding him and protecting him when he was so vulnerable. And then she studied the icon of little Jesus looking to an angel. Rather, there were two angels flanking him. In the hand of the angel on the right was a cross, and baby Jesus regarded it with resignation. The other angel, whom Jesus seemed to shun, was bearing the sponge soaked in vinegar and wormwood. It was a palliative offering Jesus would refuse from his agony on the cross.

She braced herself with the edge of the worktable as she lowered herself to the floor. "Holy Mother, only you know how dangerous it is to bring a child into a world where he will face certain death at the hands of those who should receive him with love. Please know I love my baby more than anything and want so badly to hold him. But this world isn't safe for him. I pray you take him into your arms. Your baby was to be born the Messiah, but my baby is an ordinary person like every other baby born into this wretched place. I cannot do this alone. Our Lady of Perpetual Help, please come to my aid, mother to mother."

And so the Woman dedicated each morning to her novena, praying for a miscarriage. On the second night, she lay awake feeling nothing different. Her husband had come home very late smelling of smoke, and he showered in the early morning hours. She lay in bed and wept, and when he came in, she held her tears, asking him where he had been.

"With Red. What of it?"

On day four, Saturday, she received a call from the Old Man. He told her that his garden was full of zucchini and asked if she'd like some. Hers had been devastated by borers, and she missed the taste of summer squash. He told her he'd stop by on Friday with a delivery, and she promised him more cannabis in return.

On Sunday, while her husband was down at the hotel bar, she went out to pull weeds. It was October and still very warm. The growing season had no end in sight. Warming temperatures had delayed the killing frost. There were hordes of unwanted plants suffocating all four corners of the garden. Mats upon mats of new growth had spread all around. She got down on her knees and ripped away at them.

Then a pleasant breeze passed through, and she stretched her arms wide. The air blew all about her cooling her. Through a row of coneflowers, the wind whistled until it sustained a pitch. But then the pitch began to fall and then rise until it was tuneful. It was a sweet singing, and she heard movement as something rustled branches within the globes of trees.

The Woman stood and searched all about the timber. She heard feet scurrying across limbs, the needles shaking with each step. Up in the boughs of pine, a figure jumped from tree to tree. She saw its dappled breast fluffed and ballooning under its lethal, arching beak. It walked straight across the clearing, keeping its eyes ahead. Its song tapered to a series of quick and short tones. The birds of the trees began crying and took to the sky. A goldfinch eating seeds perched atop a cosmo and barely bending its stem flittered toward safety.

The vision almost didn't register though it was in sharp focus. Even its feet were clearly visible—the high curved talons shooting from out yellow toes scaled over like reptilian skin. It merely turned to look at her with honeyed eyes as it chirped then shuffled back into the cover of pine to saunter into other treetops.

The Woman ran up to the trees, and up along the footpath. The breeze had stopped, and the day grew hot again. Songbirds soon returned to probe the depths of quiet limbs; the falcon was gone. Yet for the rest of the day, she kept her eyes to the pines.

"Grandma, have you come back for me?"

On the ninth day, after her husband had gone to work, she arose and completed her devotion to Our Lady of Perpetual Help. She was anticipating a visit from the Old Man, whose arms would carry a bounty of squash. She put herself together and went out to continue weeding. One such weed with a stem as thick as a broom handle gave her tremendous trouble. Her grandmother had called it burnweed, and the garden was full of it. She twisted and pulled to rip it from the soil, but its roots clung to something, perhaps a bit of hidden bluestone, and had latched on with all its might.

A sweet, spicy perfume began to waft from another corner of the garden. The Woman recognized the odor but could hardly believe it that late in the season. She followed it until it was so strong that it made her eyes and nose run. A faint outline could be traced from behind a smattering of milkweed. It was stark white with blushes of pink and as tall as her. It was an oriental lily in full bloom with petals bending backward on a stalk of seven buds.

She had no recollection of planting lilies there, and she had never seen a lily bloom in October. It felt strangely like an offering, as if the Holy Mother had heard her prayers and said, *Yes, child.* The Woman knelt before it and clasped her hands until at last she heard the beating of wings. A ray of sun darted through a rose-tinted cloud and pierced her breast, her womb. Then it was revealed to her in the light. An angel with topaz eyes hovered above her. It sang with a sweet, penetrating color bouncing notes on high-toned scales. It was the fleck-breasted falcon. The Woman raised her arms in exaltation, and the falcon flapped its wings. It showered the lily and the Woman in feathers. And when the final feather swiveled to the black soil, there came a powerful knock upon the whole garden.

*An earthquake!* she thought fearfully, wondering if God was angry that she had entrusted her prayers only to his mother. But then came a flurry of orange like gold and bronze and cardamom and saffron. Each flower had released its pollen—its essence—and the garden became disordered and deranged with perfume and microspores. The Woman's garden had been gilded by the hand of God.

The falcon arose and flew south. The Woman was intoxicated with all the scents of flowers and herbs. She became ecstatic, almost possessed, and ran into the shed and gathered shears and a pot. She began to hoard everything she could to trap the moment, to suspend it. Her hands were stained yellow. She worked frantically until a sudden detonating blast came from out of nowhere.

A gunshot had cracked like a whip over the divided hills and bounced off the garden shed. It brought a slight deafness to the Woman's ears as if it had been very near. A furious pain shot deep into her belly. The pot was dropped as she doubled over, moaning. She grabbed her abdomen and slid her hands down between her legs. She raised them to her face and discovered they were covered in blood. "I've been shot!"

Into the kitchen she struggled, smearing the threshold with blood and wetting the screen door handle. A car had pulled in. She heard it from the bathroom, where she had slipped off her slacks and panties. Blood was everywhere. She searched for the bullet wound until a man's voice came booming from outside the bathroom door. It was the Old Man, and with her consent, he shoved through the door and lowered himself to where she squatted on the unbalanced toilet. She explained what had happened as calmly and as deliberately as she could, and as she trusted him, she allowed him to look her over. It took only seconds. With his hands covered in her blood, he used his burnished voice to proclaim the glorious mystery: "You haven't been shot. You're miscarrying."

Later, the Woman wept with joy as she washed herself. The Old Man waited patiently in the kitchen. He picked up the zucchinis, which had fallen and rolled all over the floor. She came out with her bloodied clothes and put them in the wash. He caressed her cheek, wrapped her in his arms. He insisted she see a doctor, yet she refused. She didn't want her husband to know anything of it. She'd be diligent with pads and pretend like it was her period. Her husband didn't touch her—at least not between the legs—so he'd never know the difference.

The Old Man counseled her a while then hugged her goodbye. But he had forgotten something and went back out to his car. That's when he offered her a gift, and it had sealed the miracle for her. The moment was all so evocative like a reimagined Botticelli. Upon the checkered linoleum of the kitchenette, the Old Man bestowed his painting of oriental lilies in bloom to the Woman. Black pines peeked behind her. A fruit bowl sat empty.

After the Old Man had left and the Woman had scrubbed all traces of blood from the house, a truck came hurling into the drive. It was her husband. He was groaning as he struggled into the kitchen cupping his left eye with both hands. Surfaces she had just scrubbed were once again sullied with blood. He told her he had pulled over to take a leak on a work errand and had startled a falcon. It had clawed him blind.

The gunshot the Woman had heard was the same shot the Man with the Crooked Finger took with Buck on the Old Man's land. Falcon wings had stitched a seam in the sky that joined the garden to the acreage. For as his child slipped away from the Woman, the womb of the Elder Doe entertained new life. God worked in mysterious ways.

The Woman drove him to the medical center. She heard him screaming in pain as they doctored his wound. His vision was astonishingly untouched. All the while she sat silently in the waiting room secretly miscarrying their baby. Strong cramping was wringing the remnants out of her womb. She worked through them with breathing, keeping her face as unresponsive as she could. Inside, however, she rejoiced: *Salve Regina!*

"Grandma interceded for me to the Blessed Mother. Even in death, I think she felt she owed it to me because it was something she couldn't do for my mom."

The Woman's words to the Doe were just a continuous stream of gibberish that dripped down the walls of the shed like drops of condensation. Her talking soon died off. The room was quiet, warm; the passing moments were blissfully uneventful. Then a sigh melded into a yawn. "Think I'll rest my eyes."

But it couldn't last long. It would be too dangerous for her to fall asleep in the shed and risk her husband coming to find her. The Woman cracked her eyes to keep from drifting. They wandered to

Ava's funeral card, which was thumbtacked to the rough wall. It featured the *Ecce Homo*, the image of the scourged Christ crowned with thorns. He watched over them as they sprawled on old rugged floorboards both suffering like he.

"Saint, I've told you everything I needed to say. There's nothing left. I feel ready now."

The Woman then lay silently. After a while, it seemed as if she had nodded off. Side by side, the two shared an intimate union. The pulsing of blood through their bodies became synchronized. Their veins separated only by clothing and hair and thin layers of flesh touched. They weren't altogether different, the two of them—such that when they died someday, their hearts and ribs and femurs would be difficult to distinguish one from the other. They were but two does bedded in another bower.

The witching hour. A howl high and piercing came from the top of the hill. Such an unearthly trumpet—It heralded a call to waking as if to say, *Sleep no more!* The Doe stirred. The room was empty. The Woman had long left for bed. The Doe listened and panted. Another shriek. The she-coyote was near the shanty, maybe deeper into the little apple orchard. But as the howling continued, it shifted its character, and the Doe looked up to the footpath through the window's filmy layers in awe of its presence.

The Man with the Crooked Finger lay awake and alone. The Woman, he concluded, must have gone to sleep in the spare room. He sat up in bed sweating the bourbon out of his pores. A terrible ringing plaguing his ears climbed in pitch until he wanted to claw at the walls. Then it abated in frequency and began to wobble and fluctuate with the sound of a flickering diving board. But before he could define it, the strange sound stopped cold, cut short with a snap like a cracking knuckle.

He and the Doe were simultaneously hearing the mysterious, phantom sound. They had come to a similar conclusion at the same moment but with different intuitions attached. It was the first time

the Man had heard it, and though he was uneasy, he somehow believed it augured well for him as if triumphant destiny was inching
up on him. Whatever the sound was, they knew it was coming for
them all. At last, its will would be done.

"It's now or never," said the Woman.

The Doe had been awake some time before the Woman's arrival. She was drowsy and hungry, and she was pleased to see the Woman had come earlier than usual. But there was an agitation about the Woman. She placed a satchel aside the doorframe before bringing a bowl down to the floor. The herbal brew sloshed onto her shaky hands. It looked different that day. Bits of cold leftovers had been thrown into the brew. The Doe hadn't had anything of substance in days, and the Woman felt it was time to reintroduce solids. Nubs of carrot and chopped green beans swirled about as did a hash of cold fried rabbit and days-old cubed potatoes. The Doe lapped up the broth, grinding pappy solids into mush, the bowl reeling about her snout.

"Easy, Saint!" the Woman said while restraining the bowl with two hands.

It didn't take long for the Doe to devour the bowlful. She swished her tongue around the lining of her newly healed mouth. An unusual aftertaste lingered, that of rabbit gristle with knobs of gamey cartilage. The Woman meanwhile began untying and removing the dried tea towel from the Doe's leg. She did it with an urgency that caused the Doe pain.

"It's strange," the Woman said as she drowned the tea towel in the hot wormwood treatment, "but I'm finally ready. All I needed was your listening ear, I guess." But the Doe hadn't been listening to her troubles at least not in the manner the Woman had perceived. It had all been a bit of mindfulness in the mirror of the Doe's face.

"Not sure you're ready to walk, but when I'm gone, you've gotta go, Saint."

The tea towel reapplication was rushed. The Woman hurriedly wound it back up the Doe's leg. The butcher's knot was tighter than usual. "I gave you less cannabis. Should give you the drive to leave. Hope to hell you're far from here by afternoon." She wrung her hands like the tea towel. "Oh gosh, Saint, I'm scared. I feel like I'm becoming—becoming what? Not sure."

The Woman then stacked the bowls, cradled them in her arms, and left. Sounds of clinking earthenware and running water slipped through an open window—Soon after, the scrunch of footwork on gravel. The Woman never returned to secure the shed. Pale light cut through the cracked door as if trying to tell the Doe something, but the words were too faint.

It was a warm day, even hotter in the shed. The tight towel on the Doe's leg restricted blood flow, blunting and burning the limb. She moved it about seeking angles that would once again kickstart circulation. After a while, she chewed through the top knot of twine until blood traveled back through her veins and returned normal sensation.

The heat was stifling. No breeze entered. Her bladder was full again, making it impossible to find a comfortable position. On top of that, her stomach had begun churning and grumbling. After days without solids, the first bit of food found itself unwelcome in her gut. The stool would be loose, and she'd rather risk danger than defecate where she slept.

An hour or so went by, and the pain became excruciating. Panting was no longer effective in the little shed containing her like an oven. It was the September equinox, and though it heralded the autumn, the day blistered like high summer and scorched the bluestone outcroppings that in turn burned the feet of roving creatures.

The Doe feared putting weight on her injured leg as the pain of hyperextension was still fresh in her mind, but she had entered a critical state and desperately needed to relieve herself. She couldn't be too gentle with her limbs as there was a certain amount of force needed to gain traction on smooth flooring. There was no other way but to lean into the pain, and so she bit down as hard as she could and resolutely hoisted herself off the floor. Once she balanced her weight evenly on all four trembling legs, she was surprised to find the pain rather manageable. The leg was more functional than she had previously imagined, and she hobbled out of the shed but with relative ease.

Outside, the sun whitewashed everything and blinded her eyes, which had grown accustomed to the ill-lit shed. She staggered on the uneven ground until her vision normalized. The air slipped around her, and despite the heat, it allowed her whole body to at last breathe.

The sun scorch on the woods made everything more aromatic. The Doe smelled the garden at its peak fragrance. Near the black pines she found a giant cluster of ditch lilies long past flowering. The assemblage of blades sharp tipped like knife points were yellowed and spent. She crouched behind the mass and at last relieved herself.

Once everything had been expelled from her body, she shook her undersides and stepped out from behind the mound. The hot sun amplified the stench of her droppings as it did other odors. Something steered her senses toward the unusual black area outside the tree line. She saw it still strewn with crumbled fragments and charred wood. Sunbeams shot downward like lasers singeing the ground and releasing essences in the soil. These odors climbed high and were spirited away, odors that smelled much like the way the rabbit gristle had tasted.

She lowered her head and approached. Her insides cramped not from sickness but from instinct taking hold and twisting. The place held a sense of completion, as if she had at last reached a destination. It would be wise to turn away, she thought, to go back to the shed and lie down. To wait for the Woman and pretend this spot had never existed.

Curiosity was a strange thing, and her impulse to know had surpassed her urge to flee. Her hoof at last crossed into the dark, ashy round. It was the black leavings of a large bonfire. Fragments were scattered; some were white as ash, others mere tufts of burned fiber. Deep trenches were carved into the loam where shovels had scooped away the evidence to be discarded into the river. The Doe's legs quaked. Her nose carried the weight of truth, and it threatened to bring her down.

This black circle was the fire she'd seen glowing over the ridge the night her mother had died. It had become the bitter odor of burning that had led her past quiet, sick cornfields—the burning the sparrow had decried. But the other scents were there too bound to the dark scorch line. She sensed the doe clan very near.

She couldn't breathe, think—could only stagger on the soil. Her coat became sooty with ash kicked up by reckless hooves. She sucked it into her nostrils, opening her mouth to unintentionally swallow it and breathe it in. It choked her, and she coughed, thrashed, and bucked her limbs to shake the remaining bits of charred bone and hide from their resting places.

Just beyond her snout with bits of incineration adhered to her wet nostrils, something like white-capped mushrooms began to push upward. It was unclear at first, and she fluttered her dry, sun-blind eyes. But then with the force of a blink, it came into focus. It did not register for some time. And when it did, she began to groan and snort until she had freed her nostrils of charred animal bits. This was no mound of mushrooms before her. It was an unburned jaw lined with fat molars and bits of tough apple skin still wedged between gaps.

At last, the white-faced Doe had rejoined the herd of the Old Man's acreage. She sprawled upon them, clothing herself with their ashes and scratching her skin on their bone fragments. In the end, she had found herself still very much an outsider, but this time, it was through death's doing.

The men had paraded their bodies down Main Street before heading to the Cape Cod. It was there they piled the fresh kills high, building a pyre on which to burn them. They used the wood of the felled apple tree in their bonfire and in doing so sent the sacred tree and its conjoined doe clan into oblivion together. There was to be no reconciliation for the day they had betrayed the Doe.

And though the Doe had seen them only days earlier bounding over the hill amidst the sound of gunshots, they had neither seen nor sensed her. There would be no more sunrises for the doe clan—no more warmth, rest, or the taste of sweet fruit upon their tongues. They were now lost in limbo, fated to roam the Bluestone Woodland looped in an infinite nightfall, forever reliving the final, horrifying moments of their deaths.

And in her grieving, she saw the dark ring of the bonfire part as black waters revealing a vision northwest of the shed. It stood far beyond the ditch lilies still stinking of excrement. It was twisting and asymmetrical, branches lifting from a green field. It was the apple tree of the acreage.

She cried to it and asked it for help, yet it was silent. Grey and dusty as she was, her white spots powdered with ash, perhaps the apple tree no longer recognized her. Saliva had pooled in her mouth and was dripping in strings and dredged in ash where it dragged on the ground. The closer she crept to the tree, the heavier her body became. Her hooves plowed into the black earth as she pulled herself toward it.

It was white, bare-branched, and not large enough to be a tree. The green spread underneath it was far too flat and featureless to be the acreage's field of grass. What had appeared to her as roots at the base of a trunk was in fact the top of a skull shaved away with hide still carpeting a familiar brow. Antlers had become a smaller duplicate of apple branches, just as they had on the Old Man's canvas. And though deer bodies could not sweat, hers did as beads of blood beneath her coat. At last she collapsed on the earth under the weight of such force as if to never rise again.

The Woman had told the Doe of that night, how she had seen a poor creature whom they tossed into the bonfire while still clinging to life—how its terrified squeal sounded like an old boar at slaughter. The crown she had said still weeping warm blood. It had been the Buck. His had been the first shot the night the men had driven the Doe and her mother off the acreage. After they had sawed the antlers from his skull, the Buck had inexplicably held onto life. And before the men threw his living body into the fire, they left his rack atop a green tarp to dry in the sun.

But death could not destroy love, and while his daughter was drowning in the river, his spirit ferried her to safety. Yet the Doe couldn't remember such miracles in her desolation. She could hear only the old devil say, *Poor creature! So pitiful to be but an animal. The body is weak and born to rot. Sleep, my beloved. I know you want it. You are overcome.*

As she believed there was nothing left to live for, the Doe submitted to the voice's command and closed her eyes. And for hours as the sun shifted places in the sky, the shadow of her beloved father's crown passed over her to gently shade her where she lay.

The Doe had spent hours lying in the sun. A flock of slack-bellied vultures had finally taken notice. She was soaked in her own droplets of blood and was covered in the remnants of other deer. Streaks of excrement were matted to her fur. The sun lifted such perfume on high, drawing the birds. Hungry, they had mistaken her as carrion.

One descended, and then another. The ground was hot, and they urinated on their legs to cool themselves. As the Doe was so outside herself with sorrow, she did not hear their impressive feet with blunted talons approaching. They pranced gayly toward her as though doing a *gavotte*.

The first one, the largest of the group, readied itself to nip her. It was the vulture that had eaten her mother's eye. As such, it still had that watchful, loving energy concealed inside. With a strong plunge of its beak, it dug into her hind. Immediately, her head jolted upward, the pain renewing her with a rush of vitality. The other vulture lunged at her, the one that had eaten the Elder Doe's tongue as if to say, *Rise! There's still work to be done!*

As the flock of vultures began to swarm and snap at her, the Doe stood, kicking and bucking with such verve as to ram her way through them. She plowed straight into the garden shed for coverage and backed herself into the innermost corner, where she had spent the previous night convalescing.

A heavily dented truck speeding into the drive sent the vultures asunder. Yet it wasn't the Man with the Crooked Finger's truck. After nearly making the trip to his farm job, the Man's rig had gasped and chugged and broke down. As he investigated under the smoking hood for the source of the malfunction, he burned his hand on the hot engine; the smell of his scorched skin and hair reminiscent of deer bodies atop the pyre. It pleased him and momentarily anesthetized him—it was like sniffing gasoline fumes.

The rest of the trip he made by foot; he had called the auto shop from the farmhouse. His boss, seeing the state of his hand, saw it fit to give him the rest of the day off work. Besides, the Man never did much work. He mostly rode around on an old mule smacking cottontails with a club to bring home for supper.

After getting the truck towed to town, the Man asked the auto shop owner to drop him at home. And at present, the truck door slammed loudly as he made his way toward the house, his boots trekking furiously up the drive with its gravel-strewn mud now cracked in the heat. The Man clenched his burned left fist wrapped in an oil-stained work cloth. The mechanic hollered from the running vehicle and drove off like an old tugboat. The screen door smacked, and everything grew quiet again.

Next there came a bit of commotion inside the house—a racket of rummaging, banging, and then yelling. A phone call was made to Red. The Man shouted into the receiver, "She's trying to take us down!" which the Doe heard from inside the shed. Moments later, he returned to the deck. He flipped on an old radio. Wordless music played as he sat aside the screen door ice clinking in a glass of bourbon. The butt of his rifle tapped deck boards, keeping time with some sort of foxtrot. It went on that way second after second. The heat of afternoon didn't abate. It passed with slow, miserable hours. The Doe kept her panting as soundless as she could, feeling remorseful for having corralled herself in the shed.

The Man drank with his left hand, the ice in the tumbler soothing his burn. He grumbled and sighed between gulps. At times, he rested the gun between his knees so that he could gently rap his fist against the decaying armrest of the patio chair. The radio shorted out. It played and then went silent and oscillated with short bursts of static. A radio program managed to break through.

"Daybreak comes, brothers and sisters. I see irises in bloom. Are you ready for the Rapture? Pestilence, fires, and floods—Yes, the beast spewed out a flood, but the earth opened its mouth, swallowing it up, hurling the beast down. Woo-*ee!* Get thee behind me, Satan! Good night all, and God bl—"

Again, it seemed to tune in and out, dissipating into white noise. It behaved that way for only a few minutes until the Man could no longer stand it. It stopped making sound with one fell swoop of his fist.

There was a long space of silence. The light reddened with sunset. It was profoundly humid, and the Man was sweating about his sunburned chest and underarms. He was thirsty too, and his drink didn't slake the burning. He returned to the kitchen for more bourbon, plopping himself at the dinette table a moment and leaning against the rifle.

The Doe crept to a spot in the shed that offered a clear view of the kitchen door. Well shadowed at the back wall, she watched the Man through the distorting screen. At last, she thought, this was her chance to make a run for it. But delicate footwork suddenly sounded on the porch boards. It was even keeled without a trace of hesitation. The Doe swiveled her ears as she scanned the decking.

It was the Woman. Butcher paper was neatly folded and tucked in her shirt pocket while a red crayon rubbed between thigh skin and the beige fabric of her dungaree pocket. She rounded the corner of the house and headed for the shed. Her packed satchel was still tucked inside the entryway.

"Where you been?"

The Woman screamed. "You startled me!" She forced out a little laugh and grabbed her chest then referenced the side of the house with a shaking hand. "Where's you truck?"

"I know you saw it." The Man's voice grumbled through the door. It was low and rough and could barely phonate upon dry vocal folds. His outline through the dark screen was but a black shadow. "Going behind my back? What'd ya do? Find outside help from the law?"

"Huh?" She glanced down and saw the white cloth lashed about his hand, which shone through the screen. "What did you do to your hand?"

"Never you mind."

She watched his teeth slide beneath chapped lips—his lips like processed meat—as he finally pushed through the screen door to the deck. He beamed an ugly grin as he leaned the rifle aside the clapboard. "You put it back wrong."

"Put what back?" The Woman glanced into the shed. The wide-open door revealed the edge of her packed satchel, and her skittering eyes betrayed her discretion.

"What's in there?" he asked.

"Nothing." She feigned a smile. "Thought I heard a noise."

"*Hmm.*" A dip of chaw that had been marinating in his mouth was dislodged with his tongue and then spat out. "You told the police, didn't you?" As he said it, he pulled something from his pocket that caused the Woman to flinch. Again he grinned, flecks of tobacco clinging to his gums and teeth, a grin that gave his face many folds like the back of a vulture's head. He pulled out the serpent staff, held it up, and then chucked it to the foot of her garden. "You were rummaging, and I caught you."

While the Doe listened, a feeling began to bubble up in her—a compulsion. The fear was charging her muscles such that at any moment she would barrel out of the shed. Could the Man get to his gun fast enough? The anxiety had to go somewhere, had to be burned clean away, had to send her dashing toward peril.

The Man continued as he approached. "Wanna know how I know you snooped?" The Woman gave him a stolid shrug. "There's a pocket on each side of the gun case. You put in the wrong pocket." He quickly grabbed her by the back of the head, pulling knots of hair until she whimpered. "This is how you repay me after I spared your life for killing my baby?" He moved his hands around her throat and shook her. "Who'd you rat me out to? Some cop from the city?"

There was a wet sound as the Man strangled the Woman, of his hands squeezing into the delicate tissues of her throat and mouth, pushing her tongue up and forward in a gagging posture, her voice making little grunts like a suckling infant. The Doe immediately recognized the sound as a danger. To stay frozen in a state of panic would have been judicious in the moment, but she could no longer restrain her mind or her limbs to keep herself concealed. Without a further thought in her head, she flashed out of the shed, smoothing floorboards with her whetstone hooves, and rammed herself between the Man and the Woman as she fled past them, breaking their entanglement.

"You!" was all the Man could muster as he struggled to regain his balance. He used the Woman's back as a bracing post while she was doubled over, coughing and gasping. In a matter of seconds, he was rushing toward the side of the house to grab his propped-up rifle.

The sheer muscle power the Doe used to sprint had caused her injured leg to seize up. Spasm upon spasm twisted her body into unnatural angles until at last she collapsed. She sprawled along the ground groaning in pain, her leg thrashing about the innumerable bluestone pebbles hidden in dirt and sod.

As the Man went to reach for the rifle, he too found himself tipping over as he was suddenly forced backward. He clutched his throat and hacked as something pressed into his Adam's apple. The Woman had come up quickly from behind and pulled him back by the collar of his shirt. She then used her hands to compress his larynx. As he turned to restrain her, she drove the heel of her palm into the bridge of his nose. "I'm tired of you hurtin' me!" she cried.

A look of astonishment briefly graced his face until his eyes began to water. He then clasped her throat in return and squeezed as hard as he could to at last crush her windpipe. Somehow hooking her hand inside his mouth like a fishing lure, the Woman pulled out his cheek to rip his face. When he tried to bite her, she jabbed her thumbs into his eye sockets.

With his eyes scrunched tightly shut, the Man palmed the Woman's face then drove his knee into her groin, toppling her. And while she was down with her hands between her legs, he staggered to the house and retrieved the gun from the clapboard siding. At the eastern edge of the garden, the Doe was yet incapacitated and mewling in pain. She watched as the Man lifted the gun, the sights centered on her white patch.

But the Woman would not submit, and again she flung herself onto the Man. She grasped him around the waist and used her body as dead weight to upend him. In doing so, the rifle was dropped just out of reach. The Woman rolled herself over then struggled atop him, pinning his arms with her knees and pounding his face with her fists. She pushed her knee into his burnt hand until he cried. Yet even in his drunkenness, he was stronger than she was. Lifting his back and pivoting to one hip, he used the leverage to swing full force and punch her in the nose. Blood streamed down. She grabbed her face and attempted to stand, but she couldn't see. She tapped and dabbed the dirt around her until she felt the butt of the gun, but the Man had already stood with quite a bit of effort and managed to snatch it from her.

He pointed it at the Woman. "I've had enough of you to last a lifetime."

There was a sound in the sky of a whooshing descent, a torpedo-shaped body with wings tucked to the side cleaving the night air as it dove. Before the Man knew what was happening, the falcon, which had been watching from the pines, swooped down and clasped the front of his shirt. It fluttered its wings to keep itself buoyant and upright, cutting his chest with its talons where it held itself in place. He screamed as it took its foot to his forehead. It reopened the scar across his left eye, a razor-sharp talon unzipping its fibrous flesh. It chirruped in triumph as it took to the wing, wetting the Man in a mist of his own blood. But the rifle was still in hand, and he quickly lifted it aiming it in the bird's relative direction and blindly pulled the trigger. A burst of feathers hung suspended in the air as the falcon was shot down inside the Woman's garden.

The Woman lurched haphazardly toward him and grasped for the rifle. They each grabbed ahold of either side of the weapon and tugged, yet the Man was victorious when the gun slipped from the Woman's hands, which were too tired to grip and were damp with sweat and blood. She turned around, hoping to remount an attack from another vantage point, but it happened with such speed that there was little warning. He slammed the rifle butt as hard as he could into the back of her skull and dropped her to her knees. She stayed there a moment very prayerfully until she at last slumped to her side. Her hands had fanned out over her face to somehow shield her, but she was clubbed a final time, which emitted a crisp snap. The Woman lay on her back motionless just outside the garden fence. Her yellow hair was stuck together with blood, and it covered her face. In the scuffle, the folded butcher paper had slipped from her pocket. It rested aside the serpent staff at the foot of the garden.

The Woman hadn't gone in search of help earlier that day. She had spent the morning hours walking south to the cemetery to at last see her grandmother's headstone, to take a simple rubbing of it, and to bid it farewell. She had planned to trek north—north to freedom; the wild freedom only deer could know. But fear made her attempt an escape in two steps—baby steps, limb by limb. It wasn't an efficient plan, but it was a plan nonetheless, and she believed it would assure her follow-through.

She had to then circle back to the Cape Cod for a small number of possessions she had loaded into a satchel upon waking. On her way home from the cemetery, she had gotten lost, which ate up precious time. As soon as she heard the Man's voice through the screen door upon returning, she realized too late that she should've left that morning and never come back.

The Doe grunted to the Woman, but she didn't move. The giant slouching sunflower behind her tried to weep but had no seeds left to cry. Above them, the waning moon rose, setting the scene and casting a glow over the garden and hill.

The Man took the work cloth from his blistered hand and fashioned it as a wrap for his bleeding eye. His gun went up as he sidestepped the Woman's body, giving it a few soft kicks. He toed the butcher paper rubbing and the serpent staff only to then kick dirt onto them. He asked, "You think I like being a killer?"

The Doe struggled to stand, and once she had, she tucked her uncooperative right leg up toward her body and turned to the hills. Clouds passing over the moon stained the footpath with silhouettes which swiftly fell away. She eyed the hilltop, pointing her snout in its direction while lowering her ears to her head. She suddenly knew what she had to do. "They killed me up there," the Man said. "So what else was I to become?"

The one-eyed Man towered aside the garden like Polyphemus as he watched the Doe. In the state she was in, he wouldn't have to finish her off in a hurry. He let the gun drop down into a resting position while he adjusted his clothing, pulling up the seat of his pants with one hand—smoothing out his shirt until it lay flat, and he asked, "You know what your tree showed me, doe? That I was a monster." His face was red and distended with drunkenness and blood spatter. Mucous pooled in his nose. "Old man and me were the same kind of monster. I owed it to him to end his sickness."

His face then knotted with fury. "I kept asking myself something while I held the pillow over his face. How could he pretend to care so much about my wife and his deer and still wanna see an innocent little baby killed?" He blew his nose clear of the mucous by plugging a nostril. "I broke into his house to confront him. That's when I found him in his bed having a stroke. If that's not a sign from God, I don't know what is." He laughed, and his chin jutted out in front of his teeth, and he trembled so hard that he could barely get out the words. "When I read the abortion note he wrote for her," he nodded vaguely toward the Woman's body, "I lost it. For someone that wanted everything and everybody to live free and be safe, he sure as hell didn't try very hard to save me when I was kid. He cared more about his animals than he ever did for me. Than he ever did for my baby."

As he spoke, they crept up the footpath, but the Doe had cleared very little ground between her and the Man. She began to move with urgency, and in doing so, she kicked up an array of pebbles and dirt clumps that rolled down the path toward his boots.

"You think you're gonna outrun me, you little cunt?" He growled. "You think I'm that weak?" He spread his arms, grasping the rifle in his right hand. "I'm a beast. I'm a dragon!" He flashed his crooked, cracked smile. "And I'm the devil in the flesh!"

The rifle was then at his shoulder—cocked and aimed—and the Doe bounded as fast as she could up the footpath, pulling herself along on three legs. The reopened wound over his eye had had thick scar tissue with relatively little vasculature. It was scarcely bleeding, which spared him much difficulty. He squinted his unscathed eye over the gun's sights with the blurred image of the Doe just beyond the barrel. "Even monsters deserve a mercy kill."

But there was no gunshot. The Man was just beyond the entrance of the footpath, and the Doe was twenty or so feet ahead of him. He had stopped and was scanning the ground around his feet and the adjacent fence posts. She did not wait to see what it was that he was searching for in the tangling of plants. And as she struggled around the first curve of the footpath, she heard the Man scream. For hidden in the grasses was the rattlesnake, which had all the while been waiting for the Man. It had lifted itself off the ground, aiming its arrow tip head at his calf, and struck him, delivering a generous amount of its venom into his veins and tissue.

The Man wasted no time in firing at the snake, which was still erect, waving and hissing in exuberance to the *punji*-like music of a sudden, charmed breeze. At the sound of the gun, it quickly retreated into the cover of the garden. Another shot was attempted, but the serpent had already disappeared under the many shields of leaves and tendrils. Its hiss evaporated into the aeolian sound of the breeze that stirred the whole of the Woman's garden.

The snakebite upon his leg burned, and he had already begun to feel the effects of the venom—ice water in the veins followed by a circulation of hot blood like scalding water. Ahead, the Doe struggled around the second bend of the path. As she rounded the corner, the Man had a clear shot and lifted the rifle. She sensed the danger but could not juke his aim. Despite any injuries, his evil eye yet wielded its power. Another blast from his rifle sounded, and that time, the Doe felt a breathtaking pain in her right side. As she ventured toward the third *S* curve, she felt a warmth trickling down her previously injured leg.

The Man's roughshod stomping shook the footpath as he drew near. He was growing faint, his breathing had become labored, and his vision was poor. He blinked his uncovered eye, which unveiled the rattlesnake's unequivocal power: the footpath had been transformed into a giant serpent. Its *S* curves wriggled and breathed as it wound up the hill, beckoning him to the top.

The grade of the hill was steep, and in his failing condition, he floundered as he lost his footing on bluestone shingles—the scales of a snake's back. At times, the rifle was a trekking pole, while other times, it was an accidental abrader that scraped the white-charred flesh of his burned hand.

By the time the Man rounded the final curve of the footpath, the Doe had vanished. As a consequence of the venom, a paralysis was slowly working its way toward his diaphragm. The beginnings of pulmonary edema were leaving him breathless, and he shivered in a cold sweat. All bodily functions from the head down diminished. And as soon as he began to panic, a twig snapped, and it diverted his attention. Once more, he lifted his rifle and walked into the trees.

It'd been years since he'd returned to the shanty, and he saw his father's chair pushed against its dark back wall. "Aha," he said, as several feet aside it stood the Doe. There was blood running down the front right side of her body, and the Man saw the small, wet blotch where the bullet had entered the upper part of the leg.

She crept backward with a slight hobble, which pulled him toward her. Each time she backtracked, he advanced. Because of the Doe's impressive field of vision and her ability to see subtle movement in darkness, she caught sight of two well-concealed eyes watching and blinking from the trees.

As the Man pushed closer toward the shanty, he saw a dark outline behind the Doe. He squinted to make it out—perhaps a bush or a small tree. There were two masses side by side, one larger than the other, and this silhouette loomed behind the Doe as if she were bracing herself against it.

"I got one bullet left, and I'm gonna put it right in the middle of that white spot on your head!"

The Doe took a final step backward, which placed the Man perfectly in position. She used the exact footwork taught to her by the she-coyote: predator backs prey, prey falls into the trap. But this time the Doe used it to her advantage. And as he began to squeeze the trigger, everything grew hushed in the woods—no singing toads or chirping insects, no wind to rustle the leaves. A barely audible ringing began. It grew in volume and climbed to such a high pitch that the Man lowered his weapon and twisted his head in all directions to see from where it was coming. He realized what it was—how he had heard it in bed the previous night. The Doe too knew it well. It was that mysterious sound playing out in real time. In that moment it was being created—the origin whence it would echo backward in time, traveling in reverse to the very instant she had first heard it as a yearling back on the acreage.

The principal ringing and squealing sound was that of the old boards of the root cellar beginning to split under the massive weight of the Man. As the boards began to give way, the sound warped into its secondary wobbling character. The Man winced as the ground beneath him began buckling. The slats were smattered with the Doe's blood; the very same slats that had injured her leg in the first place.

The Man then saw clearly what stood behind the Doe. It wasn't a shrub or a small tree at all. It was the ghost of the little boy he once was, who haunted this wretched place. Standing aside him was the Old Man, who kept a protective arm around the boy.

The Man's eyes softened and he looked as though he wanted to say something. And as the boards broke, he was sent down the steps of the root cellar, his awful, hollow wailing being that of the third character of the sound sequence. And as it was always cut off by a final snap, the Man then landed in such a way that the edge of a step hit right underneath his vertebral atlas, instantly breaking his neck.

In the end, it was the Doe who was tasked with putting the Man with the Crooked Finger out of his misery—tasked with ending the long cycle of abuse from which there had been no escape, a generational string of traumas that spanned from the Man to those who had come long before him. That had been the revelation of the mysterious sound all along. Like the ghosts of the doe clan, the sound had been a singular, violent moment trapped in time and destined to travel the woodland—from past to present and back again—unveiling itself only to those meant to see and hear it.

At that spine-snapping moment, the starved she-coyote had rushed through the trees and descended into the root cellar. After tearing away at the Man's cotton shirt and tugging at his limp body, which lifted him from the steps with each pull, it gnawed through the layers of fat, muscle, ligament, and bone, which gave off a pronounced, cartilaginous, crunching noise. It then burrowed its way under his ribcage, undoing his innards with its powerful jaws to eat his heart. To the moon it howled, and to the Doe—its apt pupil—it yowled in thanksgiving, its breast and muzzle wet with the black shine of blood in the night. For its plan had come to fruition, and it had birthed its own vengeance.

There was a time-honored saying in the Bluestone Woodland that spoke to the religious beliefs of folks: "Through God, man has conquered the wilderness and tamed the beast." But now, only the night sounds endured—from the hurdy-gurdy of cicadas to the gurgling of the Man's body being disemboweled. And as an emergency siren blared as it sped along the Bluestone highway, the sparrow sang from the sugar shack: *The beast no longer holds sway!* At last, it took to the sky to drop a curl of burnt hair from its nest onto the sleeping country cemetery.

There would be no going back to the garden for the Doe. She staggered through the woods, bleeding heavily. She left a trail as she moved—smears painted on boulders used for bracing and ruby-dotted lines up ridges and down unfamiliar slopes.

She was fading in and out of consciousness. Shadows moved along the path as night began to lift. Everything grew indigo as the sun peeked above the eastern hills. One moment, she was running recklessly through a grey cornfield and blessing rows of sickly maize with her blood. The next, she was on the river's shore and coughing up sacred blood into polluted waters. In the somber break of day, the half-buried litter, once shining as pyrite, looked bleak and lusterless.

She closed her eyes and fell on the bank. A liquid pouring into her mouth cooled her scorched, dry throat and dulled her senses. It tasted of wormwood and vinegar. Time felt meaningless. When she opened her eyes, she found herself on the southern bank. Soaking and chilled, she had no recollection of crossing the river.

A small speck of light beamed in front of her in the cobalt forest of early morning. It opened and bloomed until it was a diamond glistening white. It radiated with flickering tongues of flames cool and frosty feathered. It was a downy tail, and it guided her up the dark ridge. She glided as she followed it to a knotting of trees.

At last she got a glimpse of its face. It turned back to reveal the grey snout of an old doe regal and strong, hips wide set on sturdy legs. It was the Elder Doe, and she bid her daughter to follow her into the tree cluster.

Inside was dark and empty, the Elder Doe nowhere to be found. The Doe collapsed in the center. She smelled her mother all around her. The scent shrouded her over—a maternal pall. The Doe looked up to the braided ceiling, paper-white bark peeling from poles and up-surging into a Romanesque dome. She was lying in the birch thicket.

A warmth was overtaking her. Euphoric, crushing sleepiness began to settle upon her. She felt as if she were floating in water. Her eyes closed, and she slipped away. Beyond the highway near an old familiar stump came the sound of the owl. At the break of dawn, it joined its voice with the song of the mourning dove.

At long last, the North Territory.

**M**r. Huaman said they came too late.

It was a new day and at last spring. There was a lot to get done on this precise day as the new owners of her home were coming. The Woman had to sort through storage, set aside the desirable items from the things that needed discarding. It was hard for her for as soon as she started the process, she was somehow always pulled away or lapsed into forgetting. The wounds across her face never seemed to heal. Sometimes when she brushed the hair out of her eyes, she'd find blood on her hands.

She believed her lingering mental fog was attributed to some sort of lasting brain damage from the bludgeoning rifle butt. Visions came and went as did slumber. She slept for a long time, dreaming she had been laid aside Grandma Ava in the cemetery. But then she awoke and found her way home. After that, the days were strung together in an uninterrupted haze. She couldn't even recall so much as eating an apple as cooking a supper. She was disoriented, but at least she was free. She floated atop the cool, damp earth. In a windstorm, the Man's Thin the Herd pamphlets had all blown into the garden. Long rotted away, they now served as mulch. Tender green shoots erupted through them from out the black soil.

Even the red branch of the winter dogwood had little emeralds of efflorescence. That was the beautiful thing of shifting seasons; how something as seemingly fixed as a sleeping dogwood branch from one cold, dark month to the next could suddenly and unexpectedly show signs of transformation. Then on one hot mountain spring day, it was just somehow all leafed out in green-pillowed luxury as if it had always been so.

People had this ability too she thought. How Red of all people had been the one to call the police. "It was the snakebite," he said. He still had the scar and regarded it with awe. The venom had been a truth serum and an awakening.

He spoke of how he had received strange phone calls with garbled words and static, but through it all he'd heard a phone number and a voice insisting he use it. The number even showed itself to him in the whitecaps of the river and on the foggy pane of his bathroom mirror. And when he had finally worked up the nerve to call the number, he was both astonished and unsurprised to find that it had belonged to the phone of Detective Robin Byrd, a longstanding police officer in the city.

On his first attempt, Red had shared very little information with Byrd. But after receiving the call from the Man with the Crooked Finger the afternoon everything had transpired, Red immediately hung up and dialed the detective. He told her everything and even gave her the address of the Man and the Woman, urging her that very moment to make the three-hour drive from the city to the Bluestone Woodland with backup.

Byrd herself had had dreams before receiving a call from Red. She saw her old friend, a retired physician who had moved to the Bluestone

Woodland with his partner, Fay, and each time she dreamed of him, he made one cryptic comment. She racked her brain trying to understand the message. She had even called the Old Man but found his number had been disconnected. After the first call with Red, she had asked, "Remind me of your name?" When he told her, she replied, "I'll be goddamned," for each one of her dreams had ended with the Old Man saying, "Red call."

Soon after, there had been a widespread investigation of the community by higher levels of law enforcement. Detective Byrd came to know the fate of her old friend. It was a sad affair—a murderous web that had woven and tangled everything together from the ecological concerns of local whitetail herd devastation to the murders of the Old Man, the squatter, and the grim and mysterious circumstances surrounding the death of the Man with the Crooked Finger.

All the Woman remembered from the night he had died was how brightly it shone. Not so much one giant flood of brilliance but rather a light coming from afar at first very faint but then becoming gleaming and colored. She saw the dancing and whirling even from behind her shut eyes. The reds and the blues strobed all about the facade of the pines and swirled madly over the garden. *Lully, lullay,* she had heard a robin bird singing into a two-way radio before it flew to town.

And when the town found out the truth about the Man with the Crooked Finger, they burned their Thin the Herd propaganda. It was just as the Man had believed, for they did not destroy those things because he was a killer but rather because of the secret he carried. They would have to bide their time until the next movement took its place. Different words, same intent. "They have a new thing to fear," the Woman heard Mr. Huaman say. "We Peruvians."

Yet some of the townsfolk had come to feel shame like Red. But this shame wasn't a disease; it was an incineration that burned clean away the insidious atmosphere that seemed to have combed through cornfields and penetrated the once-fertile soils. As soon as it had been dispersed and blazed away hot and fast, the whole of the area began anew. It was a virgin forest after fire. The air felt lighter as it played between the cracks and fault lines of the bluestone foundation that told stories like the rings of trees.

The little Cape Cod and land the Woman had shared with her husband were being sold to the Huaman family. It was hard to believe that anybody would want to live on the property after all that had happened there, but as it turned out, some buyers weren't superstitious or squeamish. Nobody could turn down an opportunity for affordable housing and a chance to begin with a clean slate even if it meant sharing it with the dead.

The Huamans were Peruvian immigrants who had spent the last decade in the flooded city. The name Huaman was a Quechuan word meaning hawk. And like the industrious raptor, the Huamans flew up to the mountain land in search of a new life and snatched up the surfacing opportunities like silver-backed trout from out the great river.

Mr. Huaman was to replace the Man with the Crooked Finger at his old job. Having spent the last decade kowtowing to an idle bully, the owner of the farmstead was relieved to at last have a hard worker. Mrs. Huaman was a kindred spirit of the Woman's. She knew much about herbs and canning and working the land from her childhood spent in rural, mountainous Peru.

The Huamans had three children, one of whom was a newborn, and the Woman delighted in having little ones scurrying about the place. It would be nice watching Mrs. Huaman and her children working in the garden side by side.

Of course when Mr. Huaman came to look at the property, he had found the root cellar atop the hill. Its life had come full circle; originally hollowed out by a gravedigger, it was put to rest having been refilled and reboarded by the great-great grandson of the former. However, Mr. Huaman still found it unsafe for young children— There were human remains in there after all. When he saw the large heap of wood rot and splinter from the old shanty and the upturned slats that had covered the cellar entrance, his bronzed face greyed, and he puckered his prominent brow. He had a sympathetic ringing in his ears.

"Are you okay, Mr. Huaman?"

His eyes bulged, and he spun around. "Are you here with me now, miss?"

"Yes. I have much to do before I leave."

The ruins atop the ridge and all the unknown horrors associated with the shanty certainly had left a spiritual wound on the property. Nobody was ever certain what had transpired for the Man to fall into the root cellar, and it took some time to discover his remains. Law enforcement searched the area following the blood trail leading up the hill. And when an evidence technician went to urinate around the dilapidated shanty, he noticed the upturned and splintered boards. He thus looked down the chasm to where he saw the outline of a body cleaned of much of its meat. At first glance, it looked like the scavenged remains of a deer.

When more cars were driven up the hill to collect the body from the hole and do a thorough sweep of the area, they used the entry from the neighbor's back field. The cumbersome vehicles—as it had been many years since anyone had driven up to the old shan-ty—created such a rumble in the earth that as they pulled around to the well-hidden hole, the old, decaying building caved in on itself. They all stood around to study the pile of boards that mirrored the splintered covering of the root cellar. They had barely noticed behind them on a stretcher the desiccated body of the Man, his head slumped on a broken neck with tongue dangling out his mouth—for not even hungry wild animals would eat such a disdainful tongue.

In life, he had been so imposing, but in death, he was small and fragile. And in its delicate state of decomposition, his body split apart like the many shards of bluestone that covered the woodland. A few vertebrae and other bones had slipped down into the iron-rich ground water that flooded the cellar. The edifice was in such a derelict condition that it was deemed too dangerous for crew to go fishing for remains. They opted to backfill the root cellar, leaving some of the Man's bones inside and marking it a burial.

The Woman couldn't recall what the place atop the hill was or what had happened there. All her memories became as dreams from long ago. Yet the memory of the Doe somehow persisted as unaltered and fresh as the first time they had met in her garden at red dusk. She had looked for the Doe, but nothing rustled in the forest deep, no white tail like a victory flag streaking along the black pines. Whatever had taken place that night had granted her freedom from her old life, and that was all she really needed to know.

Time had slipped away since, and the Woman remained. It seemed she was tied to the land like the many items she needed to sort through as she readied the house for the Huamans. She always said tomorrow she would separate and sift the good from the bad until things were at last in order, but too many tomorrows had turned into nearly two years.

And though this fogginess was a tremendous load to bear, she found enough strength to cradle and carry her disorientation without curving her spine dramatically. She needed to hold on only a little longer and keep working through it. The signs were everywhere. It was a new day.

For now, she needed to focus only on the moment at hand. In preparation to move on, she had to go through boxes of canning and fall storage in the pantry. The furniture, the dishes would stay in the little house. And as she made her way inside, she found it empty and couldn't remember ever having done the work. She touched her head as she tried to recall and stained her fingers red.

All traces of the things that had marked her life in the little Cape Cod had been cleaned away. The Huamans had lost most of their possessions in the endless coastal flooding, and she thought it would be a kindness to leave her items behind for them to sort through for their use. The house was to be sold as is, but she couldn't recall taking out an ad. She had heard Mr. Huaman speak as he walked down the footpath of the hill; he was a sensitive, attuned man.

"Why do you stay here?"

She was silent.

"Your belongings are gone," he said. "Don't you know you are—"

He must have been confused. Was that yesterday he had come to look at the house, or months ago? Everything had passed like sunlight moving across the garden shed floor.

Mrs. Huaman and the children would be arriving any moment. The Woman looked down to her hands but couldn't find them. It was certainly no way to greet a stranger, but she was sure Mrs. Huaman would understand. She crossed over the threshold and looked around the porch to where stood a mountain of spotted apples shriveled like old farmer's hands. They came from the little orchard up the hill, and the Woman had somehow overheard the owner say they had tasted unusual after the Man with the Crooked Finger had died in the root cellar—as if his decay had leached into the soil and made its way up the tree roots to the fruit. The horde was a welcome gift for the Huamans, so the fruit waited patiently on the porch for whatever next thing they were to become—pies or preserves, maybe fodder for animals. They were in a state of becoming like the Woman. She felt herself becoming, but what?

From the heavy tree line came a fluttering. On small gold wings weighing no more than an ounce of tansy descended a goldfinch into a pine. How long had it been since she'd seen a bird? The Woman went to the edge of the garden fence and squinted into the timber. Beyond the little yellow bird through one of the many green-black gaps of the hardwoods, the Woman saw something descending. It ambled in and out of cover until at one point it appeared as a woman crawling through the trees.

She gasped.

Emerging onto the footpath was a saint clothed in hide; her body was ever so slightly hobbling on a leg that had never healed; nor would it heal as it served as a reminder for all of her great sacrifice. Dotted behind her were two little beige splotches covered in snowflake dappling; a male and a female fawn peeking from behind her back legs.

The Doe and the twins kept some distance from the Woman, batting flies and other buzzing creatures with busy ears and tails. The whites of their fur shone against the black wash of the tree line. Atop the male fawn's crown and upon his leg was a swatch of cream-colored fur; the same type of fur that kissed the flank of the female fawn. The two babes had returned to the Doe from another time. Love was the only covenant that abided all things and bridged all space.

The moment had at last come for them to return to the acreage, the land ever-promised to them. The storm had passed, the sea was calm, and the desert was in bloom. Stretching upward was a tender shoot from out a weathered stump; the blessed apple tree was growing once more. All things rose renewed from the earth to once again climb toward the sun. Out of the garden lifted the falcon. Into the pine it ascended to perch upon the branch that it would share with the goldfinch. Not far behind it was the rattlesnake. It slunk through a gap in the garden fence so as to coil itself about the Doe's leg, which she bent at a welcoming angle for its climb.

The sudden scrunch of gravel under tires sounded from the Cape Cod drive. The Woman turned in its direction. "It's the Huamans, Saint. What do I do? My head … It never stops bleeding."

As she approached her, the Doe said, *I come with the breath of life.*

The Woman bowed her bleeding head and was made holy by the breath of the Doe; white-wispy breath as breath on a cold morning. She was healed—but her wounds would have to be carried as a mark into the life of the world to come. Such was the toll of entering paradise. The red, weeping lesions of the Woman's face and head then sprouted with white fur. From her hips, her spine pivoted until it was parallel with the ground. Now on all fours, her slender, cloven feet were again touching the earth, and she kicked them joyfully into the sod.

The voices of children bounced off tree trunks and stone outcroppings as did the slamming of car doors. The Woman turned, wondering if she shouldn't head toward the drive and greet the family. It would be rude after all to leave without saying goodbye. "I must welcome them."

The Doe cocked her head and then nodded in accord. As she trotted to the tree line with her twins in tow, she turned back a final time to baptize the Woman. Receiving the Doe's life-giving breath had been a crossing of a threshold, and the transition was complete. At that moment, she had taken the Doe's place in the Bluestone Woodland, a place of great honor. The transfigured Woman had become the white-faced Fawn.

A breeze rich with the scent of sweet grass passed through, and the whole of the forest came to life in a whirring of leaves and a creaking of boughs. The far cry of the she-coyote and the love song of the raven were heard. Before her, the rattlesnake had shed its skin to form the path that led to the acreage, and the beating of falcon wings would be the wind that propelled her onward.

*Saint*, the Fawn cried with a new tongue, *I'm right behind you!*

With that, the Fawn sped round the bend of the house. It was time to meet Mrs. Huaman and her three children, María, Rocío, and the baby, who was crying and gesturing to the hilltop with a crooked pointer finger, wiping the tears away from a little left eye slashed over with a café-au-lait spot. This baby was the one Mr. Huaman's tía back in Peru had dreamed about, the tía whose uncle had once been a powerful *curandero*. He had come to her in a dream and showed her a vision in fire. Inside the newborn's spirit, a coyote wrestled with a devil. This baby, the tía feared, had been touched by the *mal de ojo*, the evil eye.

"*Shhh, shhh*," Mrs. Huaman whispered to her crying baby. "Te voy a proteger siempre."

Upon the warped, sagging boards of the porch, the Fawn greeted Mrs. Huaman and her daughters. The baby stopped its crying to stare and reached out its fat hand with a little crooked finger pointing. And it was silent for a long time as Mrs. Huaman and the girls quietly stood watching the Fawn. It was just the sort of thing Mr. Huaman would say was an omen.

"Que hombre tan supersticioso," lamented Mrs. Huaman, interrupting the silence as she tossed a free arm up in the air. "¡Tan supersticioso!" She would call her husband at the farm when they drove back to town for supplies and firewood. Always scaring the children over nothing. There was no ghost of a murdered woman in their new Cape Cod, just a tree load of bitter apples and a white-faced fawn haunting the porch.

COBBLESTONE
PUBLISHING GROUP